In the Fool's Footsteps

A novel by
Karen Hoffman

Published by Karen Hoffman
Toronto, ON

Copyright © 2012 by Karen Hoffman

All rights reserved. No part of this book may be reproduced, scanned or distributed in any printed or electronic form without permission. Please do not participate in or encourage piracy of copyrighted materials in violation of the author's rights. Purchase only authorized editions.

ISBN-13: 978-1475267044
ISBN-10: 1475267045

Cover design by Matthew Marigold
Book concept and design by Karen Hoffman

This is a work of fiction. Names, characters, places, and incidents either are the product of the author's imagination or are used fictitiously, and any resemblance to actual persons, living or dead, businesses, companies, events, or locales is entirely coincidental.

For Bob
This book is dedicated to my brother who touched everyone he met with his generosity, zest for life and vast love for time-consuming storytelling.

Prologue

The floor creaks under the shifting weight of a girl. Her shadow stretches along the wall to be met and absorbed by the other shades—the hall tree, the curtains on the door, the umbrella stand. With a calm hand she pulls open the drawer on the table to retrieve a pencil and scrap of paper. She pushes the drawer shut, pauses when it catches, repositions it, and pushes again until it closes. The pencil scratches against the paper. The crackling of the shifting page seems deafening in the darkness, but she does not pause anymore.

I have left. Be happy for me.

She folds the paper and places it beside the lamp, in the spot that the bills and other mail usually occupy. From the table top, she grabs an envelope marked "grocery money" and tucks it inside a book. One word—Journal—is etched down the middle of the strong spine.

Centered on the front cover is a smiling boy. He strolls along a well-trodden mountain path. Over his shoulder is a sack tied to a stick, hobo-style. He looks around at the clouds, the birds, and the trees. He doesn't appear to care where he's been, and he's not paying attention to his destination. In the bottom right corner of the picture, the leather-encased foot, beribboned and jingle-belled, hovers at the edge of a cliff. The foot, with neither the consent nor the knowledge of its owner, is ready to settle into the element of air.

Turning, the girl allows her eyes to skip across the familiar shadows before reaching out to touch the cold metal of the doorknob. She grasps the knob, turns it and pulls. She steps over the threshold.

– Kimberly Harding, *Meander*

The Wanderer

"TAKE IT!"

The old woman thrust a grubby package toward me. She was curled up on her side in a snow bank off the path that meandered through the Don Valley, and it was hard to make her out in the pre-dawn gloom. Her breath hung in the cold air. I slowed my pace. By the time I reached her, she had managed to get to her knees. I crouched in front of her and she smiled.

"You'll take it, then?" she asked.

"That's alright. You keep it," I said.

"But it's yours. You're going to need it to—"

"—to find my way," I finished for her. "I know. I know. That's okay."

"Please take it!" she gasped.

I pulled Cherise's afghan from my pack and spread it across the old woman's shoulders.

"I want you to have it," I murmured to the early morning and the shivering crone, whose face clouded with anxiety.

"I want *you* to have *this*," she replied, scrambling to unwrap the dirty package. The afghan fell from her shoulders. Black tree trunks loomed around her, crowding in on the cardboard hovel she lived in. Her rags hung from her body, clothing that might have been beautiful in another era. Greasy grey strings of hair pulled at the radiance of that ancient face.

She pressed the package into my hands and nodded vigorously. I accepted it, stood and took a step back from her. My left foot landed squarely in a slush puddle.

Hours later, I retraced my steps on the path. Cherise's afghan was the only spot of colour in the miserable scene. The red-and-orange zigzags were garish against the greys and browns of the drab lean-to. It lay in a heap, unmoved since that morning.

Officers milled around the path, poking through the trees. One was on his knees inside the hut going through the old woman's few belongings, mostly rags and bits of newspaper. Another cop noted my approach with a grim nod.

"What happened?" I asked.

"You come this way much?"

"Most days," I responded. "The old woman that lives here... Did something happen to her?"

"Died of exposure. I'm C.O. Brighton. You ever talk to her? Know if she has any family that could be notified?"

I gazed on the zigzags that I had watched Cherise crochet. She liked to sit outside in the fragrant spring air, the growing afghan spread across her beautiful legs. She tucked her hair behind her ears to keep it out of her face. Her head was always slightly cocked when she crocheted, and the curve her long neck described was the most graceful thing I could remember seeing or touching.

"No," I said.

"I'll need your name and a brief statement."

"Kal Winters, but I can't tell you anything."

The body had been removed from the scene.

Later, I spread the contents of my bag in front of me. Papers, books, pencils. The package. I pulled it from the plastic bag. Rubber bands, their elasticity hardened by age, held crumpled sheets of newspaper around what appeared to be a book. The elastics cracked apart when I tried to remove them. I peeled back the layers of paper and a shiver ran through me as I gazed at my inheritance. Profound and painful recognition thudded behind my ribcage.

How did that wretch get her hands on *this* diary?

With careful fingers I turned to the back. Several pages remained blank. The last entry had been made on September 27, 2004. A lump formed in my throat and my eyes burned. Quite obviously not the crone in the valley.

The first time I had held the battered diary seemed a lifetime ago, even though it was only two years. I smelled the mildew and felt the aged mushiness of the remaining pages, about to disintegrate in my fingertips, and stained with mud, coffee, blood, who knew what else. It wasn't a large book, about two centimeters thick, but the number of pages seemed larger than the cover. Sheaves were torn out, more than twenty people had written over the decades as this diary followed its strange path, yet there was still room for more secrets. My secrets.

I opened it to the beginning. Licking dry lips, I read.

~ ~ ~

Clara Strachan

June 30, 1928

My words are gone. He tore them up and burned them because I cut off my hair. Well, my father can erase the record, but not the memory. He cannot burn my experience. I know that he only wants his little girl to stay innocent and mute like his wife. So much for my excellent essay on God's true intention for woman. My father is ignorant and afraid. It's simple. I can't forgive him and I can't stay under his roof and live by his rules. I will go somewhere where I don't have to hide my intelligence, someplace where there are people who will read my writing, not suppress it. I have seen all this village has to offer someone like me. I will live beyond the path my father has set for me. I will live outside the austerity of marriage to find the root and robustness of my true potential.

July 5, 1928

Better that he burned the words than read them. His heart would have broken to know his daughter wasn't as innocent as he'd like to think. Imagine, kissing a vagrant in a tree top! Pretty Gregory. Dull Gregory. Grumpy Gregory. Passionate Gregory. Lazy Gregory. The mere thought would turn my father's face purple. Maybe I should tell him.

I haven't seen my drifter for a few days. I must find him.

July 18, 1928

I am going to Toronto! I saw Gregory this afternoon. I went back to the tree to write and he was waiting there for me. He wanted to say good-bye. His partner has been arrested for rum-running. The fool got too drunk and crashed his car in a ditch. He wasn't hurt, but he was too pickled to flee the scene. The police found two cases of rum in the trunk. He will go to jail because he didn't wonder why he can buy a case of rum for almost nothing in one country and sell it for double the price in another. He didn't know we're dry here. Now Gregory has to get away before he's implicated for stupidity.

It took a long time to get the story out of him (he was more interested in kissing than talking), but I got his attention when I said I wanted to come with him. He didn't like the idea at first, but I explained that he needs me to buy the tickets and bring food because he can't show his face.

We're leaving tonight. We'll walk along the tracks then buy our tickets to Toronto. If we stop any sooner, someone might recognize me and then the game would be lost. I just need to elude my father until my eighteenth birthday and then I am free. We can be on the train before sunrise. I'll be halfway to Toronto before anyone knows I'm gone.

July 19, 1928

We're on the train! I've never been so tired in my life. It took us nearly seven hours to walk. We had to wait an hour for the first train, and it was terrifying. I thought for sure my father would have found me gone in the middle of the night and sent up the alarm. We were undetected, though. I purchased the first set of tickets going to America, then got off the train and purchased another set of tickets for Toronto. That way my father will think I went the other way to America.

I worry about mother. She'll be so sad and frightened for me. Maybe someday she can be happy again. I need to sleep, but we're arriving at Union Station in 20 minutes. I am too exhilarated to sleep. Not Gregory. He's snoring beside me. Now is a good time to slip away from him.

July 19, 1928

I should be hiding from Gregory, but I had to stop and record my first few breaths in this spectacular city. Union Station is enormous. It takes up an entire block and stands at least four stories high. I counted 22 immense stone pillars across the front. Inside, the ceiling is vaulted and tiled, and there are huge arched windows at each end of the main hall. Most striking, however, is the hush. Loads of people bustle through, but their conversations seem to float all the way up to the ceiling. All that is audible is a muted shuffling and clicking of heels on the floor.

Oh! It's so busy! The streets are filled with motor cars and carriages and railway cars. An enormous building is under construction across the street. An old woman not far away from me is feeding the pigeons and a man is selling sandwiches from a cart. I just saw another man kissing a woman on the mouth right here on the sidewalk. She was wearing a wedding ring, but not him!

I can scarcely believe I'm really here. I am going to drink liquor, hear poetry, smoke cigarettes, use a real typewriting machine, and get a job making my own money. I'll go to a salon to get my hair done and buy beautiful new clothes. I'm going to write about everything–the places I go, the smart, sophisticated women I meet, and all the men I kiss on the mouth in the open.

~ ~ ~

Chapter 1

The man stands behind a counter. He smiles at the girl who gazes at the items strewn there. She is dusty. Her clothes are torn and her knee is scraped. The little fool looks like she fell off a cliff. Her small suitcase lies on the floor. The man shows her a blank notebook. She nods and offers him some coins, stretching out her arm, palm up. He grasps her hand. Her slender fingers close around the coins. Behind the counter, the man's knee brushes against the other notebook.

– Kimberly Harding, *Harbinger*

The Reader

$P_{ROSPERPO'S}$ B_{OOKERY} was a writer's black hole: no shelves, no catalogue system, no priority placement for bestsellers. The store was a health hazard, a tinder-box waiting for the spark to ignite it. Teetering stacks of used books lined narrow, transient passageways. It was a librarian's nightmare. The only rhyme to be found was in a lost volume of poetry; the only reason in a stray philosophy book. The path from the door to the counter changed weekly, along with the inventory. Aisles took sharp turns, often ending abruptly at a pile of magazines or, occasionally, a wall. For Marcus Mesinger, the proprietor, it was the heart of Eden.

"Find anything?" he asked from somewhere near the back of the store.

"Maybe." I crouched in one of the passageways with one hand on the dusty floor for stability and the other massaging my aching neck. I had to turn my head sideways to read the titles. I scanned the selection of folklore and fairy tales. "I suppose shelves are out of the question?" I called.

"Phrase it right and you turn something out of the question into a question. But by doing so you turn it inside out. Is that what you want me to do to my store?"

"You mean outside in." I stood and stretched. "This early edition of Grimms... Can you dig it out for—?" My eyes fell on a book that lay on top of the pile, and I trailed off. I picked it up and blew dust from the cover. A faded picture of a boy walking along a trail emerged from the grime. No title, no author. I opened it to find the first pages were missing. What remained carried several different styles of handwriting–diary entries that started in 1928.

"You don't need the Grimms, Kal," said Marc. "The library has an older edition."

"You're just being lazy." I replaced the diary on the pile and moved to the end of the book tunnel, veered left and walked into a dead end. "You might think about putting out a bowl of breadcrumbs for clientele," I grumbled.

"I was thinking more along the lines of a golden thread," he said from just the other side of the book wall. Part of Marc's refusal to organize his store for his clients was that he preferred to organize it for himself. "Hang a right at *Another Roadside Attraction*."

My eyes scanned the piles of books. There it was, positioned at eye level, leaning against several tourism books. I swung right. The store's inventory, ever changing, held all the answers according to Marcus' kaleidoscopic reasoning, including how to get to the cash counter and how to find the front door again. You just had to know how to read the signs.

"Now where?" I asked, eyeing *Around the World in 80 Days*.

"On your left you should see a copy of *Peter Pan*. " The book was propped against a thick Jungian text. I spun around, but found myself at a loss. "Look up," Marcus said.

I did. Crude stars had been cut and pasted to the tin ceiling.

"Second star to the right," I muttered to myself and followed the directions. "Did it ever occur to you that most people lack the time it takes to buy a book here?"

He was lying across the counter, ass and feet in the air, head hanging off the other side, looking for something on a hidden shelf. He emerged with a leather pouch and landed on his feet. From the pouch he pulled a pair of pliers and coil of copper wire. With deft movements, he snipped a length of wire, folded it and began twisting it around itself.

"Not time, Kal, mental agility. And most people actually have that agility, they're just too lazy to exercise it."

"I don't know how you stay in business." I pulled up a stool.

With the pliers, he shaped the twisted wire so that it resembled a figure eight. He snipped and tucked the ends and tossed the finished lemniscate onto the counter.

Marcus practised the art of self-adornment. Head to toe, he was an array of colours, baubles and hair. A hand-knitted rainbow stocking cap hung to his waist, only slightly shorter than his blue dreadlocks. Hand-painted beads nestled in his mountain man beard and clattered against the trinkets that hung from his neck. Over a fuscia T-shirt, he wore a hand-embroidered vest. The pattern was intricate. Songbirds hid among exotic flowers. Paisleys floated down from his shoulders. His pants were a study in hand-quilted patchwork. The army boots on his feet had been painted yellow, and rhinestones stuck to them. Bells jingled at the ends of the laces. Marcus made all his clothes himself.

"What can I do for you today?" he asked. He took a roll of black ribbon from the pouch.

"It doesn't have to be today, but I would like to look at the Grimms book." I held up a hand before he could protest. "I heard you just fine. I've seen the one at the library. Now I want to see this one."

He sighed. "Help me rearrange the classics section tomorrow and I'll have it ready for you."

"Right." I stood and turned to leave. A wall of books barred my immediate departure. I looked left, then right, then down at my feet. "A map, please."

~ ~ ~

The diary lays open in front of him. The pen in his hand hovers above the page. He has not finished writing, but some emotion stops him. His brow is creased. He stares unseeing at the words he has written in the stolen journal.

– Kimberly Harding, *Harbinger*

~ ~ ~

I FOUND CHERISE in the garden. She knelt in the dirt and frost of the perennial bed, her thick, black braid hanging down her bent back. The pruners in her gloved fingers flashed in the setting sun as they snipped at the dried, dead stalks of last year's black-eyed susans. I caressed the goose flesh on one of her arms. With a startled yelp, she spun and twisted away from me. The fist that clenched the pruning shears narrowly missed my face.

"Isn't it a little early for gardening?" I asked.

She shrugged. "I'm just cleaning up a bit."

"It's cold out," I said and offered her a hand.

"I like the fresh air," she said as I hauled her to her feet and into my arms. Her smiling face was inches from mine. "Hungry? I stopped by the market on my way home."

"Anything but couscous," I teased. I had seen the box on the counter when I passed through the kitchen.

"Hmph."

She stooped to retrieve a weeding tool and trowel from the wet soil and placed them in a wicker basket along with the pruning shears and gloves. Then she dropped the basket on the patio and slumped onto the lounger.

"See what I got today?" she asked digging around in a plastic bag. She held up bunches of red and orange yarn. "It's going to be an afghan."

"Knitting? Isn't that something you do in the winter?"

"Crocheting, actually. I just felt like making something."

I sat beside her on the lounger and slung an arm around her shoulders. "How domestic of you. I didn't know you could crochet."

She grimaced and stuffed the wool back into the plastic bag. "My mother taught me when I was little. What do you think of the colours?"

"Kind of bright."

"Exactly." She kissed my nose, than sprang to her feet. "Dinner time."

I followed her in and sat at the kitchen table while she worked at the counter. Her back was straight as she chopped onions and garlic. The kettle clicked and groaned then finally whistled, lending a descant to the knock-knock of her knife against the wooden cutting board. She threw the mix into hot oil where it sizzled and popped, and rescued the kettle from the red element. The scream subsided into a lowering wail. When she tipped it to pour hot water over the waiting couscous, it whimpered a single staccato high note.

"I'm going out with the girls Saturday," she said, then pulled raisins and dried cranberries from a bag on the table.

"Your garlic is burning."

"Shit!" She grabbed the handle and flipped the contents of the pan with a flick of her wrist, then dumped it on top of the couscous. The dried fruit followed. She dug bare hands into the bottom of the bowl to fluff the couscous. Her slim fingers lifted and folded the contents until the aromas mingled.

"I don't know how you don't scald yourself," I said.

"It's in my genes." She put down two bowls of food and a pile of flatbread and joined me at the table. "Do you mind being left alone Saturday?"

"Cherise—"

"They want to take me out. You'll have me all to yourself on Sunday." With her teeth she tore into a piece of bread. Cheeks puffed out and lips pulled back, she said, "I promise."

I watched her eat. Like a trucker, but without the grace of utensils.

"How late do you think you'll be?" I asked and picked up my own piece of bread to scoop up some couscous.

She held up greasy fingers—two, then three, reluctantly four—shrugged broadly then hunched over her dinner.

"That's ok. I have work to do anyway, but I thought your parents were coming on Sunday," I said between bites.

"It's okay. I cancelled. You can meet them another time."
I didn't respond. Another time. Fine with me.

~ ~ ~

The girl raises a hand to point at something across the water. The other hand grips the rail. A breeze lifts the uneven ends of her hair. One strand catches at the corner of her smiling mouth. She stands on tiptoe with her pelvis pressed against the metal rail. The man is behind her, looking over her shoulder. His eyes follow the line of her upraised arm, and stop at her slim wrist. They travel back up the length of her arm, to her shoulder where it meets her neck. His knuckles brush against this smooth spot.

— Kimberly Harding, *Harbinger*

~ ~ ~

I ARRIVED AT *Prospero's* by noon on Saturday and met Marcus walking up the street. He juggled an armload of books, two coffees and a bagel. The bells in his hair tinkled as he dug for his keys to unlock the door. As he did so, a man approached us.

Marc smiled at the man and called out, "Hey, Arts and Crafts. How did you like it?"

"I'll know better when I see it," said the man. He looked mighty miffed. I took Marc's coffee and bagel to allow him to open the door, then followed him through the winding maze to the back counter. He dropped his armload beside the other stacks of novels.

"It's Gil, right?" Gil nodded. "I enjoyed our chat yesterday. Now, am I to assume you're not happy with your purchase?" he asked the other man.

"There must be a mix-up. The cover seems to be for a different book."

I smothered a smile. I had fallen for the same thing the first time I had ventured into Marc's bizarre universe. It had been a birthday present for Cherise. And it would have been okay, but she already had the book I mistakenly purchased.

Marc, taking his time, dug around behind the counter for a minute before emerging with razor blades and a bottle of rubber cement. He frowned. "That's odd. You didn't flip through it before deciding to buy it?"

He handed me a razor blade and slid a pile of books in front of me. He placed the bottle of rubber cement where we could both reach it. The confused customer watched as Marcus took a book from the top of the pile and opened its cover. With deft, well-rehearsed movements, he sliced down the hard seam that held the binding to the pages. Three or four quick slashes and he was halfway through the inch-thick spine. He flipped the book and repeated the motion until he had separated guts from casing. Gil was speechless.

Marc spun back to the shelves behind him—the only shelves in the whole place— and grabbed two piles: flaccid covers and elastic-bound bundled pages. He placed these in front of me. By the time Marc got the top off the glue bottle, Gil had found his voice.

"What the hell are you doing?"

The goopy brush paused between bottle and book cover. Marc's eyes flicked up, then back down to his task, which he carried out as he spoke. "I'm proactive about book covers and judgment."

Gil was flabbergasted. "Are you telling me—?"

"People, in general, are far too accustomed to purchasing the packaging without inspecting the contents. Sometimes they get home to find out they've been ripped off. They chalk it up to a lesson learned, feel embarrassed for not being a more savvy consumer, then turn around and do it again the very next day. But most of the time, they never even realize that they only bought packaging." He finished attaching the spine of the pages to the cover and pushed it aside to grab the next in line.

"Do you know where the pages that came with this cover might be?" Gil asked evenly.

Gil was growing angrier by the second. Marc had a way of pushing people's buttons. As far as I knew, though, I was the only one who had ever hit him.

I watched Gil as he and Marc sparred. I doubted Gil had ever hit anyone in his life. He looked to be in his late forties, tall and thin with a shrill voice. His wispy dust-brown hair curled up over his ears. I imagined that his wife would start nagging him to get a haircut soon.

"Oh, I'm sure they're here somewhere," said Marcus as his eyes swept the masses of books. "Feel free to look. You might even find something else you like."

"Look, I could use your help. I'm in—"

"A hurry? Suit yourself, but please, if you ever find the piece of cheese, let me know if it was worth it."

Gil's jaw fell open. Marc didn't meet his eyes, but concentrated on his task. I watched as he picked up the cover of a pulp romance depicting a long-tressed damsel swooning in the arms of a bare-chested man. The title *Eye of the Storm* blazed above their heads in raised gold lettering. He paired it with a sheaf of pages—*The Tempest*—and smirked.

"What gives you the right to waste other people's time?" Gil asked in quiet awe.

Marc sighed and set the newly re-assembled book aside. Planting both hands on the counter, he hoisted himself up to place his face inches from Gil's. His bloodshot eyes never wavered as he spoke in tones of the utmost patience. "I said, 'Suit yourself'. What gives you the right to expect me to waste my time helping you track down a book you don't need nearly as badly as you imagine? In case you didn't notice, I'm working."

"I take it customer service isn't part of your business model."

"Bingo." Marc lowered himself back to the floor and took his attention away from Gil.

"Well…uh…I would like my money back. I'm sure I can find something up the street."

Marcus raised one hand over his head to point at a sign behind him: RETURN POLICY—NONE was written in a rainbow of bubble letters and outlined in gold glitter.

"I guess I'll take a look for it, then," Gil growled and backed away from the counter shaking with indignation and plenty of spite.

"Suit yourself." As Gil disappeared down an aisle, Marc turned to me and grinned widely. "Bring back memories, Kal?"

~ ~ ~

She reclines on the red sofa. The candlelight highlights her cheekbones and jaw line. Her hair is wrapped in a scarf. Long strings of pearls drape from her neck and pool in her lap. She sips red wine, eyes closed. Her cheeks are flushed.

The man's lips move as he reads to her from a small volume. His head inclines towards the book in his hand. He looks up now and again and pauses. The book closes. His lips continue forming words and he stares at her intently. Her wine is finished. He takes the glass from her and sets it on the floor. His recitation continues.

— Kimberly Harding, *Harbinger*

~ ~ ~

THE AFTERNOON DRAGGED. We peeled and re-glued books in relative silence. Marc had a method behind deciding which cover to put with what guts, but I'll be damned if I could understand it. A few customers wandered in from the street. Most of them didn't stay long enough for the door to close behind them. Three people got lost in the winding passageways, two regulars actually bought something and a woman dropped off a sack of magazines.

Around two, Gil called out for directions out of the maze. Per usual, bewilderment had ultimately overwhelmed outrage. Marc led the poor man to the door. I grabbed a batch of books that needed homes. I surveyed my choices: there were three possible paths to take. I stepped resolutely into the middle tunnel. I inspected the books, looking up and down and side to side for empty spaces to shove books into. Before I knew it, the labyrinth had swallowed me.

It was a strange experience, scanning books based on anything but their covers, titles, authors or even subjects. I appreciated what my weirdo friend was trying to accomplish, but puzzled over how such a business idea could ever catch on with customers. Everyone *I* knew was way too busy to spend hours flipping through books until they found one they fancied. It wasn't the first time I had pondered his business model, but I couldn't deny that the place was popular.

I bumped into a handful of people wandering the pathways and tunnels, some perplexed, some smiling widely. Soon I came out of the tunnel and found myself at the back of the store again, a few feet from where I had entered the web.

A young woman stood chatting with Marcus, who appeared to be finished rearranging his inventory. She was a pretty, bookish type, or at least that was the look she was trying for with her wire-rimmed glasses and hastily tied-up hair. She suddenly gasped and placed a book on the counter as though she had forgotten she was holding it. It was the diary I had found the other day.

"How much is this?" she asked. She twirled a strand of hair that had been left out of the messy bun.

"Let's see," said Marc. He reached for the journal and flipped open the cover. "Hmm…no price. I guess it's free."

The young woman smiled politely at the stock joke. I rolled my eyes. Marcus grabbed a plastic bag from behind the counter. The bag bore the emblem of a nearby grocery store. "Just bring it back when you're finished."

The girl frowned and reached for the bag. She tucked it under her arm and dug in her purse. "I'm sorry, but I'm in a bit of a hurry. How much do I owe you?"

His spine stiffened. "I regret that you feel rushed, but as I said, it's not for sale. Just bring it back when you're done."

So the place was a library now.

She sighed and looked around the store for help. Her eyes fell on me. I shrugged and did my best to look sympathetic. Marc watched our exchange with a cocked eyebrow, then hoisted himself up to lean across the counter, as he had done with Gil. The man had no respect for personal space. He had done the same thing to me years ago when we first met. Their faces were less than a centimeter apart, noses almost touching. The woman shuffled her feet, wanting to retreat from the strangeness that is Marcus Mesinger, but she stood her ground.

"I don't have time for games," she said and set the book down. "Take your book back."

Marc was the first to break eye contact. He shook his head, then whispered something in her ear. She reddened and a slow, small smile bent her lips. She nodded and left. It seemed to me that her step was lighter. I also noticed that she had not taken the book with her.

Marc looked over at me again. "Hungry yet?" he asked.

"I could eat," I said and turned to peruse another heap that leaned against the wall. I heard the bell above the front door tinkle. I looked around. Marc had left.

I walked back into the maze and was lost within minutes. Similar passage-ways led to similar books. Eventually, the territory looked new. As I shuffled along, studying the tops of the stacks, my foot caught on the sprawling legs of an elderly woman who was snoozing in a beanbag chair tucked into a dead end of the maze. I grabbed for the bean bag chair to steady myself, but caught her leg instead. She shrieked and leapt into wakefulness, kicking as she did. I lurched backward and landed hard against the precarious tower of novels behind me.

It wobbled. I looked up. A hardbound edition teetered at the top of the pile and fell. I threw an arm in front of my face, but the corner of the book found its mark and dug into my brow.

~ ~ ~

The girl grips the pillow with both hands, claw-like. The man is propped on an elbow beside her, his body pressed against hers. Her elbows jerk and sway. His free hand is hidden beneath her skirt. He does not look at her face. Her breath comes in short bursts through wine-stained lips, quickens, gasps, holds.

He straddles her, pinning her legs to the sofa. Her back is arched, eyes open wide. He pushes her skirt up past her hips, and his hands continue up her ribcage, across her breasts, caressing her neck and jaw. His thumb brushes against her red lips. She inhales sharply and deeply. Her chest fills. He twines his fingers in the pearls at her neck. They gleam in the candlelight.

– Kimberly Harding, *Harbinger*

~ ~ ~

David Gaudrault

July 20, 1928

Most intriguing girl. You skinny little thing, perched on a ratty suitcase, pen in hand, gawking. It's not your affair, but I was kissing her for the last time. No wedding band, indeed! Who was the brute who jerked you to your feet and dragged you away? Presumably Gregory. Are you missing your confidante?

Aug. 2, 1928

Why do I keep going over your words? You are so young. Yet your face won't leave my mind. Not quite beautiful, but captivating nonetheless.

Aug. 10, 1928

Clara Strachan. You are 18 years old. A runaway from another world. How cruel to deprive your family of your fire. You left them with barely a thought. You used Gregory and ditched him in a heartbeat. You are calculating and cold.

I think not. You attract me.

Aug. 22, 1928

You contradict yourself with every breath.

Aug. 26, 1928

Your zest for life rejuvenates me and it wears me out. With dread I wait for the day that you drop me. I am losing myself in a girl. When will you become a woman?

Aug. 31, 1928

Your face, in sleep, stops me. Wet hair sticks to your cheek. Your back gleams with sweat. I was wrong. You are beautiful. I am a damned man.

~ ~ ~

Chapter 2

The sun slanting in the window illuminates half of the woman's face. One pupil contracts against the brightness while the other remains wide in the shadow. Her companion sips a beer and avoids her eyes. His hand rests on a book on the bar.

– Kimberly Harding, *Under Her Wing*

The Diviner

Marcus still hadn't returned when I regained consciousness. I knew almost immediately because, once I pulled myself into a sitting position, I could see from one end of the long, narrow store to the other. When I had slumped against the unsteady stack, I must have knocked it over, triggering a domino effect. Knee-high heaps of rare books, classics, pictorials, encyclopaedias and anthologies surrounded me and covered every inch of the floor.

Hands over my face, I hyperventilated a little.

Something moved to my left. I looked over to see an aged arm emerge from a pile of comic books. The mound heaved as the owner of the appendage struggled to be free. I scrambled over to help. Shoving aside the mangled masses of pulp, I uncovered the woman who had been sleeping. I judged her to be in her eighties. At least.

"Are you alright?" I asked as I helped her stand, kicking aside torn pages to clear some floor space.

"Fine, fine, fine." She slapped my hands away and straightened her granny-square shawl. Under the shawl, she wore purple harem pants and a black leather bustier. No kidding. She looked around the store and whistled. "Shit. Marc's gonna kill you."

We introduced ourselves.

"You're bleeding," said Rebecca, and pulled a balled-up paper towel from her pants pocket to wipe my forehead. "It was only a matter of time, I suppose. This place was a disaster waiting to happen."

Now that I could see all four walls, I realized that the store was a lot smaller than it had seemed. The woman finished wiping the blood from my face. With some aid from me, she knelt to root through the books at my feet.

"Here's the culprit," she said, lifting the bloodied bomb. It was a small volume by Kimberly Harding. "I think this book wants you to take it home."

I took the book and steadied Rebecca as she climbed back to her feet. Interestingly, the contents matched the cover.

Rebecca snatched up my free hand and splayed my fingers. "Small hands, strong fingers, flexible. That's good. You're artistic and open to new ideas." She turned my palm toward her, rubbing gently with her fingertips. I tried to retract it, but she gripped and massaged. "Relax," she said and peered at the lines.

She was lovely. Her pale skin was carved around the bright blue eyes and small mouth with a pleasing effect. This was a woman who had laughed a lot.

"Your index finger is short. You're shy, but it doesn't take a psychic to know that. Oh my, look at your little finger! The last phalange is the longest of all. You're a storyteller," she murmured and smiled. "You'll live a long life well into your eighties, but it won't always be easy. There's a break in your lifeline, just before middle age. Some kind of stress is soon going to take a heavy toll. Take care of yourself because you have a purpose in this life. See? Your fate line. Not everyone has one." She massaged the fleshy part of my palm with her thumb. "This is your Mount of Venus. It tells me about your capacity to love."

I could smell lilac, and wondered if she used scented shampoo. Her dappled-grey, still-damp braid hung over one shoulder past her knees. The last straggly foot or so was still its original red.

"You love deeply and for life. Your heart line is straight and strong, but it ends early, around thirty." She glanced up at my face and frowned. "Maybe forty." Then she turned my hand, closing my fingers to peer at the base of my little finger. "Only one long-term relationship. That's rare these days."

The bell above the front door of the store jingled. Marcus was back. He whistled when a flood of books slid out to cover his feet. "Rude," he said, and waded into the store.

~ ~ ~

She grasps a corner of the diary and tugs. He resists. She grazes his chin with the nails of her other hand and murmurs. He relents and pushes the book toward her. She picks it up, swivels in her seat and turns her full face toward the sun.

– Kimberly Harding, Under Her Wing

~ ~ ~

THE SUN HUNG LOW in the sky, and the house was dim when I got home. I had stayed a few hours at *Prospero's* to help with the clean-up. It was the least I could do after destroying the place. Determining that I was the culprit behind the avalanche, Marc elicited a promise from me to return the following Saturday to continue digging the place out. I dropped my bag and tossed my jacket on the banister.

"Cherise?"

No answer. I remembered it was Saturday. Girls' night out. I sighed and went to the kitchen where I yanked open the refrigerator door to stare blankly at the crowded shelves. Cherise's *girls* were a motley collection of shaved heads, army boots and tattoos. Loud, crude and angry, the girls often abducted her after a Saturday shift to take her to house parties and booze cans in a transparent attempt to keep her away from me. The girls detested me with every fiber of their collective being. The official excuse was a misguided joke on my part about the definition of misogyny at some time in the past year, although no one seemed to be able to recall the details. I was sure it was because Cherise loved me. No one could understand it, least of all me, but her affection for the outsider had caused a deep, abiding resentment.

I knew how it would go. They would take her somewhere after hours, get her liquored up and stoned and flirt outrageously. They would take turns buying her shots and hitting on her and continually dropping insults on my absent head. Then, some time just before dawn, Cherise would totter into the bedroom fabulously drunk and horny. She would climb on top of me and regale me with the night's laughter and insults while we had mutually unsatisfying sex. She would get frustrated, then nauseous and bolt to the bathroom to vomit up the bilious mix of scotch, beer, vodka and any number of sexually explicit shooters. I would wash her face and help her back to bed where she would sleep until noon while I cleaned the bathroom, picked up her clothes and made coffee.

I loved Cherise, but I hated girls' night out.

I puttered around for part of the evening, tidied the kitchen and picked up Cherise's tools from where she'd been rewiring an outlet. I poked my head into the upstairs bedroom to check her progress. The dry-walling was done and the crown molding lay on the floor beside a miter saw. The room was really taking shape. I found cans of paint in the newly-built closet—lavender.

The house belonged to Cherise's parents, who let her live there for free in return for the renovations. She had started it two years ago, a year before she met me, and so far, between shifts at the bar, she had finished the attic, the master bedroom and en suite bathroom. It was still unclear whether her parents planned to sell the house, move in or rent it to their daughter when the work was completed, but Cherise figured it would take at least another year. They didn't know I lived there, too.

I spent the rest of the night reading the book that had knocked me out. *Meander* by Kimberly Harding was about a runaway named Susan. The story opened in a cottage where the heroine was kept sheltered by her father. She eventually escaped and journeyed to a golden kingdom where she met the king and queen. In a public relations effort, the royals invited Susan to live with them in the castle. They taught her to read and write, and educated her about art and philosophy. She learned how to sing and play the harpsichord and was soon entertaining the courtiers and servants. She became popular in the kingdom and word spread about her great talent with music.

I got almost halfway through the story, and finally crashed sometime after midnight. Sleep came fast and hard, black oblivion free of dreams. The sun was high when I woke the following morning. Cherise's side of the bed was cold and crumpled. Her clothes were neatly laid over the chair.

I found her in the kitchen drinking coffee and reading. The book was *Meander*.

"Morning, Babe," she said. "Coffee's on."

"I didn't hear you come in last night," I croaked around my morning throat. I splashed the hot, dark liquid into a cup and gulped.

"I got in about three. You were sleeping like a rock."

"Rocks don't sleep. How are you feeling?" I slumped into a chair across from her.

"Really great," she said, smiling brightly. "It almost doesn't seem like Sunday without a hangover. Hey, this book is really good. Princess wandering the woods. Very Jungian."

"You didn't drink last night?"

"Nah, just pot. What a difference. Let's do something."

I grimaced and watched her face fall. "Can't. I have to mark papers. Sorry."

She shrugged and looked back down at the book. "S'okay. I'll start the crown."

"Cherise, I'm sorry. I meant to do it yesterday, but something came up."

"S'alright." She closed the book and stood, squeezed my shoulder as she passed by my chair. "Next time."

~ ~ ~

The tiny bloody form flops forward. Large hands cradle it, flip it, then suspend it. At the smack, it opens its mouth wide and gulps. The chest fills and the arms flail. Purple skin lightens to pink and the baby's face contorts into his first wail.

– Kimberly Harding, *Under Her Wing*

~ ~ ~

I ARRIVED AT *Prospero's* early the following Saturday morning to help with the clean-up. The door was locked, but I heard music from inside, so I knocked. To my surprise, Rebecca, the woman I had dug out of the wreckage, opened the door. I didn't recognize the place.

"Wow, you got a lot done in a week," I said.

Rebecca beamed and walked me around the store. Marcus had ripped random pages from the damaged volumes and used them as wallpaper, covering over the holes created by the crash and tumble. Tables suggested a grid pattern. Shelves leaned against the wall, waiting to be installed, the wet blue paint shining in the slats of sunlight that filtered between the sheets of paper on the windows. Marc emerged from behind the counter with an electrical cord in his hand.

"What's left?" I asked.

"All in good time. I want to show you something first." He disappeared again. I heard a click, and the store lit up. Multi-coloured lights hung in tangled bunches from the freshly painted ceiling. Red and green lights flanked the now aptly-named aisles. The counter glowed blue through its glass top. Every flat surface was outlined with tiny beacons. The effect was stunning.

"Have yourself a psychedelic Christmas," Rebecca sang. Her voice wasn't bad. Bluesy.

Marcus grinned.

"It actually looks like a book store now," I said. Marc's smile morphed into a scowl.

The three of us worked all morning. Marc danced on top of the step ladder, painting swirls and funny faces on the ceiling, singing to the music that burst out of the radio. Rebecca sanded and painted the chairs that would populate the reading nook. I organized the books by subject, author and title, of all things. I offered to catalogue them while I was at it, but Marcus scoffed. Too much too soon.

Around noon, Marc went on a coffee run. While Rebecca fiddled at a table with her tarot cards, I propped myself behind the counter to read more of *Meander*. I sat on the stool and leaned back with my feet on a crate. Rebecca sang Christmas carols as she laid out the cards. The repeated snap of cardboard against tabletop irritated me, but I kept reading.

"Hmm," said Rebecca, breaking out of *Oh Holy Night*. "The Hierophant."

I looked up to find her staring at me through narrowed eyes. "What?"

"Nothing." But she didn't look away.

Whatever. I was beginning to really like Rebecca, but she was out there. She made me nervous with her pregnant glances, even though I was sure she didn't know as much as she thought. I kept my hands in my pockets when she was close, although I didn't believe she was psychic. Marcus disagreed with me. They had apparently been acquainted for years, old family friends or something. I hadn't asked for the details.

I readjusted myself on the hard stool. I had to place my feet back on the floor to pull the stool away from the wall. That's when I noticed the book on a lower shelf underneath the counter. It was the diary that pretty girl had discarded. I picked it up and gazed at the filthy cover. I decided to keep it for awhile.

Around two o'clock, Rebecca called it a day. "Kal, come with me," she said and looped her arm in mine. "You've done enough today and I want someone to walk with." Industrial music blared from a portable stereo at Marc's feet as he busied himself with a drill and the last of the shelves.

"Marcus, we're leaving!" Rebecca bellowed over the din. He looked over his shoulder at us and winked.

We stepped outside into the bright sunshine. Rebecca bent over and grabbed handfuls of her long, filmy white skirt, then tucked the bunches into the waistband.

The hem rode around her knees. The sun turned the bristly grey hairs on her calves a shining silver.

"Mother, that racket!" she said as we continued down the street. "I'm a music fan, but I can only take so much of that stuff."

I agreed.

"So, Kal, what do you think happened last week? The books. The crash. What do you think triggered it?" she asked.

"Oh, well, I guess I must have leaned against a pile of books and they fell. Then they hit another pile and knocked them over."

"Really." She turned to fondle a cantaloupe at the fruit stand we were passing. "Humph. Too ripe." She dropped the melon.

"Do you have another theory?" I asked as we resumed walking.

"I suppose not, but don't you think it's odd that all the books were arranged just so? Every single one of them ended up on the floor. That's quite a chain reaction."

"It is a hell of a coincidence," I answered.

We turned down a side street and walked in silence for a few blocks. Tall and narrow Victorian townhouses, all painted in bright shades of blue, yellow and burgundy lined the street. Crocuses poked through the last crispy wisps of snow, purple, yellow and white, in tiny front gardens. We took another right and the gardens stretched farther back from the sidewalk. Bright yellow forsythias flanked elegant walkways, and the houses, all detached, became larger and statelier as we strolled.

"Well, here I am," Rebecca said after a time. "I'm having tea with a friend. Thanks for the escort."

She left me standing on the street feeling as if I had missed something.

~ ~ ~

The diary lays open in the woman's lap, but she does not read. Her blue dressing gown falls open to reveal a red slip beneath. She is contemplative, her face serene, her eyes far away. She doesn't respond to the knock. The second rap at the door breaks into her reverie, and she starts. The book slides from her knees. She stands, leaving the journal on the floor, and moves to the door.

– Kimberly Harding, *Under Her Wing*

~ ~ ~

REBECCA'S WORDS ABOUT fate stayed with me. Within days, two books had come to me under the weirdest of circumstances. I camped at the library for a couple of evenings, scouring the internet, combing through birth and death certificates, maps of Ontario, newspaper archives and legal databases. I slept little, saw Cherise only in passing. Curiosity quickly turned to obsession.

Clara Strachan was born in 1910 in rural Southern Ontario. Her parents, Hans and Ada, were second-generation immigrants from Germany. She had two brothers, born 1900 and 1902. Two younger sisters had died in infancy. On June 27, 1928, Clara Strachan had disappeared without a trace. Her mother died five years later from pneumonia. Her brothers took wives in the meantime. One moved to Berlin, Ontario, now called Kitchener; the other to Saskatchewan. The family property was sold when the father died in 1955.

Clara Strachan, the would-be writer, never published anything. She never made the newspaper. She had never been to court, never owned a house, never married. Besides the diary itself, her trail went cold as soon as she left home. Clara Strachan seemed to have dropped off the face of the earth.

I turned my attention to Kimberly Harding.

~ ~ ~

The hollow-eyed man shivers in the freezing November rain. A bassinet with a blanket thrown over it dangles from one hand. The woman ushers him into the house and takes the basket from his wet, white-knuckled grip. She pulls the sopping blanket off the bassinet and kneels. Reaching inside, she lifts the sleeping child and cradles him. The woman's eyes meet the man's. She nods, tight-lipped, and he leaves.

— Kimberly Harding, *Under Her Wing*

~ ~ ~

Daniel

April 13, 1941
Peter is my given name. My last name doesn't count bec
have just learned that Beth is not my real mother,

April 27, 1941
Beth is not the name she was given at birth. She says
temporary until we're old enough to listen for and
Universe. I haven't heard mine yet, but Beth says

May 7, 1941
I may hear it in a dream, or a whisper in my ea
book or see it on a sign. It is never the same fo

May 15, 1941
Beth gave me this diary to work out my tho
mysterious birth. She said that it is natural to fe
emotions, but to write about them so I can
control me. I am not angry and I don't see

June 3, 1941
The woman I thought was my mother is no
anything, it is sadness. I am melancholy th
those are traits that I would like to inherit

June 6, 1941
The sadness is fading. Now, I find that I
woman and man who wrote in this diary
answer. She said that Clara and David w

June 30, 1941
She often speaks vaguely. I thought I shou
have more experience. I may understand
one question per day, so I have to save th

July 17, 1941
I have been reading about other children
by accident. Oedipus murdered his fat
was their son. When he learned the tru
eyes.

August 5, 1941
Moses, from the Christian Bible, was put
river. He grew up to lead his people out
my life when I grow older.

August 11, 1941
I think Beth is a witch. I saw he
didn't understand. At first I thoug
in her throat. She poured the liqui
jar. That's not all, though.

September 10, 1941
The ugly duckling grew up to beco
found another swan and went
beautiful.

September 12, 1941
Rapunzel was stolen from her pare
greens in a witch's garden. Her lov
cut off.

September 28, 1941
Rumpelstilzken wanted the princ
gold. He made a deal with her
guess his real name. I wond
my name.

October 13, 1941
I am frightened. I woke u
was standing over me wi
name spell.

October 31, 1941
My birthday is in two weeks.
warrior, or leader. I don't
have decided on Dani

~ ~ ~

Chapter 3

A breeze ripples the tall grass of the field. The naked girl shivers beside her sleeping lover. He stirs but doesn't wake. With a tentative hand she breaks the stem of a daisy that grows close to where his tousled head rests. She watches his eyelashes flutter against his cheeks as she brushes the flower head against the pinkening skin of his chest. In sleep, he swats at the bloom.

– Karl Hanson, *Genetrix*

The Mother

"Kal, pack up. We're closing." Debbie, the librarian, thumped a hand on the back of my chair.

"Right now?" I asked, still reading.

"Now. Let's go."

"Nice customer service." I slammed the book shut and glared at her. I knew I was on thin ice with her, but I couldn't help myself. She irked me. She bustled around with that big bum of hers, sighing and tut-tutting, scolding and eye-rolling. Queen of the stacks. I was sure she was the reason I couldn't find half the books I needed for my course work and research. She crossed her arms and tapped a foot.

"Alright, I'm going." I had completely lost track of time. Three hours curled in a chair at the library reading the odd diary. Cherise would be angry that I had missed dinner again, but I just couldn't put it down. Something about it seemed so familiar.

The first intact page bore the date June 27, 1928 and the signature of Clara Strachan, a foolish runaway who had come seeking fame in Toronto. The next entry after her last was made one day later by a man calling himself David Gaudrault. I inferred from his writings that he had stolen the diary from the steps of Union Station on the day of Clara's arrival in Toronto. In just over a month, he found her again, welcomed her to the city and seduced her. The next few pages were printed in a child's hand, but the pages were ripped down the middle making it difficult to piece together.

Since then, more than twenty different people had written in Clara's diary. Over seven decades, Clara's first impressions in her grand adventure passed from person to person, were read and added to.

At first I thought the contributors to Clara's diary no better than graffiti artists, reading and defacing private property. But, the progression from one story to the next, one style of handwriting beside another, one person's pain to another's joy developed a rhythm in my mind. The writing wasn't particularly good, and the stories weren't immediately vivid, but the collection bore a simple honesty that hinted at truths.

On my way out the door, with Debbie on my heels, I glanced at the clock. Past nine. Cherise was going to be very upset with me.

~ ~ ~

The girl drops the flower and pushes a blonde lock behind her ear. She braces herself on an elbow and reaches across the prostrate boy to feel under his clothes lying in the grass. She locates the leather case. Her fingers fumble with the buckle, but she soon opens it and pulls out the journal.

– Karl Hanson, *Genetrix*

~ ~ ~

CHERISE WAS IN BED reading when I got home. I stood at the foot of the bed and pulled off my clothes. She didn't look up from her book, something about Eastern philosophy.

"You're in bed early," I said as I crawled in beside her. I put my head on her shoulder. She turned the page. "How was your day, love?"

She shrugged and shifted. My head hit the mattress. I found her shoulder and nuzzled. "Ross is pushing me pretty hard about my thesis topic. I have to hunker down."

I felt her stiffen beside me. "You're still coming to the art show with me, right?" Art show? Right. One of the *girls* was a sculptor. We had agreed a week ago to attend. I expected loads of lumpy, unfinished female nudes.

"We'll see." I reached out to pull her to me, but she bolted upright and flung the covers from my naked body. "Cherise—"

"Surely you can take a couple of hours off to spend with me. Jesus, Kal! You're not even writing the damn thing yet." She was on her feet, pacing. I watched her shadow move back and forth on the moonlit wall. "What's it going to be like when you start doing some real work?"

"*Real* work?" I sat up. "You think I've been fucking around?"

"How would I know what the hell you've been doing? I never see you." She gathered the blankets into her arms and left the room. "I'll be on the couch."

"Cherise!"

Heavy footsteps on the stairs.

"Cherise! I'll come to the damned show, okay? Come back to bed."

I heard the couch springs squeak, blankets rustle, then muffled sobbing.

"Cherise?"

~ ~ ~

The girl lies on her back, alone in the snowy field. The diary, wrapped in plastic, balances on her pregnant belly. Her gloved fingers are laced, palms cradling that precious roundness. Radiating from her body in the whiteness is the impression of a snow angel. A set of footprints track her path to this spot, deep blue imprints in the glowing expanse. A shadow darkens her face and shoulders.

– Karl Hanson, *Genetrix*

~ ~ ~

"I HOPE YOU have good news for me, Winters."

Professor Ross reclined behind his desk. He had his feet elevated and tapped at a keyboard in his lap. His vast face glowed from the rays coming out of his computer screen.

"Literacy rates are improving among school children," I offered as I seated myself in front of my thesis adviser.

"Have you got a topic for me to approve?"

Nail picking. "Archetypal imagery. Maybe."

"Specifically…?"

"Generally."

He sighed, lowered his feet to the floor, leaned his meaty elbows on the desk and glared at me. "*Generally* isn't specific enough."

"Come on, Michael. I'm still exploring my options." I tweezed a hangnail with my fingernails and yanked. Instant burning and a bead of blood that eased into the edges of the nail bed. I stuck the finger in my mouth.

"Kal, you've been exploring for two years. I need something more concrete from you. A study of archetypal figures is a start, but so was water imagery in 20th century literature. Any of the dozen topics you've suggested are fine, but you really need to focus. I can understand your hesitation, Kal. I've been there, but it's getting ridiculous. Most people have something in mind before they start a Ph.D."

"I couldn't think of anything original to say about water." Still sucking.

"How about archetypes? There is an abundance of information out there. I hope you don't pour your heart into research, then decide that it's all been said before. Kal, I need you to get serious and soon. Come back in two weeks with a proposal. That will be your topic. No backing out. Are we clear?"

I lowered my hand and watched a drop of blood soak into my pants. "Two weeks?"

"Do you have the essays marked yet?"

"About half of them. I thought you didn't need them until next week."

"On my desk in the morning." He leaned back again and put his feet up. Meeting adjourned.

~ ~ ~

The girl lifts a hand to her eyes and squints. The red hair of the woman who stands over her glows with a halo of sunrays. The girl struggles into a sitting position and lifts the book, offering it up to the woman.

– Karl Hanson, *Genetrix*

~ ~ ~

WHEN I GOT HOME, Cherise was dusting. Never a good sign.

"When are they coming?" I asked when she turned to flash me her sweetest smile.

"Who?"

"Your parents."

The feather duster flitted across the top of the television and down the sides. "What makes you think they're coming?"

I didn't bother to respond. This was a familiar game, but I didn't feel like playing. She flicked the chicken feathers over the coffee table, the bookstand and the baseboards. The kettle whistled in the kitchen. I moved to get it, and passed Cherise where she bent over the couch to catch the cobwebs with her snare. She glanced up at me through thick lashes and quickly away. I goosed her as I passed.

I grabbed the kettle from the element and turned off the stove. Her cup was ready on the counter, beside the box of teabags: *St. John's Wort flavoured with mint. Effective for mild anxiety.* That meant they were coming today. I poured the boiling water over the bag, then walked back into the living room.

Cherise had climbed the bookshelf to run the duster across the aged crown molding. I caressed her ankle and ran my hand up the inside of her calf.

"Don't let them get to you, okay? You know I love you."

"Mm-hmm," she said and started to hum.

"I'll get out of here," I said to save her the trouble of trumping up an excuse for me to leave the house. "We'll go to the art show on the weekend and have a great time together. Your tea is steeping on the counter." She tiptoed across the shelf, holding on with one hand, and stretched to reach the corner. "Don't wait up for me."

She was still humming when I went back through the front door. It slammed more loudly than I intended.

~ ~ ~

By the end of the week I had exhausted my options at the library. I had sat up all night reading Kimberly Harding's *Under Her Wing* and only slept for a couple hours before an idea pried me out of sleep. I wandered down to the kitchen and dug the phone book out of the drawer. I assumed that Gaudrault was dead and I didn't know Peter's last name, but the next writer, Myrtle Ellerington, was listed as M.W. Ellerington. I jotted down the address, chugged a pot of coffee and went to see her.

The house was set back from the road, mostly hidden by a large cedar hedge. As I passed through the front gate, I avoided the eyes of a man who walked his dog on the sidewalk in front of the house. I ducked behind the hedge and shut the gate behind me.

The front lawn was an expansive clutter of trellises held vertical by knotted, dying vines, rusted metal sculptures of dancing children, and decayed wooden compost bins. The hedge, I thought, was for the neighbours rather than the homeowner. I went to the front door and rapped my stinging knuckles on it.

I didn't wait long before the door flew open. The foyer was dark to my contracted eyes, and I couldn't see who had answered my knock. I squinted and made out a staircase, a mirror, and a hall tree heavy with coats.

"Hello?" I heard a small voice ask from somewhere about waist level. I looked down and met the brown eyes of a child. She twirled her skirt and fidgeted on her feet, rolling onto her ankles, then onto the soles of her black patent shoes, then back onto her ankles. She sucked in her cheeks and bit down, flashing fish lips at me while she waited for me to speak.

"I'm looking for Myrtle Ellerington," I said. I was never good with children.

"Wait here," the little girl told me and flung the door shut in my face.

I waited. Ten minutes passed before Myrtle opened the door. From the dates in the diary I knew she had to be in her seventies, but she looked much younger. Her short blond hair had barely begun to fade. Her movements were lithe and her dress draped from still-firm curves. I introduced myself.

"What can I do for you?" she asked.

"Do you know Clara Strachan?"

"Well," she said. "Well, well, well."

"You do know her, then?" I pressed.

"Clara Strachan," she said. Her mouth formed the name slowly, and it came out on a breath.

I shrugged out of my backpack and plunked it onto the porch. I dug out the diary and held it up to her. "Do you remember this book?"

She gasped and reached for the book and me with both arms. She ushered me into the foyer and closed the front door. She took the diary and ran gentle fingers over the cover.

"Have you written in it yet?" she asked

"Why would I?"

"That's what it's for, dear."

She took me by the elbow and led me through the house into the kitchen. It was the old-fashioned kind, with a cast-iron stove, a butcher's block and copper pots hanging from the ceiling. She pulled an apron from a hook and tied it at her waist.

"The little girl that answered the door... Is that your granddaughter?" I asked. Myrtle stirred something on the stove.

"Great granddaughter," she said. From the counter beside her she grabbed a handful of chopped herbs and sprinkled them into the pot, still stirring. She looked over her shoulder at me and winked. "I love the sound of that: *great* granddaughter. Do you have children, Kal?"

"No."

"Not yet."

"Not ever."

She left the stove and retrieved a bowl from a rustic-looking china hutch. Into the bowl, she ladled soup from her cooking pot and placed it in front of me. She gave me a spoon, and ripped a chunk of bread from a loaf that sat on the table. "You don't like children?" she asked and placed the bread in front of me.

"It's not that—"

"It never is, dear. Eat your soup."

She left me alone while I slurped. Her soup was delicious. I gathered that she had grown the herbs and vegetables herself, since I could see a large greenhouse out of the kitchen window. During the brief trip from front door to kitchen, I had glanced into different rooms and seen that the house was littered with plants of all varieties. Most of the plants were in hanging baskets, since every available surface was covered with framed photographs.

The photos in the kitchen all featured children. I plucked one picture from the china hutch and placed it on the table in front of me so I could study it while I ate. I recognized Myrtle, much younger, and very pregnant. She sat in a garden, with a little boy in her lap and a girl, older than the boy, standing to the side, clutching Myrtle's arm. It was black and white, probably taken in the fifties judging by the dress Myrtle wore. She was radiant, but her daughter scowled at the camera. I thought it was an odd choice for framing.

Myrtle returned just as I gulped down the last mouthful of soup. She took my bowl, handed me a serviette and sat down across from me. She folded her hands on the tabletop and said, "What would you like to know, Kal?"

"What was she like?"

"Who?"

"Clara."

Myrtle frowned and shrugged. "I never met her."

"How did you get the diary, then?"

"I stole it." She chuckled. "My boyfriend Danny always had it with him, but wouldn't let me read it. So I took it one day. That's the way I was back then. Spoiled rotten. He thought he lost it."

"Do you know who he got it from?"

"No, I don't."

I reached for the book and turned to the end of Myrtle's writing. I spun the book and pushed it toward her. "Did you give it to Dr. van Horne when you were finished with it?"

She gasped and sat forward, peering at the markings on the page in front of her. "Derek van Horne? He wrote in there? Well, I'll be... I looked after his son for a little while after his wife died. Shame what happened to that poor boy."

"You knew him, but you didn't give him the diary? How did he get it?"

She shook her head and clucked. "So many questions, Kal. And you haven't added your own story. Does it matter how it came to us? Or what became of Clara? Some mysteries are beautiful."

"You can't tell me?"

"I can tell you only what I know. A woman came to me, just before my daughter was born. She said she was Daniel's guardian and asked me to give the diary back. I handed it over and never saw it again. Until now, of course."

"Wasn't Daniel the father?"

"It's possible, but I never told him. The situation was…difficult."

I thanked her for lunch and walked back through the hallway to the front door. She patted me on the shoulder as I stepped outside and said, "Write down your story, Kal. You never know who may benefit from your experience."

~ ~ ~

Myrtle

May 5, 1944

Oh! If only the story of Clara and David had an ending! Perhaps Danny was that ending. I'm sure he would be embarrassed to know I read his childish worries. But I am held in thrall by this magic book and will not give it back. I believe it was meant to change hands. My hands are as deserving as any.

What shall I write about? Certainly not my own dreary life! Shall I invent my own escape from drudgery as did Clara? That does sound silly, doesn't it? How can I hope to compare to that free-spirit, born with the courage to choose her own way in life, to follow her own path when the one set out for her was so dull?

But, what an awful start! An adventure story should not start with lamentations. I believe it should start with a quest, a goal, a determination to prevail. I'll have to turn to my mathematics now, and think about a better way to begin my epic.

May 8, 1944

There once lived a princess who locked herself in a high tower and held her breath until everyone left her alone….

That's a better beginning. Let the princess save herself for once, I say. Let her become Queen without having to first marry a prince. Oh, I do wish I could have read Clara's essay about God's true intention for woman. If only I could ask her about it. I'm sure we have much in common.

She didn't want to get married, and neither do I. She had an overbearing father, and so do I. She wanted to be a writer, and she followed that goal. I, too, want something very badly, but for the first time, it isn't something I can ask Father to buy for me.

I want a baby.

May 16, 1944

I will have a baby. I found a medical book in the library today. My goodness. It turns out that I'm on the right track with Daniel.

July 19, 1944

I'm starting to worry that Danny may not be my best choice. Although Danny is good-looking and sweet, he is superstitious and has an awful temper. I'm sure he will try to take a dominant role in my child's life. I cannot have that. I will not have it.

July 31, 1944

This morning, the gardener (Frederick?) ogled me. At breakfast, Chester's eyes were less than innocent as he leaned over to take my plate. Neither will do. Frederick is dull and Chester has the weakest chin I've ever seen on a man.

My tutors are even less appealing. Mr. Pendleton is too old. Mr. Nielson is too fat. Mr. Williams is married. Mr. Hayes smells terrible and never combs his hair. Mr. Gooding has a horribly pasty complexion that I fear hints at a bad heart. Mr. Silverman is far too serious and has no imagination. Finally, Mr. Elliott always smells like liquor.

August 3, 1944

I am a dolt! I cannot believe that I forgot M. Valeur, the French tutor! The moment he arrived today, I wanted to pinch myself. He is perfect. He is handsome, quiet and sensitive. I believe that he must have a poetic nature with such soulful eyes.

I have decided to hide a note for him in my next set of lessons. The note must be perfect so he doesn't think I have a silly crush on him, and not too forward so he won't think me loose. I am sure, though, that with the right amount of flirtation, I will have my stud.

August 18, 1944

Success! I found a reply to my note (en francais!) in my lessons. It took me nearly an hour to interpret it, but the message is clear now. We met yesterday afternoon at his apartment.

August 30, 1944

Perfect success! I am pregnant! I am so happy. I want to tell the world that I am going to be a mother. I have to contain myself. I have four months before I start to show, and in that time, I must get rid of M. Valeur. I wonder if he misses France?

September 20, 1944

I feel ill just about every day between 10:30 and noon, but I really don't mind. For the time being, I am able to hide any signs that I am pregnant. I have also noticed that my breasts are tender, and the nipples have darkened a little.

October 14, 1944

I might be crazy, but I'm sure I felt Clara moving today. (Yes, I am going to name my little girl after the one who inspired her conception.)

November 4, 1944

Already it seems that my clothes are fitting tighter. I will have to tell Mother and Father very soon that I am carrying a child. I will not marry. I want my own life.

November 25, 1944

I told them today. Father was angrier than I've ever seen him. Instead of yelling, he grew quiet and pale. Mother went into a flutter and needed help into a chair.

I breathed not a syllable of the father's name nor of my own conviction to remain a spinster.

December 16, 1944

The past few weeks have seen this house turn to mayhem. My belly grows wider and fatter with each passing day. Along with it grows Father's determination. He has interviewed the male staff three times apiece. M. Valeur performed admirably.

Only Danny squirmed, and not right away. My pregnancy was not obvious during the first interview, three weeks ago. Yesterday, however, Father called Danny into the study for a third interrogation. For the first time, Danny saw my belly. Father noticed Danny's reaction.

I do not know why, but I began to weep. I begged Father not to dismiss Danny, and insisted hysterically that Danny was not the one. Father set the wedding date. Danny left the study. Now I sit, locked in my room.

January 3, 1945

The wedding passed yesterday. I stood in white before the minister, with wet cheeks and a heaving belly. I fainted and Father had a maid prop me. We waited an hour for the groom. I have not changed my name. I am not chained to another person. I am not married.

Danny could not be found. Oh, Danny, I shall miss you, and I can never thank you enough for not loving me the way I thought you did.

January 9, 1945

Father dismissed the rest of my tutors. He confiscated my books, and I am not allowed to leave the estate. His attempt at tenderness was to revoke the order that kept me locked in my room, but I have not left.

I had my first visit from Dr. Bondi yesterday. He says the baby is too large. I have done everything to ensure the baby's health, but he is from an old school. Large babies are dangerous to the mother. I am hungry most of the time. Mother is softening towards me, and will have some food sent.

March 19, 1945

My interest in writing has waned in the past weeks. I listen inward, wrapped in Clara's silent messages to me through the blood we share, and the cord that connects us. She kicks most frequently in the morning after breakfast, and very often in the deep night, waking me from dreams of Danny. During the day, I imagine that I feel Clara's heartbeat. I feel her fingers exploring the walls of my womb. People are blurred. Dr. Bondi's advice drifts toward me, but I am barely cognizant of his frowning face. Soon, I will be a mother. Soon, I will have to defend my child against those who want to take her from me.

April 8, 1945

My daughter, Clara Andrea Ellerington is one week old. She arrived three weeks earlier than expected. She is beautiful, fat and healthy. No one tried to take her from me. Father has fallen in love, and Mother is so enamoured that she no longer cares what her friends think. It seems that Father might have been correct about something, however. Clara looks nothing like me. She is a duplicate of her father. She has his eyes, his nose and his strong jaw. She will be tall like him; tall, handsome and noble. Just like Danny.

~ ~ ~

Chapter 4

The father steps in front of the coffin, leans over it. He rests a hand on the lifeless fingers of his wife and kisses her ashen cheek. His eyes are closed. The little boy approaches and tugs on the man's jacket. The man sighs, then hoists the boy so that the child may see his mother.

– Karl Hanson, *Sire*

The Father

I TILTED MY HEAD and eased my ear closer to my shoulder. The tendons of my neck ached, but I pushed until I heard the satisfying pop in my neck, then relaxed my shoulders and repositioned the mouse pad.

I clicked on a promising link.

Kimberly Harding published her first short story in 1930 in the small literary journal, *Light Reading*. The story, called *Mark My Words*, went largely unnoticed at the time. She continued writing for the journal, and in 1932, the book that had struck me was released (a small collection of short stories, all based on a character named Susan). Harding's writing was marked by its strong fairy tale elements and impetuous characters. In 1938 her second book, *Harbinger*, hit the stands to mixed reviews. The critics couldn't pin her down, and they resented her experimental style. From one story to the next, something about her style changed. One critic dubbed her "the inky chameleon" and vowed never to touch another Harding publication. In 1943, she published *Under Her Wing*, her third and final book.

Three papers had been published on the subject of Harding's writing: an inadequate stylistic analysis, a foggy semiological interpretation, and a comparative psychological exploration. Several annotated versions of her short stories barely existed. The merit of her work remains undecided in literary circles, an annoying footnote to Canadian literature.

Little is known about Harding outside of her writing. She never gave an interview, never attended public readings, and never released any statements in rebuttal to the critics. She posed for a single publicity shot in 1932 after the modest success of her novel. This photograph, a full-length view of her reclining on a large tree branch, half of her face in shadow, appears on all of her book jackets. It is the only known photograph of the reclusive writer.

It may have been the only photograph Clara ever had taken. By now I was sure that Clara Strachan had changed her name to Kimberly Harding. I supposed it was to retain anonymity from a family that would never understand her choices. Each of the three books she had written corresponded beyond chance to the first three contributors to the diary, details lifted from its pages.

The first set of stories was autobiographical. *Meander* had to be about rejection notices from publishers. The other stories contained details of her experiences leaving home, ditching Gregory and kissing a man on the mouth in the street, among other moments that probably happened after she lost her diary.

My theory was that David Gaudrault, after having made the girl his lover, gave the diary back to her. The relationship turned sour. She left, probably angry. Then, I imagined, an idea formed and she picked up her pen.

Harbinger was about a Don Juan. He conducted walking tours of the city, meeting each group at Union Station. From the sightseers he handpicked pretty innocents that he later seduced with wine and poetry, then strangled.

I had no doubt that her affair with David had left Clara bitter.

Her last book, *Under Her Wing* told the story of a changeling raised by a witch. After David's entries, there was a thirteen-year gap before a boy called Peter began writing. This section of the diary was mangled. The ragged bits of paper that clung to the binding were blotted with what looked like mud. Only scattered phrases and the odd date were visible, but the few remaining words supported my thesis. His entries, made during several months in 1941, studied myths and legends that dealt with mysterious births, soothsayers and destiny. I was unsure how the diary fell into his hands, but I had a hunch that Clara had met him and was interested in his story. The success of her experience with using David's writings may have inspired her to loan the journal to Peter for him to pour out his heart. She reclaimed the book and turned the scribblings into a novel.

The diary's grip on me intensified and my preoccupation with it developed its own pulse. The thrill of making the connection between Clara and Kimberly Harding beat in the soles of my feet, surged behind my eyes. What I couldn't explain was why Kimberly Harding stopped writing when the diary kept on.

My internet search had so far yielded little more than frustration. Looking for Kimberly Harding, I had found personal web pages that belonged to a quilter in California, an Alpaca breeder in Massachusetts, a Scottish dominatrix, all of whom shared the writer's name. I had also come across a mind-boggling number of organizations trying to get my credit card number.

I drummed my fingers and waited for the next page to load.

"Come on, Kal," said Debbie behind me. "I've asked you a dozen times not to eat at the computer. You'll get crumbs in the keyboard."

I jammed the rest of my pizza slice into my mouth and chewed. Then I lifted the keyboard, flipped it and gave it a shake. I wiped the bits of fluff and crumbs from the desktop onto the floor and flashed Debbie a doughy grin. "Better?" I asked around my soggy mouthful and set the keyboard down.

Debbie sighed and put her hands on her bulbous hips. "You've just moved the mess."

"Whatever, Fusspot. I'm busy." I waved a dismissive hand. The hard drive had finished groaning and the page was loaded. It looked good.

Debbie turned on a heel and waddled away.

I refocused on the computer monitor. Kimberly Harding peered at me from the shadows of the tree she embraced. I scrolled down the page and learned that it had been mounted as a tribute to a misunderstood writer. It contained quotations from the author's stories, citations of literary references to her work, and a gushy essay by the web site owner outlining her harebrained interpretations of Harding's stories. At the end was a list of every piece Harding published. I recognized all but one of the titles: *Genetrix*.

I found it in the library catalogue. As I suspected, Kimberly Harding was not the author. I pulled the book from the stacks and gave it a glance. I could understand the web site owner's mistake in thinking Harding had written it. The simple style was similar and the fairy tale themes consistent. I figured that the author, Karl Hanson, had been influenced by Harding. I flipped through a few more pages, ready to replace the book on the shelf, when my eyes settled on a peculiar phrase: *She turned her attention inward, wrapped in the unborn child's silent messages to her through the blood they shared, the cord that connected them.*

I compared the passage to the diary, then perused more of *Genetrix*. The story was Myrtle's. The details exactly matched the entries she had made in the diary in the forties.

I went back to the catalogue and looked under the authors section for more works by Hanson. After *Genetrix* he wrote *Sire*, *The Minstrel* and *The Marriage*. I found *Sire* in the stacks and placed the other two on hold.

~ ~ ~

The woman crouches and speaks softly. She holds out a hand, but the little boy ducks behind his father's legs. Stern words and a rough grasp on the child's arm. The boy drags his feet, frowns, blinks wet eyelashes. He pulls against his father's hold and finally drops, kicking on his stomach, screaming into the floorboards. Calling for his mother.

– Karl Hanson, *Sire*

~ ~ ~

DR. VAN HORNE was sleeping when the nurse led me into the room. I backed up a few steps to leave, but the nurse stopped me with a wave.

"He'll wake up in a few minutes," she said. The old doctor snored in a chair by the window. He had proved harder to find than Myrtle. He wasn't listed in the phone book and seemed to have no family, but the staff at the hospital where he had worked for forty-three years had been helpful. "If you don't mind waiting, he'll be happy to have a visitor." She placed a blanket from the bed around his shoulders then breezed past me and out of the room.

I took a step farther into the room and looked around. It was small and tidy, befitting a nursing home. The pale yellow walls bore dozens of framed degrees, certificates and awards for years of work in the medical community. They gave the chamber the feel of a waiting room.

Opposite the pristinely tucked and turned bed was a wall filled with medical texts, journals and periodicals. I stepped toward it and dropped my bag. I perused the titles–*The Anatomy of This*, *The Biology of That*–and stopped at what appeared to be the only novel. *Sire*. I reached for it. My fingers were about to make contact with the leather binding when the old doctor coughed. I turned.

"May I help you?" he gasped around the phlegm in his airway, and resumed sputtering.

"Dr. van Horne. I'm Kal Winters."

I walked to his chair and we shook hands. He indicated that I should take a seat at the end of the bed.

"Ah, yes. The biography," he murmured. He turned to look out the window. "I think you'll be very pleased to know that I have prepared myself for this interview. It should run quite smoothly."

My stomach flipped over when the lie I had told the hospital staff settled back on me. It had seemed harmless at the time, a way to assuage their concern for the beloved old practitioner. Now, though, confronted with having to tell another fib to cover the first, and having to tell it to a feeble old man who had done only good in his life, I felt guilty.

He fumbled with the blanket. "Blasted nurse. It's too warm in here as it is."

"Shall we start with your relationship with the writer, Karl Hanson?" I didn't look him in the eye.

The doctor frowned and shifted in his seat. With a shaky hand he plucked a pair of glasses from the windowsill and positioned them on his nose. He lowered his chin and squinted at me above the rims.

"I'm sorry. Who?"

I went back to the shelf and grabbed the book. The leather cover felt warm in my hands, the metal corner protectors shone under the fluorescent lights, and the gold lettering glinted.

"The author of this novel," I said and placed the book in his lap.

He adjusted his glasses and picked it up. "Karl Hanson," he read. He handed it back to me. "It must have been a gift."

I opened the front cover. The first gold-trimmed page bore a penciled message: *May this offering to your son's memory serve to help you find the balance between will and ego, so that your empire may flourish. –K.*

"Do you remember who gave it to you?" I asked.

"Oh, my, no. I received any number of gifts over the years. Several books. I used to collect them, you see."

"You don't anymore?"

"Many of them were destroyed in a fire." He jerked in his chair and looked out the window again. His head wobbled over his shoulders and he worked his false teeth, in and out, sucking and popping. His wheezing grew louder.

I showed him the diary next. "Do you remember this book, sir? Was it part of your collection?"

He turned back to me, and I noticed that his eyes and cheeks were moist. When he saw the diary, his mouth dropped open and gaped in a silent sob. He reached shaking arms for it and hugged it to his chest. The blanket slipped to the floor as he rocked with the diary. Alarmed, I jumped toward him and put a hand on the book he cradled. I pried at his fingers, but they would not loosen.

The nurse came back.

A truncated scream escaped her when she saw me over the old man struggling with him, and she sprang forward and yanked me back by my shoulders. "What happened?" she barked.

"I showed him a book. He won't let go of it."

She checked him over, looking for injuries. "That's all?"

"I swear."

Dr. van Horne cried. The howl found its way out of him and filled the room. Two orderlies in white bustled in, and the nurse stepped aside for them. They wrestled the book from the old man and hoisted him up and onto the bed. Another nurse entered tapping a syringe.

The first nurse held the diary toward me. "You'll have to leave now," she said. Her eyes were hard.

"I didn't do anything to him."

"Just go. We'll handle this."

I accepted the book and shoved it back into my pack. Dr. van Horne quieted. The orderlies backed away from the bed. The needle exited his vein. "What did you give him?" I demanded.

The first nurse ushered me into the hallway, her fingers digging into my arm. "A sedative. He'll be fine," she said and closed the door in my face.

The library microfiche answered at least some of my questions. I found a handful of newspaper articles from the 1950s and 60s that mentioned Derek van Horne's appointments to various boards and committees, his involvement in charities, and other achievements. One article, dated August 11, 1971 caught my interest: *Doctor's son dead in fire. Arson suspected.*

~ ~ ~

The boy peeks from behind a curtain. One eye settles on his father at the big desk. He watches the man pause in his writing, grimace and drop the pen. The man drops his head onto his arms. His shoulders shake.

– Karl Hanson, *Sire*

~ ~ ~

SIRE, BY KARL HANSON, was a tired and transparent cautionary tale of an emperor, his golden heir and how their empire burned to the ground. It just about put me to sleep, but I read the whole thing, scouring it for signs of Clara or any of the other writers. It appeared to be an allegory for van Horne's tenuous relationship with his son. My mood darkened with each page turned. It was full of typographical and grammatical mistakes, the characters were devoid of emotion, motivation, or any qualities that could be called characteristics and the plot was a meticulous study in pissing off the reader. The repetition alone made me want to find the writer and beat him with a thesaurus. But I was sure Hanson and Harding were the same person, despite the devastating drop in quality. It wasn't unheard of for a writer to release a bad book.

With only a week to go before Ross started demanding my proposal again, this was frustrating. I had been hoping to find something in the diary that could lead me to a thesis. However, a string of badly written books under a series of pseudonyms had not yielded an academic line of inquiry. And I had wasted an entire week of research time. I knew I had to set it aside and concentrate on my school work, but I didn't want to.

~ ~ ~

Dr. van Horne

September 9, 1948

I buried my wife last week. How do you say good-bye to your heart? My dearest. What will Simon and I do without you? I was blind to the seriousness of the situation. I have lost you. Simon is excessively distressed by your sudden absence. He eats only a little, certainly not enough to sustain his young growing body. He calls for you repeatedly in the night and nothing will subdue him. We both suffer terribly from lack of sleep. I shall have to take a leave from the hospital until we two lonely souls can find a workable routine.

September 19, 1948

Angela, it's silly for me to address these notes to you, but I find comfort in it. This morning I did not reach for you when I awakened. So soon the body forgets. The hospital has generously granted me one month's leave, although I still attend various committee meetings in the afternoons. Simon does not like having me home during the day. He reminds me constantly of the way you handled the house, and is as helpful as he is angry. Next week I intend to interview nannies. So many applicants! It will take several days to check references.

October 8, 1948

After a string of depressingly inappropriate candidates, I have narrowed the list to three. Simon got into the habit of hovering during the interviews. I felt it important to see how the applicants got on with him. He disliked them all. Oh, if you were here to tell me how to handle his horrendous tantrums. I've never seen such an unruly child. Some days I cannot believe he is the same boy I call my son. I do hope it passes with his anguish.

October 30, 1948

We have been through no fewer than six nannies in the past weeks. I returned last week to my duties at the hospital, but cannot settle back into my routine. Every day I am called home to discipline the boy. Most times it is warranted, but twice, the calls were due to hysteria only. I fired those nannies on the spot, having to cancel my remaining appointments. The other four resigned after only a few days each. We cannot go on like this. Simon is a constant worry and he is wearing me out.

November 2, 1948

I am sending the child to boarding school. He is bit young for school, but the Director assures me that it will do the child good to occupy his mind with learning and a new environment, away from reminders of the mother he lost.

November 9, 1948

I feel so helpless in the face of my son's grief. He is home from school, crying in his room. He expected you to be here when he came back. The Lord only knows how the mind of a child works. Myrtle assures me that she can work with him and that it's good for him to be around other children. I can't escape the feeling that I am shirking my duties as a father, but I cannot fulfill my duties as a doctor as long as Simon is at home.

November 30, 1948

We have struck a deal, Simon and I. I will bring him back home when he is old enough to start at the public school. He has promised to do his best to curb his anger and I have promised to spend every Sunday, all day with him doing whatever he wants. He wants to visit you.

December 2, 1948

I took him to the cemetery today. I think he finally understands.

~ ~ ~

Chapter 5

The man sits in his chair with both hands raised. In one he holds a microphone. Across from him sit two younger men. He holds them rapt as he speaks into the microphone. Behind him lights blink and the tape rolls from one large reel to another.

— Karl Hanson, *The Minstrel*

The Expositor

After another frustrating morning at the library where I spent more time bickering with Debbie than actual research, I gave up and wandered with my newly borrowed book to *Prospero's*. Marc sat at the counter thumbing through a book and scribbling on the odd page. He looked up when the bells above the door tinkled.

"What fresh hell is this?"

"Dorothy Parker," I replied. "What are you doing?" I leaned on the counter to look at the book he had open before him.

"Scavenger hunt," he said. "You write something cute or pose a riddle, then say what page to turn to for more." He flipped several pages, smiled wickedly and wrote something upside down in tiny print. His tongue stuck out between pursed lips. I squinted: *There is only one 's' in Christopher Reeve.* Okay.

I left him to his 'work' and flopped into a beanbag chair in the reading nook. I pulled out the book I had signed out of the library. "Do you have the time?" I asked.

"Uh, four-something, I think," Marc answered. Five hours before I was supposed to meet Cherise at the art show. I hadn't bothered going home because I knew she was working. Five hours in which I could be writing a thesis proposal. It wouldn't hurt to read for half an hour before I got started. The book was *The Minstrel,* in which Karl Hanson presented the rise and fall of a rock star. The singer filtered the word of God to the masses. No one recognized the music as gospel. No one claimed the singer had the voice of an angel. No one could even remember the singer's name, yet the lyrics left a positive and lasting impression. Right. How could Hanson refer to the protagonist as a rock *star* when no one had heard of him? I sighed.

Two hours later, I finished the last cheesy page with a sniff just as Marc returned and placed a coffee on the counter. I snapped the book shut and unknowingly placed it in such a way that the coffee shop logo on the paper cup lined up with the author's name.

Koffee Haus
Karl Hanson
K.H.

"Gotta fly!" I rounded the counter and sprinted out the door and down the street. I burst into the library and just about squashed a toddler who was playing with a magazine rack. I tossed an apology to the presumed mother as I dashed past her, then skidded around the stacks and halted at the index cards. I flung open the drawer marked "H." I shook my hands to steady them. As I did so, I glanced at the tables in the centre of the room. People gaped at me. I dove into the drawer and picked through the index cards, pausing only to get a pencil and paper from a table. The list I compiled of authors with the initials K.H. and their bodies of work filled eight pages. I had a lot of reading to do, but it could wait.

At the library's computer, I surfed the internet to find information on Mr. Nigel Foster, who wrote in the journal in 1954. Foster had been a radio personality since the mid-1940s, working for various stations across the country. He made a name for himself as a storyteller, presenting and discussing folk tales from around the world and across time. In the 1950s, he switched his focus to the beat scene, preferring material with political and social commentary. The move caused him to lose most of his audience and he had serious trouble finding new listeners.

On March 23, 1954, Nigel Foster had a meltdown on the air. The station dropped him, and he retired from the public ear for two years. His comeback was less than fiery. For ten years, Foster paid the bills by doing voice work for commercials before an upstart station gave him a show in 1966. He returned to his roots, bringing tales from around the world to Toronto listeners. His popularity was attributed to making difficult material accessible and appealing to regular folk by highlighting sex and violence.

The parallel between Foster's career and that of the so-called rock star in *The Minstrel* was shaky, but worth checking out in light of the author's initials. I reached Mr. Foster by telephone at the talk radio station where he currently worked. He was eager to discuss the diary, but he had a stipulation.

"On the air?" I asked.

"Yes," he replied. His voice was deep and kind. "This is just the sort of thing my listeners would be interested in. That diary is living evidence of the oral tradition."

"But it isn't oral," I pointed out.

"No, but it passes from person to person the way a story does, and it speaks of truth and divinity and the mysteries of life." He had me there. "Can you come by the station tonight?"

"Sure." Shit, the art show. "Would I be finished by 9:00?"

"I think we can manage that," he said. "I have to run it by the station manager, but I don't anticipate any problems. Come around 7:30."

I agreed. "Should I prepare anything?"

"No, you leave all that up to me."

~ ~ ~

The man sips a drink in his home. Torn packing paper covers his lap. Nestled in the brown layers is a volume of hand-written pages. He sets down the drink and lifts the book. A single page slips out and flutters to the floor.

– Karl Hanson, *The Minstrel*

~ ~ ~

THE RADIO STATION was dim and deserted when I arrived. The receptionist's desk was empty. I waited and poked around the lobby. By 8:00 no one had come to collect me. I stepped through an unlocked door into a hallway. Black-and-white head shots lined both walls. Most of the personalities were unknown to me, and somewhat homely. A fluorescent light flickered above my head where I paused in front of one photograph. A young Nigel Foster smiled at me from behind the glass. His dark eyes were large and set deep beneath fine eyebrows. The long, prominent nose swept straight and wide down to full lips.

I heard Foster's voice through speakers hung from the ceiling. The show had started without me.

"Welcome to *The Hearth*. I'm Nigel Foster. As promised, tonight we are going to discuss the incarnations of Shakespeare's *The Tempest*. I'll play for you an excerpt, then take your calls so that we can get to the bottom of what the bard was trying to tell us. So, call your friends, gather your children, halloo out the window to passers-by, and tell them to tune in."

Had he forgotten about me? I walked the length of the hall to stand under an illuminated "On Air" sign and debated whether or not to knock on the door. A gravelly voice crackled through the speakers, the bookstore's namesake calling on the powers of nature. My fist hovered by the door.

"Can I help you?" came a woman's voice from down the hall. I dropped my hand and turned. She strode toward me frowning. She looked like an executive on a budget, belted and buckled into place but frayed around the edges.

"I'm supposed to have an interview with Nigel Foster tonight. Kal Winters." She stopped a few feet away and sized me up. Her grey hair was pulled back into a face-lifting bun, and her lips were puckered so severely that her cheekbones appeared ready to pop out of the brittle skin. I held out my hand, but she ignored it.

"I do hope you weren't about to knock on that door."

I looked from her to the door and back again. "Well, no one was here, and the show started."

She pointed to the sign above my head. "When that light goes out, someone will be out to help you." She spun on a heel to leave me.

"Is this how you treat all your guests? Because this is ridiculous. I had an appointment. I don't expect wine and cheese, but someone to meet me at the door and offer me a seat isn't too much to ask."

She stopped and turned back to face me. The pucker loosened just enough to turn up at the corners into a nasty smile. "Would you like me to show you to the green room?" I nodded. She indicated the floor. "You're welcome to take a seat anywhere you like. Mr. Foster will be with you when he's ready. Do *not* knock on that door." She left.

I sat on the floor and stared at the door. I should have left, and even considered it, but I really wanted to hear what Foster had to say about the diary. Who gave it to him. How it left his hands. I would just have to be late for the art show. I hoped that Cherise would understand. Forty minutes later, the door opened and Nigel Foster entered the hallway.

His wide, round eyes were accentuated, to say the least, by the thick glasses perched on his nose. Nigel's hair was so thick, there was no room left on his scalp for the curls. At one point in the day, I imagined it had been parted in the middle, and perhaps lying down, but at this late hour, gravity and pomade meant nothing to the mane. The part looked more like a parting of the sea, two frothy grey-and-white waves straining to join and embrace each other again. Only a god could keep them apart much longer.

"I understand that you met Olivia, the station manager. Isn't she a peach?" His chuckle rumbled and beat from deep within his barrel chest. "Come with me," he said and led me through the door.

The tiny, cluttered booth smelled like cooked cabbage, burnt cauliflower soup or wet feet. I wasn't sure which. A young man who was contained behind a Plexiglas window glanced at me and raised an eyebrow at my escort. Nigel offered me a wooden chair that was jammed in beside his own padded and wheeled affair. After shuffling some papers, he winked at me. "Here are your headphones. Speak into this microphone clearly, but don't shout. All set?"

I glanced over at the Plexiglas cage and watched the young man count down on his fingers. The last finger disappeared into his fist, then quickly reappeared to point at Nigel. Foster's voice rolled out of him with a slight English affectation as he introduced me.

"Today, I came across a wanderer, a breath of fresh air for our little radio show. You well know that wanderers have the best stories to tell. This minstrel put up a fight, but I believe I have won, and that we will hear a tale this evening. Tell us your name, Wanderer." He pointed a spindly finger at me and winked.

My chest tightened and my tongue felt thick. The heavy pause fattened, and Foster's finger wavered in the air inches from my face. He raised an eyebrow. I licked my lips. The radio booth was quiet, but I imagined the hum that reached into homes across the city. Finally, I overcame my fear. "Kal Winters," I slurred.

"Kal Winters." His repetition clambered over my last syllable. He spat out my first name like a cough, but he savoured my surname, drawing it out into a hiss. He paused again, breathed in through his nose and out through his mouth twice, and closed his eyes. I wondered if it was my turn to speak, but he didn't point to me. I looked to the producer for guidance. The skinny hairball only shrugged. Foster appeared to be weighing his words, and I wondered how anyone could think this was good radio. Finally, he spoke again.

"Strong name. Fine and simple. Kal Winters. It rolls off the tongue, doesn't it? Kal Winters. With a surname like Winters, one might assume you to be the frosty sort. Pure of thought and icy of emotion. Would you say you're that sort of character, Kal?"

I was taken aback again, this time by the switch in his timbre. He became authoritative and piercing. His delivery was all business and no nonsense, and I didn't know what to say to him. I hesitated a second, then jumped in my chair when he pounded his fist on the table-top.

"I've never thought about—"

He jumped on my words again, cutting me off as soon as it became apparent I had nothing to add. "K-A-L, just one letter away from the German *kalt*, meaning 'cold.' And Winters. Well, that needs no elaboration. Are you telling me, Kal, that you're warm and snuggly?" It sounded like an accusation.

"Well…no—"

"Of course winter doesn't need to imply cold. It can also allude to death. Where do you stand on death, Kal?" He shifted gears again. He reached his hands across the desk, leaned on his elbows, and glared at me.

"M-my death?" I stammered.

"Yours or someone else's. Are you a bringer of death, Kal Winters?"

"Of course not!"

"Okay." He pushed away from the desk and spun in his chair. He had to pull his feet up to avoid hitting the shelving unit. When the chair faced me, he stopped it by placing a foot on the ground. He winked at me again, chuckled and continued, "So this story isn't a thriller, horror or murder mystery. Are you a welcomer of death?"

It was my turn to pause. I made him wait while I sized him up. I considered leaving, but I wanted to ask him about the diary. If he wanted it to be on the air, so be it. "I am neither a bringer nor a welcomer of death, Mr. Foster. It's true we all have to die someday, but—"

"A waiter! Of course–that's another implication we get from a name like Winters–not the literal, but the metaphorical hibernation. Kal here is wintering, fast asleep in a cave until the snow melts and the blooms of truth turn their faces to the sun. Wonderful! Kal, what is it you're waiting for?"

"I am waiting to ask you about this diary," I said into the mic. "But if you want to play games first—"

"Ah, stasis. You're waiting to act, waiting for a sign, waiting for the proper motive. What is your motive in wanting to speak with me, Kal?"

I didn't answer him. The man was pissing me off. His little show depended on my co-operation, but I was determined to make him earn it. We squared off in silence for yet another moment before he set his jaw and turned back to the microphone.

"The diary that Kal refers to, ladies and gentleman, is a very old book. The cover is faded and torn, but I can still make out part of the picture. A young person, probably a boy, with a sack on a stick is strolling along a path. There are tall slopes of rock in the background. The sun is shining. The trees are in full green. A dog chomps at the hobo's heels, but he doesn't seem to notice." Nigel threw an earnest glance in my direction. "Are you the hobo, Kal?"

"No."

"Do you know where you're going?"

"Nowhere."

He frowned at my one-word answers, but pursued his line of thought. "Literal-minded. Nothing wrong with that. Let me ask you another way. Do you know what your goal is?"

I drew a breath and crossed my arms. Nigel's eyes pleaded with me to play along. I smirked and spoke clearly without shouting. "I want to find the origin of this diary. Do you recognize it? I found your name inside."

"1954, wasn't it?"

"That's right. April."

"This book led you here."

"So far, yes."

"Where will you go next?"

"Wherever the diary takes me, I guess."

Nigel laughed, short and strong. "Spoken like a true adventurer. I think you *are* the hobo, Kal. You're on a quest and this diary is the only clue. I wonder if you'll recognize the end of the path when you reach it? More with Kal Winters and the Diary Quest after this."

The producer signaled to Nigel that we were clear. Foster shuffled some pages. "Ad spots," he muttered.

"Did you ever meet Clara Strachan?" I asked.

"I did not," Nigel answered. "The book was left at the station shortly after I was fired. They sent it along to me."

"Who left it there?"

"It seems, Winters, that we both want questions answered. Since you came to me, I believe I have the edge, here." He wouldn't look at me. I couldn't believe the difference between the man I had spoken with on the phone and this jackass.

"We're back in ten." The producer's voice crackled through speakers into the booth.

Foster met my eyes. I stared back at him with a faint frown. I guessed that his motivation was a combination of boredom and a flagging career. I could find answers without him, but curiosity kept my butt in the hard seat.

"Fine," I said.

He chuckled, took a breath and launched into the second portion of the show at the producer's signal.

"Good evening, listeners. I surprised you tonight with an unexpected guest, Kal Winters. So far we have an idea about Kal's character and the hint of a fatal flaw. We've discussed character motivation, but we haven't had any action yet. No conflict. No complications. Kal, help us out here. Maybe start by telling us where you got that diary." He punctuated the speech with a smirk.

"I found it."

"Where?"

"At a friend's place."

Foster's head snapped up at my words. He narrowed his eyes at me, but his voice remained pleasant and smooth. "It is an old book. I'm sure many of the people who wrote in it are dead by now. How did your friend come by it?"

"I don't know. He didn't tell me."

"Intrigue," Nigel breathed into the microphone. "Have you written in it?"

"No." The word rushed out of me. Not yet.

"I'm afraid there is a flaw in this plot, Kal."

"A flaw?"

"Yes." He leveled a triumphant gaze on me, and laced his fingers behind his head. "The origin of the diary is obviously the first person to write in it. Why don't you go straight there? Why track everyone else down and bother them in their homes, at work, on the street? Why bother at all?"

"Why not?"

"That's a disappointing answer. I'm afraid it lacks the eloquence our audience is accustomed to." His words contained a threat. He would not answer my questions as long as I refused to act out the scene. I prickled at his arrogance, and pushed my microphone away. I scraped my chair across the floor until we were knee-to-knee, then reached out and grabbed his mic away from him.

"What does the name Kimberly Harding mean to you?" No answer. "How about Karl Hanson?"

"Absolutely nothing," he said as the producer indicated that we were gone to commercial.

"Who was the woman that asked for a story?"

"I beg your pardon?"

"In the diary. You wrote about a sumptuous woman."

"That is none of your business. I think it's best if you leave, now."

~ ~ ~

Nigel Foster

April 12, 1954

"Tell me a story," she said to me, that most sumptuous of women. "Tell me a story," said she to me, then kissed me full on the mouth before vanishing into a crowd of frumps and vagrants.

"I want to," I whispered to the mob. "I want to tell you the best story ever uttered. I want to teach you about love and hatred, war, heaven, hell, and flood. I want to tell you dirty stories, sweet stories, stories for children and kings. Every story I know, find, imagine or dream. I want to. But you asked me to stop."

If you will not listen, I will not talk.
Nigel Foster

June 7, 1954

The Story: An Autobiography
It is late, or early by another's standards. The garbage men outside thrash and bash tins at the curb, and the birds have begun to sing. I have hovered since dusk, floating above blank pages that will soon be my home. I have reflected on what defines me, and why people accept or reject me. The sky is now lightening. I take that as my cue to come alive.

I began with a wild beast and a man. One would be dinner; both were determined to dine. In prehistoric hovels, the hunt left me enough to scratch my way into existence. I grunted and screamed my way into the consciousness of half-men.

I traveled from cave to cave, then into villages. Horses carried me to farther countries, kingdoms and empires. I lived through tempests, comforting, soothing, warning and explaining things the people could not otherwise understand.

I was heard by kings, gods and horrific monsters. I became the bridge between the divine and the earthly. Whole armies and singular shining-eyed women surrendered to me. The elite tried to claim me, elevate me, shape me. I was examined, pulled apart and criticized. Where I would not bend, I was burned, maimed and disowned.

I was born with man, and I shall die with him. With no soul to soothe, I am powerless. With no ears to hear me, I am mute. With no child to ask for me, I am dead. I am a story. But, if no one will listen, I am not.

June 30, 1954

The Story: A Reflection
I am...
...a collection of words following the movements of one or more characters through a series of related events.
...a series of scenes engineered and ordered to teach a lesson.
...an anthropomorphic tale constructed to explain natural phenomena.
...greater than the sum of my parts.

I enlighten, entertain, and lull children to sleep. Who thought of me first? More importantly, who *heard* me first? Did they lean forward, breathing quick, heart pounding, at the first sounds I made? How vain of me to insist I bring people to a new self-awareness. When did I start craving adulation? I exist, and that should be enough. I have gotten away from myself.

~ ~ ~

Chapter 6

The man squints against the smoke in the dark bar as he pushes his way through a crowd. He reaches a table at the back where a young woman dabs at her eyes with a handkerchief. He stands in front of her, coughs, and places a book on the table. Her make-up is smeared under her brown eyes. The man hands her a pen and walks back through the throng.

– Karl Hanson, *The Marriage*

The Union

I SPRINTED UP the steps to the gallery and paused at the top doubled-over to catch my breath. The doors opened to release a flood of people. I remained bent and staring at the pavement as the crowd parted and converged around me. A familiar pair of Doc Martens planted themselves under my nose. My eyes tracked up the polka-dot tights and paused until fingers gripped my chin and whipped it up. Cherise sneered at me.

"You're late."

"I know, I'm—"

"The show is over."

"Cherise, I—"

"Luckily for you, I know the curator and some of the artists." She grabbed my elbow and dragged me through the doors into the show. "But, don't think this gets you off the hook."

The first piece when we walked in was a cast-iron claw-foot tub standing in pipe-cleaner grass and surrounded by pâpier mâché trees. Cotton-ball clouds hung from the ceiling and the outside of the tub was covered in plastic and silk flowers, individually glued in place. A soft female voice beckoned from a speaker hidden in the groundcover. "Go on. Get in. Relax in my embrace." The tub was filled to the brim with concrete.

"Wow, how did they get that in here? It must weigh a ton," I commented.

"Dollies and lots of ropes and pulleys."

I turned to see the artist, hands planted on hips, feet wide. "Grace," I said.

"Kal. You're late."

"Yeah, I got tied up. This piece is..."

"Heavy?" She waved a hand. "Don't bother. I know what it means."

Among the entire show there wasn't a single female nude. I was surprised and whispered as much to Cherise. She replied by glaring at me and didn't say a word to me all the way the home.

~ ~ ~

"I'M SORRY. You have the wrong number."

Click.

I lowered the receiver from my aching ear. I slashed out the name and moved to the next number in the phone book. It was the last listing under Ashby. I wasn't feeling optimistic.

I had punched the first three digits when Debbie descended on me.

"Kal, you've been on the phone for two hours! Don't you think—"

I finished dialing and waved Debbie off when it began to ring on the other end.

"I mean it, Kal!"

"Shh!" Saliva foamed through my teeth.

"Hello?"

I wiped my bottom lip and glowered at Debbie. "May I speak with Carole Ashby, please?"

"That's the most polite I've ever heard you, Kal," said Debbie. "You know, I—"

I sliced at the air with a taut hand to silence her.

"I'm sorry, but no one by that name lives here," said the childish voice.

"Is she a relative of yours?" I asked for the fifty-eighth time.

"No. Bye."

Click.

Carole Ashby must have married and changed her name. No one who shared her name knew who she was. "L. Simmons" appeared ten times.

If I had had a more productive way to spend my time, I might have been disappointed or at least discouraged, but it was a rainy Sunday. *Prospero's* was closed. Ross had been satisfied with my idea to investigate living archetypes as compared to literary archetypes as long as I had an outline for him by mid-July. I had found and scanned every book on my list and matched nineteen of them to the diary. The process had carried me through May, June and the early days of July. I had pages of notes, one box full of marked-up napkins and another of photocopied newspaper clippings, journal articles and citations. I was almost ready. I had hoped to speak to more of the writers, but I had just over a week to write up my outline.

I dialed three numbers before Leo Simmons answered.

"This is Leo," he said. His voice was self-assured and friendly.

"Mr. Simmons, my name is Kal Winters. I recently found a diary that might have belonged to you at one time." Letters from Leo Simmons to his sweetheart Carole Ashby had been pasted into the journal, but they were forty-three years old. Would he remember?

"A diary? No, sorry. I've never kept a diary." He chortled at the suggestion.

"It contains letters from 1956 to someone named Carole."

The laughing stopped. "Well, I'll be—Carole *Ashby?*"

"Yes," I said as my stomach flipped. "The letters are yours?"

"They must be."

"Sir, this diary has belonged to several people over the years. I'm trying to talk to as many of those people as I can to trace the path of the book. I realize it was some time ago, but do you have any ideas about how I might reach Ms. Ashby? Friends? Family?"

"Yes, I think I can help," he said. "She's my wife."

I hung up the phone and put my hands on my hips. "All done," I said to Debbie. She grabbed a cloth from the counter and swiped at the pizza crumbs I had dropped there. The phone rang. She threw me a bitchy look and answered it. I stuffed my papers and books into my bag, blew her a kiss and strolled out into the rain.

The circumstances of Karl Hanson's *The Marriage* had little to do with Leo's missives from school in Montreal, but both were about lovers. The connection was small, but every step I had followed so far was based more on hunch than undeniable evidence.

Leo and Carole lived only a few blocks away from the house Cherise and I shared, to the south, where the homes grew wider and the lots deeper. A flagstone walkway led up to the wrap-around porch, and the branches of a maple tree brushed against the upper windows. Carole answered the door and ushered me into the living room with a pleasant greeting.

"Leo will be in soon. He's puttering in the garden—weeding, I think. Labour intensive, but he insists on doing it himself."

She seated me on the sofa and offered me cookies and juice from a tray on the coffee table. The room was cozy with sage-coloured walls and high ceilings. Botanical prints hung on the walls, and tropical plants crowded each corner. Above the fireplace was a black-and-white photo of the couple on their wedding day. Leo, tall and handsome, gazed at his bride with adoration. Someone must have said something amusing just before the shutter snapped on the camera because Carole, rather than meeting her husband's eyes, looked up at the sky, her mouth open in a wide smile.

"May I see it?" asked Carole.

"Of course." I handed her the diary.

She steadied the book in her lap, and let it fall open to Leo's letters. She covered her mouth with one hand and her eyes misted as she read the faded words. I sipped at my juice.

"Oh my, he did love me all that time," she whispered and looked up at me. She noted my surprise with a nod. "I knew it, of course, but never appreciated it. I mean *really* appreciated it. I never loved him that way."

I choked on my juice. My eyes watered and I had to cough to clear my airway. "Mrs. Simmons, I'm not sure—"

"Isn't that why you're here? To get to the bottom of all these stories?" She moved to sit beside me on the couch and pat my back while I had another coughing spell. "I've been dying to talk to someone about it all these years. Please, take a moment with me before Leo comes in."

I breathed deeply and nodded around my juice glass.

"We grew up together, Leo and I. I always thought of him as a big brother even though we're the same age. Everyone teased us about getting married some day. Our parents, our teachers, the kids at school. We were best friends.

"They say that friends make the best lovers, and I don't imagine they're wrong in most cases. We kissed the first time when we were twelve, hidden in the bushes behind my father's house." She chuckled at the memory and shook her head. "You should have seen him. The tall, skinny thing, dancing under the stars and howling at the moon. He believed he was truly a man, and couldn't wait to try again.

"Our next kiss didn't happen until just before he went away to school. We were nineteen and one of us was in love. I knew I would miss him while he was gone, but I looked forward to the opportunity to meet other boys. They all stayed away, you see, because they figured I was Leo's girl. Well, the kiss was nice, wetter than I would have liked, but still, it didn't... I didn't...." She searched my face, waiting for me to finish her sentence. I shifted in my seat, uncomfortable with the image she raised.

"No fireworks?" I offered.

"Exactly," she breathed. "No passion. No tingling. I didn't know what to say. He told me I made him dizzy and he offered to stay behind, to study in Toronto instead of going to Montreal. I thought I would go crazy. I couldn't imagine pretending to share his feelings, but worse was the idea of hurting him."

The creak of rusty hinges sounded from the back of the house. Carole glanced around and frowned. "That's Leo now. He must be finished in the yard. He'll still be a few more minutes cleaning his tools."

"Why did you marry him?" I asked, hushed.

"I finally told him how I felt the first Christmas he came home. It was awful. We both cried. But I convinced him it was best. The next year, he brought a girlfriend for me to meet." She still looked toward the back of the house, listening to the clink of her husband's tools.

"Is that when you realized you loved him, after all?"

She turned back to me, then, and dropped her eyes to her hands. They rested on the diary. "No. That is not when I realized I loved him. His girlfriend was a horrible person. She only wanted his money, what little of it there was. She flirted with every man she met over the few days she was here and I even caught her with Leo's brother. In the bathroom at Christmas dinner. Leo showed me the ring he planned to give her. I couldn't let him do it. I respected him too much to let that trash ruin his life."

Leo's footsteps shuffled a few rooms away. We heard the creak of stairs. Carole fidgeted with the curled corner of one of Leo's love letters to her.

"Did you tell him what happened?"

"I did, but he wouldn't believe me. Finally, I said I made it up to cover my jealousy. We were engaged a month later."

I leaned forward to place my juice glass back on the tray. I didn't know what to say to a woman who sacrificed her own passion for a man she didn't love. I couldn't look at her. I felt neither pity nor compassion for her. I wondered why she thought Leo would never find someone better than his first small attempts at love, but could not voice it to her. I had just met her, after all.

"I know him better than he knows himself," she said as her husband's footfall descended the stairs. "I love him every bit as much as he loves me. Just differently. I want him to be happy, and being with me makes him happy."

Leo entered the room and took us in. He strode forward with his hand outstretched. "Did you tell the story of our first kiss?" he asked.

"I was just explaining how we were meant to be together," said Carole and tipped her face for a peck on the cheek.

~ ~ ~

"WHAT IS THIS?" I showed Marc the diary.

This was right up his alley—he loved books because they held words and Marc loved words. He lived his life by them. He wooed lovers with them. He feathered his nest with them. Marc embraced, devoured and absorbed words. He occasionally stole them. He often left me at a loss for them. His favourite kinds of words were the obscure ones.

"A diary." He shrugged and slid it back to me.

"You're holding out on me." I clenched my teeth. Nothing was ever straightforward with Marcus.

"You found this here? It's in deplorable shape. I wouldn't recommend restoration. The result would be disappointing."

"I don't want to restore it," I said. "Just tell me about it."

"It's worthless. Anything else?"

"I'm not interested in its worth," I replied. "I'm just curious about it."

He sighed and flipped it open.

"The paper is badly deteriorated. Oil from people's fingers—*many* people's fingers—coffee, humidity, dust, blood."

Blood?

He pinched the corner of a page between his thumb and middle finger. With a light twist, a triangle of brittle paper pulled away cleanly. "I'd put its age in the early part of the 20th century."

"Like around 1928?"

He glanced at the first page. "June 27, 1928," he read. "Sure, why not? The book could be a few years older. Mass produced, shitty binding, blank pages. Probably went for a few cents at a dime store."

"Could something like this be reproduced now?" I asked.

"You mean like a phony? Why would anyone want to do that?"

"I don't know. An evil marketing ploy?"

He rolled his eyes. "They could come close, I guess, but this paper is the real thing. They make it differently now, with chemicals and preservatives. Polymers."

"What about from a specialty paper store? I thought you could get anything. Or handmade."

He set the book down and placed his palms on the counter. "I repeat: Why would anyone want to do that?"

"Could they if they wanted to?" I was losing patience.

"Yeah, okay, sure. But in this case, it's doubtful. That's my expert opinion, Kal. For free." He had a strange look on his face. One finger reached to trace the faded pathway on the book's cover.

"What *is* it worth?" This book of other people's secrets had to be worth something.

"What price would you put on someone else's diary?"

~ ~ ~

Leo Simmons

September 14, 1953

Dear Carole:

I'm all moved into my room in the dormitories. My new roommate, Andrew, is something strange! I can't decide if you would like him or not. He has an imagination that he prefers to use as a black art. I don't dislike him, but I don't really trust him, either. If you were here, I'm sure you'd have him figured out in an hour! I miss you so much already, Carole. How will I last until Thanksgiving to see you?

Your first letter was waiting for me when I got here! How sweet of you to write before I even left. Every day, I've gone to a different restaurant to try the coffee and the atmosphere, just as you suggested. The best one is just a short walk away. I have yet to find the best tavern, there are so many to choose from, but Andrew assures me we will find it.

You know me so well, Carole, and take such good care of me, even when you are in Toronto and I am in Montreal. I am dearly looking forward to your next letter.

Love,
Leo.

September 21, 1953

Dear Carole:
I have decided that you would like Andrew very much…but you would probably rather die than admit to it. He is very handsome to begin with. And I know that you always say that you don't care what a man looks like, that it's what's in his head and his heart that matters, but I know that his smile and wink would put you off balance. No one can help themselves around him—not even men.

And he is fun, Carole. He has roped me into going out with him every night this week. I have the best intentions to do my school work, then he wheedles and jokes until I just can't concentrate. I sneak off to the restaurant between my last class and dinner so I can at least keep up with my reading. I miss you, Carole.

Love,
Leo.

September 28, 1953

Dear Carole:
School is getting tough. Even Andrew is starting to hunker down. I have been helping him with Chemistry this week. His self-esteem gets in the way of serious studying. Luckily, it's still the beginning of the semester. I struck a deal with him: If he earns all Bs on his midterm reports, then I will do anything at all that he suggests.

Mother wrote and told me about the dance at the Fishers' last weekend. You didn't tell me that you danced with David Macleod. Naughty girl! Mother said you laughed at him for the whole dance. Mean! I was glad to hear that you are laughing, though.

Love,
Leo.

October 5, 1953

Dear Carole:
I'm getting bored with my studies. Andrew has taken our deal quite seriously and isn't nearly the fun he was before. We haven't gone out to the tavern for nearly two weeks! I need something to entertain me, my classes are so dull. You see, I have to wait until next year to declare my major area of interest, so until then, the school is forcing me to take general science courses. I say, "Bring on the BUGS!" But they say, "You must study hard and learn chemistry, physics, and botany first. You must be a well-rounded student." Come and visit to alleviate this crushing boredom.

Love,
Leo.

October 12, 1953

Dear Carole:
Everyone here is talking about Hallowe'en! Can you believe it? It's so childish, but all my friends are positively buzzing. What do you think I should wear?

Short letter. Midterm exams start tomorrow and I have a lot of work to do.

Love,
Leo.

October 19, 1953

Dear Carole:
You haven't written for awhile. Are you tired of me? Has David Macleod stolen away what little piece I had of your heart? You know I'm teasing.

Please write to me, soon, though. I enjoy all of your letters.

Love,
Leo.

October 26, 1953

Dear Carole,
Good news! Andrew met his goal of straight Bs on his midterm report. He hasn't named his price yet. I am afraid. He can be quite insane.

Since you haven't written to me with a suggestion for my Hallowe'en costume, I have had to come up with one on my own. I shall be a praying mantis for the party. What do you think of that?

Love,
Leo.

November 14, 1953

Dear Carole:
Still no letters from my dearest one? Mother wrote that she hasn't seen much of you lately. Are you avoiding my whole family, Busy Bee? I have a surprise for you when I come home at Christmas! Don't bother guessing because I'm not going to tell you.

Love,
Leo.

P.S. If you don't write to me soon, you may not get your surprise!

November 21, 1953

Dear Carole:
At last a letter from my butterfly! But I couldn't tell if you miss me? You've stayed so busy with all the parties and shows. Have I a right to be jealous? On second thought,

you better not visit me in Montreal. Andrew might steal you away from me. I will see you in less than a month!

Love,
Leo.

December 5, 1953

Dear Carole:
Mother says that you are spending a lot of time with Timothy Brown, but I won't say any more about that, because I'm very excited about the surprise I have for you at Christmas.

I'll be on the 8:35 train on December 15. Father is picking me up at the train station. Will you go with him to meet me?

Love,
Leo.

~ ~ ~

Chapter 7

The muscled forearms ripple with exertion as the man slides the rag over the smooth chrome. He polishes it until the sleek, cold metal glitters in the brilliant sunlight. He switches cloths and rubs cream into the supple leather of the seat and arm rests, bringing up a different kind of shine. Dropping the rag onto the grass, the driver hoists himself onto his chariot. He adjusts his legs in the footrests, then reaches down to caress the slick wheels. He pumps. The axle shivers and screeches as the wheelchair lurches forward.

– Kass Holbrook, Rock and a Hard Place

The Dilemma

SANDRA DARLING had about her the air of a china-doll on a shelf, pretty and prim and solitary. Her plump face puckered into a vague sadness when I showed her the diary. I was seated on a delicate loveseat in her calm blue salon, curling my toes into the cream-coloured shag rug to hide the holes in my socks. Perched on the edge of a neat, winged chair, she served up tea. Only when the tranquil liquid was distributed would she answer any questions about the diary on the coffee table.

In 1958, Kurt Darling lost the use of his legs in a single-car accident. Kurt and Sandra's only child, a promising boy of eight, died in the same accident. Kurt was drunk at the wheel. I had found the brief newspaper article on microfiche. It contained few details. Kurt was given a fine and sent home to recuperate. He never did. Two years later, he was found with his head in the gas stove, asphyxiated.

"He thought I blamed him. He thought I hated him," she said between sips. "I loved him, though. I thanked God every night for taking the child instead of Kurt."

My cup clattered against the saucer. Hot tea hit my leg, soaked into my jeans, burned and cooled. The stain mingled with the rest. Sandra's eyes rested on the diary, strangely serene after such a devastating confession.

"You've read it," she commented. "I never did. I just bundled it up with the rest of his things and donated it to charity. I've wondered about it, from time to time, but it was private."

She fell silent. The mantle clock ticked, and I detected a music box playing from somewhere in the back of the house. The phone rang, and I jumped, spilling more tea into my lap. I leaned toward the coffee table, rid myself of the cup and saucer, and waited. The phone rang several times more, but Sandra made no move to answer it. The caller gave up, and the house fell quiet again, except for the tick-tock of the glass-domed clock.

I had questions, but I was reluctant to throw my voice into the weird vacuum of the room. The widowed Mrs. Darling's depression had oozed into the bricks and mortar of the house, insulating the pretty rooms with melancholy. I could almost smell its sweetness floating up from the loveseat to envelop me.

"Have you ever had to choose between bad and worse?" she asked after a time. I wasn't sure she'd spoken, her voice was so quiet. I glanced at her, and realized for the first time that I had lowered my eyes to stare at the diary. She didn't wait for a response. "The hardest part is wondering if you chose rightly."

Her bottom lip quivered and her hands began to shake. I took her cup and saucer and placed them on the table.

"I'm sorry to bring all this up, Mrs. Darling. All I really wanted to know was where your husband got the diary. Did someone give it to him? Did he find it?" My jaw felt tight. I was desperate to change the subject. It was too cold, this woman's pain.

"He wanted me to leave him. Here in the house, so I wouldn't have to see him die."

"He killed himself." Whispered.

She took steady breaths, in through the nose, out through the mouth, then shook her head. "Not exactly," she said.

"Stop." I turned away from her, scrambled to gather my things. "Don't say anymore." This was too much, what she was about to tell me. I hesitated before snatching the diary from the coffee table, wondered if she had the right to read her dead husband's words. There was nothing in there to help her now.

Suddenly, she laughed. She raised a finger and pointed it at me, her breasts jiggling under her dress. Her face lifted and I could see the fillings in her back molars through the gaping grin. "What's the matter, Kal? Never met a murderer before?"

"I-I'm sorry?" I stammered.

"That's what you think, isn't it? That I euthanized my husband?"

"You didn't?"

She guffawed and slapped her knee. "He died in an accident," she said and stopped giggling. "But I don't expect that's exciting enough for whatever book you're writing about all of us."

I leaned back on the sofa and regarded her, trying to figure out her game. "Mrs. Darling, I'm not writing a book about any of you. Someone beat me to it."

Her mouth opened and shut. She frowned. "I beg your pardon?" she finally said.

"When did you meet Clara, Mrs. Darling?"

"Clara. The girl who started the diary? I never—"

"She may have called herself Kimberly. Or Kass?"

"I'm sorry, but I don't know what you're talking about."

"Have you read *Rock and a Hard Place*? It's pretty good. It's about making difficult choices." She shook her head. Not laughing anymore. I pulled the novel from my bag and handed it to her. "You've never seen this before?"

"No." She opened it and read a little from the first page. "Is this supposed to be about me?"

"I was hoping you could tell me."

She closed the book and tossed it onto the couch beside me. "I've never heard of it or Kass Holbrook or that other name you mentioned."

"Clara Strachan."

"Right."

"Really." I stood and put the book back into my knapsack. "You also said you never read the diary, am I right?"

She nodded and raised her hands, palms up. "I'm sorry I couldn't help you more. Why is it again that you want to know all this?"

"I'm a literature student," I replied. "Um, Mrs. Darling, if you never read the diary, then how do you know Clara started it?"

Her eyes narrowed a hint and her mouth puckered into a tight, forced smile. "Kurt told me, of course. It's an intriguing story, don't you think? What do you suppose became of the foolish girl?"

"That's what I was hoping you could tell me," I said then shook her hand. "Thank you for your time."

~ ~ ~

THE PUBLISHING HOUSE looked more like a coffee house. Scattered around the long, narrow, third-floor space, rather than cubicles and desks, were bistro tables. A handful of youngish staff sat at these, sipping coffee and marking up manuscripts. Laptop computers reflected in the lenses of horn-rimmed, tortoise-shell spectacles.

One corner of the space was dedicated to the evils of office work: a fax machine, photocopier and mini-fridge. Each was decorated with gold star-and-moon stickers that glittered in the sun slanting in just under slate-grey blinds. The blinds covered a wall of ceiling-to-floor windows. The opposite wall was made of crumbling, red brick, and patched with rough mortar. Poster-sized cover art flanked a huge hand-painted portrait of Shakespeare.

The exposed ductwork was painted light blue and white to blend with the skyscape mural on the ceiling. At the far end, a storm of Renaissance brilliance loomed. Under this huddled the only office in the place, a glass-walled cubby. I turned toward it. A pale, spike-haired girl stopped me.

"Excuse me?" she said. "Are you an author?"

"I have an appointment with Mr. Denby," I said, and watched her take in my disheveled appearance. I shrugged. "Hangover."

The hip young thing in front of me frowned.

"It looks worse than it is," I said. "Is Mr. Denby in?"

"He is," she said. "Your name, please?"

"Winters."

"Oh, yeah. I'm sorry. I thought you were one of our vagabond writers."

"Well, you got part of it, right."

She giggled, and I smiled at the sound. Not unlike Cherise. She walked me through the room, slinging greetings to her go-getting colleagues. I glanced around at the editors, all of them under 35, and took them in from their sleek heads to their platformed feet. I wondered if I would be among them in a few months. Or if my ivory tower was destined to shatter.

Bruce Denby watched our approach through his glass walls, and was on his feet by the time we reached his door. He appeared confused as he looked from the cat to what she had dragged in.

"Frannie?" he asked my escort.

"Kal Winters," she answered.

"Of course," he said, and laughed. "Sorry, I was expecting..."

"Kal is feeling under the weather," Frannie said in a stage whisper and winked.

"Sorry to hear that." He rounded the desk and showed me a seat. "What can I do for you?"

As he spoke, he closed the door on Frannie and dropped the blinds on his glass walls. He was a tall man with salt-and-pepper hair and a craggy face. He was, no doubt, the editor-in-chief, the distinguished leader imparting the tricks of the paper trade to his dedicated staff. Before the last blind dropped, I caught an image of his angel-faced workers in their stylish factory-converted workplace, and thought of Fagan.

"In my email I gave you the name of a writer you published several years ago," I said.

"Kendra Horne," he said. "I did some digging. I didn't remember the name right away, but I recall now. Two books with disappointing sales. They're both out of print now. I can't tell you anymore. I never met the woman. But, that was a while ago. I've worked for three other companies since then."

"What about the other names I gave you?"

"Never heard of any of them. Except for Kimberly Harding, of course. Interesting, though, that they all have the same initials."

"I think so."

"Do you have a theory, Kal?"

"I do," I said, and dumped the contents of my pack on his desk. Six books, all by one K.H. or another spilled out. On top of the pile was a seventh book: the diary.

He picked up the diary, thumbed through it, and placed it back on his desk. "A diary," he said, and crossed his arms. We stared at each other. I searched his face for signs of recognition, but he looked expectant. He was the first to break the silence. "So, what's your theory?"

"I think these other books are all by the same author. Have you ever met Clara Strachan?"

"No," he replied, and gathered all the novels into a pile, which he put back into my knapsack. "I'm afraid I can't help you. If I think of anything, I'll email you." He handed me my pack, and moved toward the door.

I stood and shouldered my bag. As I turned to face him, I scooped the diary from his desk. "Oops," I said, my eyes locked on his. "Almost forgot this."

He shrugged, and I limped out underneath the storm clouds.

~ ~ ~

THE PARTY WAS jumping by the time I arrived. Music pounded through the townhouse. I hoisted my case of beer over my head and wound my way through groups of wobbling, chattering guests. Cherise and Marcus were on the back patio with the smokers.

"You made it!" Cherise hooted and launched herself at me. With awkward abandon, she hugged me and the case of beer. Giggling.

"Had a bit to drink, love?" I said into her hair.

She backed off and looped her arm around Marc. "Marcus convinced me that I needed to unwind."

"Chick Pea!" hollered a guy from nearby who moved to join us. He leaned over Cherise and leered at me. "Is this your chick pea?"

"Kal," said Cherise. "This is Dean, a childhood friend of Marc's. Can you believe Marc was ever a little boy?" More giggles.

Dean pumped my hand and punctuated the greeting with an eyebrow-raising squeeze, then slung an arm around my girlfriend's shoulders. The three of them looked like a kick-line. I yanked a beer from the case and flicked the cap over Dean's head.

"Are you the host?" I asked.

"Sure am."

"What's the occasion?"

"Dean never needs an excuse to celebrate," Marc said. He extracted himself from Cherise to pull a joint from a pouch on his hip. He licked it, lit it, took a haul and passed it to Cherise. Who accepted it. Dean's arm tightened around her.

"Oh, I see," I said, then, "Dean…washroom?"

"Top of the stairs, Chick Pea."

Dean, I found out later, was in sales. The upscale furniture, top of the line stereo equipment and expensive art proved he was a talented huckster. I passed the washroom to poke my head into the rooms on the second floor.

The office was done up to look like a Victorian library with a large oak desk in the middle of the floor and built-in bookcases around the perimeter. The books had a decorator sameness to them, worn leather covers in various browns and beiges, and I guessed Dean had them there for aesthetics rather than any effort at self-improvement.

The bedroom languished behind a heavily carved oak door, and had the same aura of pretension as the office. The four-poster king-size bed was swathed in dark velvet curtains and laden with pillows. At the foot was a hinged, gilded floor mirror. Fancy guy.

I finished my beer and left it on the bedside table, then pulled open the top drawer for a quick peek. A blindfold, handcuffs and an instant camera nestled beside a stack of porn. I hurried back downstairs to find Cherise.

She was seated on the couch. Marcus snuggled beside her and talked quietly into her ear. I followed their eyes to Dean, who had a flirty, overstuffed woman backed into a corner. Cherise pulled my attention by laughing out loud. She slapped Marcus on the arm and said, "You're making it up! I don't believe you." Tales of Dean's exploits, no doubt. I felt better. Marcus would keep Cherise safe.

They made a nice picture, two friends chatting drunkenly. Cherise looked radiant. Her hair was parted into two braids that hung over her bare brown shoulders. She sat cross-legged with her red skirt hiked and bunched between her thighs.

I drank a bunch more beer and suffered gushy conversations with Dean's guests, waiting for Cherise to join me, to share her glow. But Marcus held her stoned attention on the couch. I double-checked Dean's progress with tits-du-jour, satisfied myself that he was occupied and stumbled away from the party.

~ ~ ~

Kurt Darling

February 10, 1959

Interesting book. Don't know what I can add, but here goes. Hope Clara found her hearts' desire, but doubt it. Life is tough–tougher for a runaway. Hope David was good to her. Men ought to be good to women, appreciate what they add to the world, all they do for us. I have a wonderful wife. Sandra. She's beautiful. No words for how much I love her. She got the short end of the stick when she married me. Kurt Darling. 34 years old. Born and raised in Toronto. Used to be a roofer. Alcoholic. Killed our little boy in an accident last year. Jack. Eight years old and he wanted to be a hockey player. I lost my legs. Sandra says she forgives me and loves me, but I know she deserves better. She should leave me. Don't know why she doesn't.

February 13

Sandra never complains. Takes care of me, helps fix the house for the wheelchair–ramps, moved bedroom downstairs. My best friend Allan helps, too. They call my chair the chariot and laugh. That's good. I like it when Sandra is happy. I try to laugh, too, but it's hard. I miss Jack. He would be nine tomorrow. My boy.

February 14

Sandra put away Jack's pictures today. Get on with life, she said. How? How? We had a birthday cake with candles. Shaped like a heart for Valentine's day. Last birthday, she said. Only us now.

February 20

Chariot squeaks. Driving us crazy. I wish I was dead. Sandra would be better off. Think about doing myself in, trouble is insurance don't pay out for suicides.

February 26

Allan moving in with us. Says he can bring money in and help renovate. Doors too narrow for chair. I think it's a good idea. Maybe when I'm gone, Allan and Sandra will fall in love. He's a solid man, treats her with respect.

May 3

Renos done. I asked Sandra for a divorce. She said no and cried and cried. For better or worse, she said. She thought I stopped loving her. Never. Divorce would give her better life without me. I told Allan about it. Said he'd slug me if I weren't a cripple.

May 11

I can make it look like an accident and Sandra will get insurance. Allan will take care of her when it happens.

~ ~ ~

Chapter 8

In the photograph, a pretty girl hugs a lion at the circus. The boy's mouth is agape as he hands the snapshot back to the man. The man chuckles, puts the picture back on the shelf, then leads the boy past fish tanks and bird cages to a cardboard box. The man reaches into the box and pulls out a kitten. The boy accepts the tiny creature and holds it under his chin. The storekeeper kneels in front of the boy, and wipes at his bloody nose with a kerchief. A woman hovers over them, clutching a book to her chest.

— Kass Holbrook, *Steadfast*

Fortitude

"Can't you read?" barked the man in the doorway. I stood on the slanted porch of a rundown row-house. Each unit leaned eastward against its neighbour. The end house, where I braced myself on the exhausted porch, bore the weight of the rest. Rain pelted me through holes in the verandah's roof. The man's head was down. He appeared to be scowling at my footwear which indeed deserved his disdain. He jerked a thumb to his right, indicating a sign propped behind the cracked, dirty glass of the front window: NO SELICITERS. The hand-drawn letters were bleached almost to the colour of the brittle cardboard, and crammed against the edge of the page as the writer ran out of space.

"I'm not selling anything. Are you Milos Andropoulos?"

"Do I know you?" He still glared at my feet.

"My name is Kal Winters. I'm conducting preliminary research for a graduate thesis and I'd like to ask you a few questions." I had decided, after the veiled nastiness of my last interview, to be forthright. Hopefully honesty would beget honesty.

"Nope." He yanked on the door to close it, but I caught it with my elbow and pulled the diary from my jacket.

"Do you recognize this? Please just take a minute to look at it." During the brief tug of war with the door, his fingers closed around the journal.

"It's a book," he growled, and let go of the door. Without looking at it, he opened it and traced the quilted pages with a feather touch. "Hand written?" He looked up at this, and searched out my face through milky eyes.

"You're blind!" I blurted.

"Is this a…diary?" he demanded. He took an involuntary step back. I moved over the threshold.

"It is you. Milos. You wrote in there when you were eight. You *do* remember."

"Who are you and where did you get this?" He backed farther away, and hugged the diary to his broad chest. I advanced on him.

"I'm a literature student. I'm trying to trace the path of that book."

His thigh knocked a table. A lamp rocked and crashed to the floor. He stopped at the sound and took a deep breath. "Close the door on your way out," he said and turned. A black curtain hung at the end of the hall. He and the diary disappeared behind it.

"Hey!" I shouted and launched myself after him. My foot skidded on the lamp shards and I ended up in crude splits. I turned an ankle and felt glass bite into my knee, but I scrambled up and shoved the curtain aside. Momentum slammed me into a wall that I couldn't see in the blackness of the room. I fumbled around in the dark, running my hands along the wall in search of a light switch. I tripped over shoes and fell into a hall tree. Coats fell to the floor and my feet quickly tangled in them. My fingers came across the square smoothness of a switch plate. I found the switch and flipped it. Nothing but a loud click.

"Milos?" I called and listened for the sounds of movement. The blackness was absolute. The windows must have been blocked. I shuffled along the perimeter of the room, feeling my way along a couch, a credenza, past an armchair. The rustling of my clothes seemed deafening in the stillness of the house.

My own breathing filled my ears. At once the room closed in around me and expanded and stretched beyond my grasp. My body felt oddly out of proportion: tiny fingers, stubby things at the end of spindly arms; my feet great weights on thick, stumpy legs. The real trouble, however, was with my head. Heavy throbbing, growing with every breath of stale air, ears ringing, eyes watering, desperate to see, nose stinging and tingling in the dust.

A floorboard creaked somewhere above and to my right.

"Milos?" Silence. "Milos?" My voice was a shrill whisper. I imagined faces and forms in the dark, tendrils reaching for me or hovering inches from the tingling flesh of my neck. I found an opening in the wall, a doorway to more darkness. I stumbled and drew a sharp, shallow breath, shuffled forward, hands raised ahead of me.

"Milos!"

My foot hit something solid. I crouched and stuck my fingers into the void. Wood. A lip. Vertical bars. Stairs. I crawled up and ahead.

"Milos, I'm coming up. I just want the diary. Give it back and I'll leave you alone."

With my right hand on the rail, I walked up the stairs. I felt ahead with a foot and kicked each riser before stepping up. I reached the top and stopped to run my hands along the wall on my left. A door. Behind me, I guessed was a hallway. I would check each room. I found the knob and turned just as I heard heavy steps rushing up behind me. Milos slammed into me. We toppled into the room and landed on a hard mattress on the floor.

I was on my stomach with one arm pinned underneath me. Milos lay on my back, but hoisted himself into a kneeling position with a knee on my spine. I pushed against the mattress with my free hand and tried to roll away from him, but he found the appendage and with a firm grip on my wrist, twisted my arm behind me until I stopped struggling.

I gasped for air and gagged on the stench from the mattress under my nose. He loosened his grip and moved away from me while I coughed. I flipped over and caught my breath. I could no longer tell if he was in the room. I crawled towards the door.

"Are you going to leave or do I have to call the police?"

"Just give me the diary and I'll be on my way." I reached the door on my hands and knees. My fingers touched his foot and I drew back.

"What right do you have to it?" he asked.

"It was a gift." Again with the lies.

"From who?" His voice was husky.

His presence in the room gave me better bearing in the darkness. I stood to be on more equal footing with him, although he was a foot taller than me.

"Does that matter?" I decided to follow a hunch. "She thought I needed it, so she passed it on to me."

Wind whistled around the house, and rain pattered on the roof above us. I smelled mildew in the room, a musty undertone to the reeking mattress behind me. In front of me, Milos' heat touched my cheeks. He stirred and moved into the hallway. The dampness of the neglected room enveloped me. I shuffled forward, mindful of the staircase to my right.

"Wait here," he said.

I felt his hand brush across my face before he descended the stairs. His warmth flitted past and away, pulling me after him. I swayed in the dark and vertigo swirled in my head. I crouched and found the top step to sit. The house creaked. The wind whined.

Milos appeared at the bottom of the stairs with a candle and beckoned to me. He had the diary tucked under an arm.

The light of the candle hurt my eyes, but I met him at the bottom and followed him into the shabby living room. The credenza, sofa and armchair I had passed were pushed against bare walls, and an empty china cabinet loomed in a corner. No rug adorned the floor. I looked up to the ceiling to see a dusty, vacant light fixture. The bulb had been removed long ago. The single window was painted black and no curtains softened the edges of the dark square.

Milos set the candle and the diary on the credenza. The light from the flame flickered along the wall, sending the sketchy shadows of cobwebs dancing in the corners of the room. He sat in the armchair; I on the couch.

"Did I hurt you?" he asked. He looked young in the dim light, with wide eyes.

"No."

He let out a breath and relaxed his bulk into the chair. He was well over six feet tall and in great shape. Barrel chest, flat stomach, thick sturdy thighs. He could have done a number on me if he'd been inclined.

"You said you needed my help."

"I'm studying the journal for a Ph.D. thesis," I said. I chose my words carefully. So far, nobody was willing to talk about the book. "Is there anything you can tell me about it?"

He rubbed a hand across his face before leaning forward in the chair again. He braced his elbows on his knees and laced his fingers behind his neck, head down in dejection. "Did you read it?" he asked from this position.

"Yes."

"And what will you write about me for your thesis?"

"I don't know yet. Maybe nothing. I was hoping to use you and the others as sources. I'm trying to find Clara."

"Who is Clara?" he asked.

"The girl who started the whole thing."

He snorted into his lap. "You're chasing a ghost. She'd be... What? Ninety years old? A hundred?"

"Ninety-four. Did you ever meet her? Did she give you the book?"

"I went blind," he whispered to his knees. Each word dropped in the stillness of the room and clattered on the bare boards of the floor. He lowered his hands to rub at his thighs, then shook his head. "I'm sorry. It was a long time ago. I was just a kid. I don't think I can tell you anything."

"Who gave it to you?" I asked. I was losing him. "You wrote about a woman who came to your school. Did she give it to you?"

He swallowed, still shaking his head slowly. "It's hard to remember."

"Would it help jog your memory if I read to you what you wrote?"

"I don't think that would help anyone." He was shutting down on me. He was withdrawing, closing himself off, the battered little boy. I changed tactics.

"Your father abused you when you were small. Is that why the woman gave you the diary? So you could write it down?"

"My father," he whispered and raised his head to stare unseeing at the ceiling. "This is the house where I grew up. It's awful, I know, but..."

"But what?"

He ran his hands up and down his thighs, more quickly now, rubbing at the denim. "I don't understand why you need to know all this. I don't mean to be rude, but I don't see where it's any of your business."

"You're right, it probably isn't," I said quickly. "But I'm drawn to this diary. I can't explain it, but I need to know more about it before–"

"Before you add to it?" he interrupted. "Afraid it's cursed, maybe? Maybe by writing in it your nightmares will come true? Like me writing about Oedipus, then going blind myself. It's hereditary. My father went blind before me, and his father before him."

"Of course not. I don't believe in witches and curses. I was going to say before I can write the proposal for my thesis."

"What do you hope to accomplish?" he asked. His hands stilled and he turned his face toward me. "What is your thesis?"

I paused. An odd feeling started in my gut and skittered up into my throat. I didn't want to tell him. It was clear, however, that if I didn't answer his questions, he wouldn't answer mine. And why should he? "I think Clara Strachan is still alive, or was recently. I think she wrote books under an assumed name. Several assumed names."

"You think she turned out to be a famous writer and you want to expose her to the literary world." He nodded. "Good thesis."

"I hope so," I said, moving to the edge of my seat. "So, can you tell me who gave you the diary? Was it Clara?"

"I told you, I don't know who the woman was. I don't think that would help you anyway."

"Why not?"

"Because you'll never find her that way."

"How will I find her?" I was getting the feeling that he knew where she was. He knew more than he was telling me, anyway.

"You said she writes under an assumed name. I would start there."

"The most recent name is Korine Horner, but biographical information on her is hard to come by."

"Who published the book?"

"That's not as easy as it sounds," I replied.

"Too bad. I'm sorry I couldn't be more help. The book is beside the candle. I have no use for it. As you can see, I don't have a bookshelf to keep it on." He waved his hand to take in the dilapidated surroundings. "Take it. Leave the candle in the front hall. Please blow it out before you leave."

"But Milos..."

"It's Kal, right?" He stood. "Kal, I understand your fascination with the diary. But, *you* have to understand something. The things we all wrote in there–it was a way to get rid of them. You see? Nobody is going to welcome you in and give you the answers you're looking for. I'm sorry."

~ ~ ~

CHERISE SLEPT LATE. I tiptoed through the kitchen, careful not to slam the fridge and cupboard doors. Toast and strong coffee lubricated my hangover. I popped some aspirin but it did little to ease the pain around my eyes.

I curled up on the couch to glance over *Steadfast*. Thankfully, the story about inner strength over adversity was better than the previous two written under the name Holbrook, and I found myself drawn in by a small boy's determination to survive. After an hour or so, I set the book aside and pulled out the diary.

I went for a walk to clear my head. When I returned home half an hour later, Cherise still hadn't come downstairs. She couldn't hold her booze and I knew how hard Marc could go. I took a tray to the bedroom. A breeze blew the curtains, allowing the late afternoon light to filter across the bed. Cherise lay curled in a ball with her face to the wall. Her hair spread over her shoulders and out behind her on the pillow. She was on top of the blankets wrapped in a thick terry robe, although the August air was heaviest upstairs.

"I brought tofu," I said and set the tray on the bed. I kneeled to lean over her. "Did you have fun at the party?" I asked.

She shifted and stretched her legs, but didn't answer me.

"I think someone has a hangover," I teased. I brushed the hair from her face and tugged at the collar of the robe to kiss the spot where shoulder meets neck. With my puckered lips inches from her skin I stopped.

"Are you working today?" she whispered thickly.

The hickey, purple and mottled, was the size of a kiwi slice.

"I thought we could spend the evening together," I said, and brushed her robe back in place. I smelled rosemary in her hair. She must have showered before bed. Washing away her sins.

"I don't feel well." Her voice was muffled by the pillow.

"I'll go to the library then. Your dinner is here. Drink some water." I backed away from her and off the bed, eyes on the terry cloth that covered her neck.

"Okay." The second syllable dissolved into a whimper.

"Is there something you want to tell me?" Calm.

She turned her face farther into the pillow. I left the room, but paused outside the bedroom door, at a loss. I heard the bed sheets rustle and my throat tightened.

~ ~ ~

Milos Andropoulos

Monday

My name is Milos Andropoulos. I'm eight years old. Today at school a lady told us a story about a baby boy who got gave away so bad things wouldn't happen to him. They were a king and queen.

I wish my parents had gave me away. I don't want to be blind.

Tuesday

Today the lady who told us the story yesterday came back again. She waited for me outside at recess. She said she left out part of the story, and she wanted to fix her mistake. The baby boy who grew up and turned blind because bad things happened to him. The lady said that she forgot he was really born without his eyes and the bad things didn't make him blind. She said the bad things happened because he was already blind. I guess she wants me to tell our class her mistake. She's a nice lady.

Wednesday

Today at the pet store I saw a kitten that didn't have his eyes open yet. The man who owns the store said all cats are born like that. But then their eyes open when they get bigger. Then the mother cat bit the baby on its neck and picked it up by its fur. The man said it didn't hurt the baby, but I know it hurt him a lot. He can still feel things even with his eyes closed. I asked Mom and she said the man was right. She said that's how mother cats take care of their babies. She said it helps them grow up from baby kittens into strong cats.

I forget what day it is. I think I've been away for a week, but I slept a lot so I don't know for sure. I'm supposed to be at school today, but Dad won't let me go until my cheek heals better. He's afraid it will get infected and ugly and make a scar on my face that I'll have forever. It doesn't hurt as much as my shoulder, though. Mom gives me stuff that makes me sleep so I can't feel it. The Doctor didn't believe me when I told him I hit a car when I was on my bike. He asked me what the car looked like, but I couldn't remember. My eyes were closed when I hit it. He said be more careful but he said it to my Mom. When I woke up one day, she was beside me and she was crying. I told her it didn't hurt. I don't like when she cries.

Thursday

I know what day it is because I went back to school. I was hoping the nice lady would be there, but she wasn't. I asked the teacher but the teacher said the lady is too busy to tell us more stories. I want to give her book back. I want to hear more stories.

Friday

I don't have anything to say. Nothing happened at school and I didn't go anywhere after school. I have to come straight home from now on says Dad. He says I bother the man in the pet store but he's wrong. He smiled a lot the whole time I was there. People don't smile when you're bothering them, do they? The kittens are all gone now anyway. They went to stay in all different houses with all different families. I hope nothing bad happens to them. I wish I could stay in a different house. But Mom might cry, so I better stay here until I'm big enough to get my own house. I have to go now. My part is boring. I'm sorry.

~ ~ ~

Chapter 9

The woman holds a lantern aloft, searching the darkness. Snow swirls around her, clinging to her purple shawl. Flakes hit the heated globe of her light and sizzle away into nothing. She steps to the edge of the porch, but her foot hits something. She stumbles. Her other hand grasps the railing and she steadies herself. Her eyes scan the almost-empty street and hit upon a retreating grey figure. A rising wind catches at the figure's hood and pulls it away from her face. Shining dark hair whips around her head and shoulders. The figure passes through a yellow pool of light on the road and away into the cold shadows. The woman on the porch calls out, but there is no reply. She stoops to investigate the object her foot caught on. A thin skiff of snow has already collected on the package that lies at her feet. She lifts it, turns, and with her lantern lighting the way, shuffles back into her solitude.

– Kevin Herbert, *The Sage*

The Recluse

Marcus was nowhere to be found when I stormed into the store. A guy in a suit stood at the counter with a pile of books. He drummed his fingers and heaved an exasperated sigh. When I approached, he whirled on me.

"You work here? I've been waiting for 15 minutes!" A line of sweat stretched from his temple to his earlobe.

"Not usually." I sidestepped him and moved behind the counter to punch at the cash register buttons. "He locked it. You'll have to wait."

"Oh, for God's sake," he spat under his breath. "Here. I have exact change. Just take it."

"There's tax," I lied and pushed the money away. I figured I'd take out my frustration on this prick until Marc returned.

"Look, I'm in a hurry here."

"I can see that."

"What kind of place is this?"

"Nobody knows, sir."

"Are you getting smart with me?"

"How would you know if I was?"

Not very original, but it did the trick all the same. His face turned white, then red, and his eyes darkened. The tendons in his neck and jaw pulsed beneath his skin as he took deep breaths. I imagined the wheels squeaking behind his forehead as he tried to find a zinger to floor me with. "You rude little–" He stopped and smacked a palm on the counter. "That's it. You just lost a sale," he said then stormed away.

"Have a nice day," I called, remembering my manners.

He bumped shoulders with Marc in the doorway. "You work here?" he demanded.

Marc, arms full of grocery bags, took a step back to regard the puddle of rage in front of him. "Nope," he said and walked back to join me.

The man slammed the door as he left.

"Asshole," Marc and I said in unison before Marc dropped his bags and grabbed the stack of books.

"Huh, self-help garbage," he said as he flipped through the pages. "Maybe I should call him back."

"Have fun at the party?" I asked.

"Yeah, you should've stayed longer." He took the books to replace them on the shelves.

"Something happen after I left?"

He crouched behind a table and out of sight. "Don't know."

I waited for him to reappear. "You don't know? Did you leave, too?"

"Nope. Passed out on the couch. Weird."

"What did Cherise do? Did she just leave you there?"

"She passed out before me. Dean carried her upstairs since I was in no shape to take her home."

"She slept in his bed?"

Marcus looked up, surprised, as I rounded the counter. "Oh, come on, Kal. How many times has she crashed at my place? When did you turn Baptist?"

"She's never come home with a hickey before." I clenched my fists. "I can't believe you left her alone with that shark."

"Whoah." He reached for my shoulders. "First off, I've known Dean—"

"Hands off!" I shoved him. He stumbled backwards into a shelf. I planted myself.

"Kal!" he hollered. "I am not her keeper. She's a grown woman who makes her own decisions. Your problem is with Cherise, not me."

I let out my breath and dropped my head. He was right. Marc took a step toward me and placed a hand on my arm. "You haven't even asked her about it, have you?"

"I don't have to."

He squeezed my arm and gave it a gentle shake. I looked into his eyes.

"Yes, you do," he said.

~ ~ ~

THE TINY BUNGALOW huddled in the shadows of the tall apartment buildings that surrounded it. Cedars snugged up against its fieldstone walls and swayed against the leaded-glass of the front window. Multi-coloured paint peeled from the gingerbread trim on the roofline and porch. The yard was a mass of desiccated weeds.

My research of Ivy Redding, the cottage's owner and the tenth writer in the diary had unearthed a legal battle over this property in the late 1950s. Land developers had tried to force her to sell in the name of progress. They had tried to have her declared insane and a menace to her future neighbours. They had tried to prove she was running a common bawdy house, that the house was unsafe and various other ridiculous claims. The house had been in her family since the days of York, and in the end, Ivy had it declared an historical site. She could live there until the end of her days. The house would then pass to her heirs. In the absence of descendants, the house would be turned over to the city and turned into a museum. Tenacious lady.

I rapped on the front door.

"Who is that nibbling on my house?" came a voice from inside, then the door swung open.

Ivy Redding, five foot two, no more than ninety pounds, wiry white hair to her shoulders, brown, leathery cheeks hanging below her jaw, and dressed in nothing but an orange thread-bare towel shook with laughter, presumably at the look on my face.

"M-miss Redding?" I stammered.

"That's me," she said, arms wide to usher me in. "Where is it?"

"I have it with me, but first I want to thank you for answering my letter. And for seeing me."

She chortled as we entered the kitchen. Still wrapped in her towel, Ivy puttered around the stove. She put on some water to boil and dug around in a lower cupboard. The towel did its best, but when she bent over, I caught glimpses of the folds of skin that lay against the backs of her thighs.

"Would you like to take a minute to get dressed?" I asked. "I don't mind waiting."

She straightened and faced me. "One of the benefits of being a hermit is the amount of money saved on a wardrobe." She turned again and hunkered down in front of the cupboard. "Now, where is that damned mint?" She hiked the towel above her thighs and climbed headfirst into the cupboard. I averted my eyes.

"Miss Redding, do you remember how you got the diary?"

"Yes," came her muffled voice from deep inside the cabinet. "A woman gave it to me at a very rough time in my life. She said it would help to talk to someone."

"What was her name?"

"Don't know."

"What did she look like?"

"I don't see what difference that makes. A-ha!" She backed out of the cupboard with a tin clutched to her chest. The towel slipped and drifted into a heap on the worn planks of the floor. She braced herself on the counter-top and pulled herself up. The towel stayed on the floor for the remainder of the interview.

As she busied herself making us a pot of mint tea, we bandied back and forth. I asked direct questions, she provided vague answers.

"Was her name Clara?"

"Could be. Or Emily or Darla."

"How old was she?"

"Oh, you know. Not old. Not young. Kind of in between."

"How did you know her?"

"I didn't."

"What would make her think the diary would help you?"

"I don't know what she might have thought about anything."

"Do you know any of the other people who wrote in the diary?"

"Do we ever really know anyone?"

"Did you meet any of them?"

"I've met lots of people. Who's to say whether it was any of them or not?"

When the tea was steeped and ready to drink, she brought the cups to the table and sat. She planted her elbows and rested her chin in cupped hands. Ivy Redding regarded me with a faint smile and twinkling eyes while I took a tentative sip of the steaming liquid.

"I should have company more often," she said. "This is fun."

I swallowed the tea and stared at her. The batty old thing was playing with me. "Are you going to tell me anything about the diary?"

She dropped her hands to her tea cup and held the cup under her nose. She inhaled deeply two times before sipping. "The scent is the best part. Very relaxing. You should try it. It enhances the flavour of the tea."

"Miss Redding, I—"

"Just take a moment to breathe. Inhale and exhale."

I sighed.

"That's a good start. Now breathe in."

I picked up my tea cup and held it a couple inches from my nose. I sniffed. The smell of mint tickled and stung at the same time. It burned and cooled through my nasal passage and down the back of my throat. My sinuses tingled and opened.

"Now take a sip."

I sipped. The flavour was altogether different. The bitterness I first detected gave way to a refreshing sweetness. The hair on my scalp stood up and a shiver ran through me before my shoulders and neck relaxed. I took another breath and realized that I had closed my eyes.

"It's very nice," I said. "Do you grow the mint yourself?"

"I do," said Ivy. "I keep it in a barrel so it doesn't take over the rest of the herbs."

That was the first direct answer she'd provided since I arrived. I opened my eyes and smiled across the table at her. "Is there anything you would like to know about me?" I asked.

"A multitude, honey," she replied. "But, not until you're ready to share. I presume that you've read the diary."

"Yes."

"What are your thoughts?"

I launched into my theory, but she reached across the table to pat my hand. "Breathe," she whispered.

I set down the tea cup and hauled my bag into my lap to get the journal. I laid the book, closed, on the table between us, and hugged my bag to my chest. We regarded the book without speaking, the silence broken only by the odd slurp.

I tried to recall my initial impression of the book. Was it burning curiosity to learn the secrets of the well-traveled tome? Or did that come later? When I first gazed upon it, guilt and curiosity had battled in my mind and heart. The years of dust and mildew only added to its allure. I cradled history in my hands and I yearned to dive into it, to read about private lives before my own. I wondered if I had the right, but I opened the book and read before I could come up with an answer.

I remembered the tenderness I felt toward the foolhardy Clara, and the outrage at David for using her private thoughts written down for no one's eyes to take advantage of her. The changeling boy, Myrtle and her baby, and all the others. All of them worked out their personal triumphs and crises on the musty pages of Clara's lost diary. It must have touched her, I thought.

"You haven't written," said Ivy. "What are you waiting for?"

Her fingers had slid to the book to caress the face of the boy on the cover. I never intended to add my own story to the collection. I shrugged.

"What did you think of my story?" she asked.

"I'm not sure I understand it," I replied.

"What's not to understand? It's about my passage into womanhood."

"But, you were in your—what, forties?—when you wrote it."

"I never felt like a woman until then," she replied. "That's when I met my Nan. She's no longer with us."

"I'm sorry," I mumbled. "When did she die?"

"I don't know. I don't keep track of time. It was right before I got the diary."

"1965. Is that when you became a hermit?" I asked.

She chuckled and tucked her hands into her armpits. Her long breasts plumped with the pressure of her arms. "No, honey. I've always had those tendencies. That's why it took so long for Nan to find me. She came to the door one evening to sell me lipstick. We were together a long time after that. We both got grey hair and a few wrinkles. Then she died of cancer and that woman brought me this book."

"Did it help?" I asked around the sudden lump in my throat. "To write? Did writing it all down help the pain?"

She frowned and shook her head at me. Her hair brushed back and forth on her bony shoulders, and her jowls jiggled. "You didn't get the book the same way, did you? Where did you get it?"

I swallowed hard and asked again, "Did it help?"

Her face softened when she noticed the tear slip down my cheek. "Yes, honey. It helped. It helped me to say good-bye." She pushed the book toward me, then got up and crossed the kitchen to a cupboard. Standing on tiptoes, she reached up and pulled down another book, which she opened up and placed on the table in front of me. As I started to read a passage from *The Sage,* she retrieved her towel from the floor. Trailing it behind her, she left me alone.

~ ~ ~

Ivy Redding

A child once lived in a small cottage with an old woman who called herself Grandmother. She cooked for the child, washed the clothes and bedding and baked wonderful cookies and pies. Every autumn Grandmother gave the child a new knitted sweater and hood. "For you birthday," Grandmother always said.

One year as the leaves began to turn and fall, the child wondered about the anticipated sweater. Would it be blue with red zigzags? Or maybe a wonderful bright yellow, with purple at the neck and cuffs. Last year's sweater had been the best yet–stripes of every colour and little birds embroidered on top–but last year's sweater was now too small, of course. The day drew near, and the child lay in bed at night listening for the click of the knitting needles. There was, however, only the sound of Grandmother snuffling her nose. Perhaps she finished it early this year, the child thought, and fell asleep satisfied.

The big day came and the child shuffled into the kitchen, ready for a feast of raisin bread and donuts–birthday fare. Grandmother raised her head from the stove and said, "Go chop some wood, child, then come in for your sausages."

Chop the wood? Sausages? This was not birthday stuff. This was not special. Well, sausages were a little special, but certainly not birthday special. Sausages were not donuts.

The child frowned at Grandmother's back, then went out to chop the wood. Each stroke of the axe raised the child's temper another notch. Whack! *Chop the wood?* Whack! *On my birthday!* Whack! *Silly old woman.* Whack! *Gone senile, is what.* Whack! *I'm walking around with holes in a sweater that's too small.* Whack!

The wood chopping went quicker than usual.

The child struggled into the cottage with an armful of wood, and dropped it clumsily by the fireplace.

"Thank you, child," the old woman said and smiled, then she placed breakfast on the table. Sausages and sour-dough bread. Burned! All of it!

"Are you well, this morning, Grandmother?" the child ventured, tearing at the tough bread with frustrated teeth.

"Oh, as well as I can be under the circumstances. I'm an old woman and my strength is going from me," she replied and broke off a bit of too-crisp sausage.

The child was worried. Grandmother had never talked liked that before.

"Do you know how old you are this year, child?" the old woman asked after the breakfast dishes had been cleared away.

"I think about 12 years old?" the child replied. They had never kept track of such things before.

"You are 13 years old today," then, "Ah, you thought I forgot your sweater and special raisin bread."

The old woman chuckled and went to the chest of drawers. She pulled out—not a sweater!—but a full coat of grey and black wool. No bright colours, no birds or lambs embroidered on it.

"You are getting too old for a child's sweaters," she said, and wrapped the coat around the child's shoulders. It was dull, but oh so warm. And far too big.

The child stood up to model the coat. The sleeves hung almost to the knees, the hem dragged on the floor and the shoulders drooped. The old woman rolled up the sleeves, and tied the belt, blousing the coat so that the hem lifted above the floor.

"You'll grow into it," she said, and the child was suddenly afraid.

Grow into it? But I've always outgrown things, and it was okay because a new one would be knitted.

"But this isn't your real birthday present," the old woman said, leading the child to the door of the cottage. She swung open the door and pointed into the thick trees. "Your real present is out there."

She hid my sweater and raisin bread in the woods? the child wondered. She is getting too old. I shall have her teach me to knit when I get back. I'll have to do the knitting from now on. And the cooking, too, from the looks of things.

The child kissed Grandmother and turned toward the path leading into the trees.

"It's not on that path," said Grandmother. 'You have to find your own."

The child nodded and set off in the opposite direction. Grandmother waved and closed the door. The child didn't see her brush away a tear.

The child walked for many hours, searching behind rocks and in the branches of the trees for the birthday sweater, but it was nowhere to be found. As it grew dark, the child was glad for the too-big coat, even if it was ugly and plain. The child sat down to think and eventually fell asleep.

By morning, the child realized that the trees all looked the same, and that the cottage was lost somewhere among them. Fear rippled in, but gently and without panic. Follow the sun, and the village will appear presently. In the meantime, there was a present waiting to be found. For breakfast, the child ate berries and for dinner a small rabbit roasted over flames.

Years passed this way. The child grew into the coat, but by then it was tattered and dirty. The child wandered into and out of villages looking for the birthday sweater. Silly, by now, because it would be far too small. The child often thought of Grandmother, wondering how she was making out, realizing she was probably dead and gone.

The child's hair grew and legs lengthened. The child became wiser within the trees and knew where to find the best berries, how to ward against wolves in the night, and how to build a fire even in the rain.

Around this time, the child was molested by a thief in the night. The thief had no coat and thought to take the child's. In the struggle, the child got a cut that bled and bled for nearly a week. The child thought it might die. Weakened, the child crawled to a nearby stream to drink. Faint from the loss of blood, the child saw a vision reflected in the water. A beautiful woman, with bright lips and pale skin. Some message in the vision's eyes gave the child the strength to stand, the inspiration to keep moving forward.

Eventually the wound mended. Without a coat, the child decided to find a way back to the cottage. There was no sweater in these woods.

Along the way, a prince on his horse rode down the child, and attacked. The child fought back by grabbing at the prince's satchel and knocking him over the head with it. Leaving the prince behind, the child climbed into a tree to examine the contents of the satchel. *Perhaps a knife to cut my hair or a pair of breeches without holes.* But there were only some coins and a looking glass. And in the looking glass…

…the vision from the stream. A beautiful young woman with wise eyes and a full smile.

"Oh, Grandmother. Thank you," the child–the *woman*–said to the trees and birds. Then she climbed down to see if the prince was alive or dead.

He was propped up under a tree when she returned. He apologized for attacking her. He had mistaken her for a thief that had stolen one of his horses. He then offered to escort her through the woods. The woman said politely, "No, thank you, I shall find my own way."

"But a young woman alone in the woods—" he began, then stopped to rub his forehead. "Yes, alright."

The young woman never found the cottage. It was as though it had never existed. And she never saw the prince again. And she lived happily ever after, straying from as many paths as she could find.

~ ~ ~

Chapter 10

The fading stripes turn from mustard yellow to greyish green as a cloud passes in front the sun. The wind quickens, nudging at the pen, pushing and turning it until it rolls off the book, falls through the bench slats and lands in the grass below. The rain comes, large and heavy, pelting the cardboard book cover and pinging off the garden trowel left beside it on the bench. Next door, a lace curtain sways in the just-closed window.

– Konstantin Horowitz, *The Weird Sister*

The Turn

I AVOIDED THE HOUSE. For two nights, I slept on the floor of the office I shared with the other grad students, my head under the desk and my feet wedged under the chair. I wasn't ready to discuss anything with Cherise. I knew what expression her pretty face would crumple into as she hiccuped her way through an explanation. She was drunk and stoned and I had left her there without a word. Things had been strained between us, I knew that, and her infidelity came out of her loneliness and anger. That's what she would tell me when I got up the nerve to confront her. The tables would turn. I would have to make promises. Then I would go ahead and break those promises.

I couldn't do it. Not yet. At least not until the hickey had faded. Easier to forgive her and admit my own guilt without the evidence glaring at me from her neck.

Through email Ross had demanded sources and a timeline to support my thesis, so I threw myself into detective work and documentation. I begged off the undergraduate tutorials I was supposed to cover and went over my growing pile of notes around the diary.

Everyone I had spoken with denied any knowledge of Clara, Harding, Hanson, or any of the novels based on the diary. Surely, if someone learned there had been a book written about them without their permission, there would have been some sort of lawsuit. I ran all the names through an online legal database and found nothing. Nobody I had talked to was forthcoming about their involvement in this strange diary, whether to tell me how they got it or who they passed it along to. I had the distinct impression that these people were hiding something, but what? Perhaps they were merely embarrassed to be confronted with their own pasts. So, why write it all down in the first place and then go ahead and sign it? What or who compelled them?

~ ~ ~

ON MONDAY, I TRACKED down Ross in the food court. I hadn't seen him in person for a few weeks now. We had corresponded through email; I answered his questions and took on more and more of a work load from him while he consistently ignored every question I posed about progress on my thesis. I found him stuffing a microwaved burrito into his face.

"Mm, Kal," he said around a mouthful of flatbread and beans. "I saw your proposal."

I sat across from him. "What did you think?" I asked.

"Well, if you'd done any research at all on Kimberly Harding, you'd know that she disappeared a number of years ago. I'm afraid that connecting authors by their initials is a very shaky thesis, not at all at the level of a Ph.D. candidate." He jammed the last third of the burrito into his mouth and crumpled up the wrapper, chuckling. "Really, Kal. Were you drunk when you came up with it?"

"Are you saying the idea has no merit at all?" I asked, keeping my eyes on the balled up tissue he had thrown on the table.

"Not as it stands, no." He pushed away from the table and pulled himself to his feet, leaning heavily on the table as he did so. "It reads like a pulp mystery novel. There's nothing academic about it."

"I'm still working on it. I had thought to do a comparative stylistic analysis of the novels," I said, standing to follow him, but he held up a hand to stop me.

"Then, you'll have to work on it on your time. The last idea was better. Go back to it. In the meantime, fulfilling your TA obligations should be your priority. I'm still waiting for the second-year Brit Lit midterms. Really, Kal, if you want to be a mystery writer, perhaps you should reconsider grad school, hmm?"

He left me fuming in the food court.

~ ~ ~

MY BOLDEST IDEAS happen over a pint of beer. The darker and chewier the beer, the darker and chewier the idea. On this bright summer Wednesday, I had treated myself to a beverage on a patio. Normally, I preferred the anonymity of darkened, empty dives, but when I stepped out of the mausoleum that was my home now, I yearned for some warmth.

I had returned home to a sullen Cherise after sleeping in my office for a week. I had decided to allow her to bring up the topic if she wished rather than hurling accusations. Her hickey was gone, so at least I could look at her now.

I turned my feet towards Harbord St. I knew it would be busy with summer students cutting class and writing term papers with liquid inspiration. I even knew I might see some faces from my classes, but I strolled on. Change jingled in my pocket.

I took a seat on the first patio I found. Chairs and tables were crammed together on the narrow strip fenced off from the sidewalk. Fashionably grubby youngsters crowded around tiny tables, laughing from behind round sunglasses and hoisting beverages of various shades of gold, amber and brown. I ordered my Guinness and remembered Cherise telling me it matched my eyes. I actually smiled to myself, then chuckled when I realized how strange, but comfortable the expression felt to my atrophied facial muscles.

I leaned back in the plastic chair and unbuttoned my vest. A warm breeze sent gentle fingers through my hair. Moments after the chipper waitress dropped off my beer, I, still smiling, offered the empty chair at my table to a lone woman. She turned the chair a few degrees away from me by way of apology for invading the space of my table. I told her not to bother herself, to make herself comfortable, that I didn't mind the company. Me.

Yes, I did.

The woman across from me pulled out Milton's *Paradise Lost*. I pulled out *The Weird Sister* by Horowitz. We nodded at each other's choice in reading. She flipped open her book. Penciled inside the cover was her name, Jan Dawson, her phone number and her student I.D. number. I guessed she was a fourth-year lit critter, and that, although she had never heard of Horowitz, she assessed me as someone advanced enough in academia to pretend otherwise. I positioned the book on my lap, my elbow on the table, and my brow on my fingertips. I studied Jan through the fence of my fingers, and winced when she dug a pink highlighter from her studded leather purse and slaked it across the page.

"You'll regret doing that," I said to her before I could stop myself.

"Pardon?"

I kept my fingers in front of my face and nailed my eyes to my book. "Nothing," I muttered. "Sorry."

"Regret what?"

I lowered my arm and took a few sips of my beer. When I looked at her, she was leaning in, twirling the pink marker. Her eyebrows, badly plucked into clownish half-circles, were raised. With heavy-handed black, she had outlined her pale blue eyes, and filled in the banished eyebrows with frosted purple powder. Her stringy hair was a dull, flat black that absorbed the life from her complexion. I would have bet my beer she had an Ann Rice novel in that bag of hers.

"Might as well use your eyeliner pencil to black out the rest of the book. This is the last time you'll look at it, anyway."

"I don't understand," she said and pondered the pink pen in her hand.

"Never mind. You probably have a paper to write. Don't let me bother you."

"No. I'm curious."

I sighed and closed my book. I turned my shoulders so I could face her fully. The server came by and I ordered another beer. "You've bought used books for your courses, right? I bet they're underlined and highlighted. When you open them to any page, where does your eye go? Straight to a passage that someone else has decided contains the only important words on that page. You don't know why he chose that paragraph. Maybe it reminded him of home, or maybe he was writing an essay about the colour yellow. Whatever it was, it has no meaning for you because you weren't the one who highlighted it."

"But, this is my book," she said with a sniff. "I'm not going to sell it."

"Oh. How long do you think you'll have it?" She shrugged. "Ten years? Thirty? Do you really think you'll be the same person thirty years from now? All I'm saying is, don't wreck the book for the next person who reads it—you."

"Well. Okay," she said and capped the highlighter. From experience, and the look on her white face, I knew she was trying not to agitate me. "Highlighters are bad."

"No, they're just lazy and permanent," I responded. "If you like a passage, write it down somewhere. Just remember to cite your source."

She dropped the pen into her bag and nodded at me with puckered lips and rounded brows. I finished my first beer with a gulp and turned away from her. I noted with odd relief that the shadow had crept back over the old part of me. Good riddance good mood.

My second drink arrived. My mood improved, but just a little.

Somewhere in the bottom third of my fifth pint, or maybe it was my sixth, the idea hit me. I flagged down the waitress, grumbled about my bill when she brought it, and paid it. I waved good-bye to Jan and climbed over the wrought-iron barrier onto the sidewalk. I took a few lock-kneed brisk steps in the direction of the university campus, then stopped and turned just in time to see a flash of pink in Jan's black-nailed fingers.

By the time I reached the campus, my strolling gait had become a purposeful stride. I no longer felt jovial under the summer sun, but I smiled. I composed my entrance line in the elevator. My jaw set and eyebrow raised, I barged into Michael

Ross's office. His massive face registered huge surprise. Gobs of flesh quivered as he lumbered to his feet. A pimply undergraduate seated in front of the desk quaked.

"It's okay, George," said Ross to the undergrad before addressing me. "Kal?"

"Beat it, George," I snarled. "Professor Ross will meet with you later."

"No, George, stay—"

But the kid hit the ground at a scamper. He scurried by me and was out the door before Ross could finish the sentence. The professor fell back into his padded chair with a mighty ripple and placed his large paws flat on the desk. "What are you doing, Kal?" he asked.

"Did you shit on my proposal because it deserved it? Or was it for personal reasons?" I answered. I waited for him to say something, but he only breathed, rather heavily. His lungs had a big job to do, oxygenating that body.

"Really, Mike, if you can't see past your problems with me to give it a fair assessment as an academic, then I need to know that. I need to decide how to proceed. It's a good theory, Mike. It has merit and I have proof."

He had lowered his eyes to his fidgeting fingers. He wouldn't look at me, but I knew I was getting to him. I slouched to let my bag slide from my shoulder to the floor. "I'll show you," I said, and bent to unzip the knapsack. But I noticed a book on his desk and straightened. It was *Meander* by Kimberly Harding. I raised my eyes to his and noticed his hand waver, as if to throw something over the book.

"I think you should go now, Kal. We'll talk later about this when you've sobered up. And about your future here." His eyes were narrowed and he licked his lips nervously.

"Yeah, Mike. We'll do that," I said. I whirled around and staggered out of his office. George leaned against the wall in the hallway. He backed away from me as I passed by cursing under my breath. The bastard was going to steal my idea.

~ ~ ~

I NEVER FOUND MOIRA. Her diary entry was short and cryptic, scribbled in hard, rushed script. She fulfilled some obligation by leaving her hurried mark, then turned her back on whatever circumstances brought the journal to her. She wrote and ran.

Her short note stood out from the rest. She was the only one to leave out her surname and other personal details. She was singularly unimpressed with the book and its creator, and her entry hinted at directives given to her with the diary.

I cursed my luck that the one person likely to provide me with useful information was untraceable. Whatever twist of fate had released Moira from her personal difficulty chose not to smile on me.

"Five minutes to closing, Kal. Pack up," said Debbie from the circulation desk.

I tossed a glance over my shoulder and grunted my assent. It was time to quit anyway. Since noon I'd stared at my notes, the diary and library reference materials, but no flash of insight had leapt from the jumble of pages. It was nearly eight now, and my brain was turning off. I gathered together the mess and jammed it into my backpack.

I was missing something. The diary was all the evidence I needed to connect Clara Strachan to Kimberly Harding and the other various pseudonyms she used after shedding the first. I had to keep looking, to complete the picture, to flesh out the rest of the characters that were involved before Ross beat me to it. I was growing more interested in the truth behind the fiction. My intellectual curiosity was satisfied. It was something else that drove me now.

Nobody wanted to talk about their part in the diary or the books that were based on their honest pain and triumphs. It didn't make sense to me that these people shared private thoughts in a public forum, allowed it to be fictionalized, then refused to talk about it all these years later. They no longer had anything to hide. Yet, they were hiding something.

I stood and walked to the door. I waved a neutral good-bye to Debbie, and she smiled. Lately, we'd had a truce of sorts. I noted with interest that when I made an effort to be nicer to people, they made an effort not to bug me so much.

The air outside was moist with light rain and smelled of soil and worms. The lawns on the street had turned from green to brown, and leafy plants drooped over the matted mulch in flower beds. The sun was orange as it began its descent behind the rooflines of the neighbourhood. The combination of simultaneous sun and rain cast a greenish glow on the damp pavement.

I was unsure of what to do next. I had connected each contributor to Clara/Kimberly. I had read the diary and each book based on the entries in it. I knew who was still living, and those who had passed, I knew where to find their relatives. I had talked to a few people and I had hit a wall with each of them. I could go back and try to talk to them again, or I could keep plugging ahead and talk to the rest of the writers and hope to uncover something significant. I could stick with the evidence I had and publish the diary with my findings, or I could abandon the project altogether.

The last option repulsed me, whereas the idea of cashing in an advance cheque was tempting. I decided to start writing, and to continue interviewing people.

~ ~ ~

Moira

Thursday, 1955

Ding dong! The witch is dead!

…and I have no intention of hanging around this dump one day longer.

My situation has changed drastically since I picked up this little book. Yesterday, I read it cover to cover and felt ridiculously sorry for myself and curiously inspired by all these people who have found their own way. Oh, to be able to drop all obligations and do just as one pleases, except maybe for that one little boy. But then, I don't suppose he's a little boy any longer. So perhaps, he too is doing whatever he damn well pleases.

Well, I am not a lost little boy, and I am not a beautiful woman lost in the woods.

I have been snared all my life in a trap that was not of my own making.

Sometimes things just happen and some of us end up getting dealt crap and we just have to make the best and wait and wait for all the nonsense to clear so that we can get on with our lives. Sometimes it never clears and there are people who waste their whole precious time on this planet cleaning up after everyone else.

Well, the waiting is done. I'm out of here. My story is just beginning and I don't intend to waste time writing it all down. The End.

~ ~ ~

Chapter 11

Water streams down the pane of glass. The face behind it is distorted, rippled by endless dirty rivulets. Metal strikes metal with a squeal and the face winces. A jolt. Her head jerks as the bus is thrown into gear and lurches forward. She leans her forehead on the glass, eyes closed. Drizzle mixes with the exhaust from the bus. Brake pads squeal and the bus slows to a stop, waiting to turn onto the busy street. Pedestrians huddle together on the corner, halted by the red light and miserable in the damp cold. The bus window slides open an inch and the corner of a flat, rectangular package pokes through the opening. The light turns green, and the book tips out of the window.

– Konrad Heuslegger, *The Scales*

Deserts

Andrew Murray lived on the top floor of a Victorian house in Kensington Market. Unlike many of his neighbours, Andrew wasn't a poor artist stretching his budget to live in the popular area. He wasn't an actor, wasn't a painter, wasn't even a psychic. Andrew was a lawyer. He was a very good lawyer, but, unlike many of his colleagues, Andrew Murray wasn't in it for the money. Not anymore, anyway.

"I don't think intellectual property is an issue here, but I would have to know more about it," he said to me on his balcony. I pulled my eyes from where two drunken lovers screamed at each other in the street. I had asked his opinion about Ross stealing my idea. Without telling him exactly what the idea was, of course. "Sorry, but from the little bit you told me, you don't have a case. Without more information I would have to say your best bet is to publish before he does. Another drink?"

He stood and picked his way over the plants and bags of potting soil that cluttered the tiny balcony. His hand hovered over the white mug I held. I gave it to him and he climbed with it back through his bedroom window, a commendable feat for a man in his seventies. The angry couple had disappeared around the corner by now, but I could still hear the woman's strident voice.

I heard the clink of ice on glass from inside Andrew's home, followed by the caramel splash of seven-year-old Scotch. One of his priorities, I figured, judging by the state of his apartment.

It was a strange home. He had given me a tour when I arrived, with soft eyes and proud gestures for the four minutes it took us to walk through the three rooms. His taste leaned towards minimalist. The kitchen, bath and great room that served as his bedroom were all painted white. Linens, curtains and dishes were white. It couldn't be called monochromatic, however, due to the splashes of colour in the oddest places. The door hinges, for instance, were all peacock blue. The screws that held together the white wooden bed were crimson, and the brackets underneath the white kitchen shelves were buttercup yellow. I found it an interesting choice to highlight the hardware most people who cared about that kind of thing opted to camouflage.

Andrew returned and handed the mugs to me through the window, then climbed out after disentangling himself from the bleached muslin curtain. I ducked my head to sip my Scotch. The chill of the ice cube against my top lip sent a tingle through my jaw. I wanted to ask him more about the diary. He had been vague earlier when I brought it up. Before I could frame the question, however, a screech pierced the relative quiet of the night. Andrew and I jumped to the railing in unison. The female portion of the inebriated couple emerged from an alley up the block and ran toward us down the middle of the street. She waved her arms over her head, and as she passed through the circle of light under a street lamp, her smeary face reflected horror.

I glanced back up the street to the alley and saw the boyfriend stagger from the lane and onto the sidewalk. He fell to his knees behind a car. Beyond the hood, I saw his shadowed form. He struggled to pull himself to his feet. The woman's screams echoed off the dark brick faces of the buildings as the man's hands scrambled over the car to get a grip on the bumper. He hauled himself up and sauntered with only a slight sway. His girlfriend ran past us, her hysterics subsided by now to whimpering. After a few minutes, the man's careful footsteps carried him into the wash of light in front of Andrew's building.

Our collective gasp floated down to the man, and his eyes turned to us before he collapsed. The broken beer bottle stuck out of his stomach at a right angle. Blood soaked the front of his shirt and darkened the corners of his mouth.

Andrew scrambled over me to crawl in the window.

"I'm going down!" he shouted over his shoulder. "Call 911!"

~ ~ ~

HOURS LATER, AFTER the police and ambulance had come and gone, and the night was quiet again, Andrew told me his story over the bottom half of the bottle of Scotch. We sat inside now. The window was still open, but only a crack. The temperature outside had dropped while we stood on the sidelines to watch the paramedics work on the hapless lover, and give our statements to the police.

"You think my turning point was the diary, don't you?" he asked.

"It wasn't?"

He shifted and yanked a white pillow from underneath his thigh. He was in a chair across from the bed where I sat cross-legged.

"The diary was no more than a 'to-do' list for me."

"Then why write it down if wasn't significant?"

"I didn't say it wasn't significant. It was. I just didn't know it. I was plotting my own demise as a corporate lawyer."

I shrugged.

"After my part in the diary ended, I accepted a job and moved downtown into a very swanky space. I spent weeks packing. I was orderly and meticulous about editing my life–letters, papers from school, photographs that wouldn't fit into my new lifestyle. I sent change of address cards and took the opportunity to edit my contacts. Those who didn't fit didn't get a card. Finally, as moving day approached, I dismantled the big items. My designer furniture, bookshelves and dinette set. I put all the screws and brackets in labeled envelopes which I then put in a box." He stopped to uncap the bottle and hand it to me. "Do you see?"

I took a pull from the bottle and passed it back. "No. I don't."

"The contents of that single box held together my whole life." Andrew leaned forward and smiled. I stared at him blankly. "The movers lost *that* box."

~ ~ ~

I TIPTOED INTO the house. It was only four in the afternoon, but if Cherise was napping I didn't want to wake her. I checked all the rooms, but she wasn't home. The answering machine flashed in the kitchen. I got a beer from the fridge and hit the button.

"Hey, Cherise, it's Dean. Just checking in to see if you're okay. Call me."

I guzzled from the bottle as Dean's voice rhymed off the phone number. The machine beeped and the next message played.

"Cherise, it's me again. Dean. You should call me, soon. To talk. You have the number."

The door slammed as the next message played.

"Cherise, hi. I just talked to Marcus. What the hell did you say to Kal? I don't know what you think happened after the party, but we need to talk. Call me."

The floor creaked in the living room. Keys jingled. The machine beeped again.

"Look Cherise. I've been waiting around all day for you to call me. I don't know what kind of game you're playing, but if you tell anyone what we did together—*together*—I'll find you." I looked to the doorway where Cherise braced herself. She gaped at the answering machine. Dean's voiced snarled between us. "You had a lot to drink and toke. That's no excuse, baby. I never heard the word "no" come out of your pretty mouth. There's no going back, now, darling."

Her knees buckled and she went down with a wail. I went to her, gripped her arms and tried to pull her to her feet, but she fought me shrieking, "No! No! Get off me!"

I scrambled with her on the kitchen floor. "Cherise, stop it! Calm down, please, honey, calm down. It's just me." But she was possessed. She caught me in the jaw with an elbow and rolled away, curled in a ball. The same way I had found her the morning after the party. She rocked and sobbed. I couldn't get near her without sending her into another frenzy.

I stood. My heart pounded and I heard thunder in my ears. The messages finished with a beep. I picked up the phone and dialed.

Dean answered on the first ring. I heard clattering as he fumbled with the phone. "Cherise?" His voice was tight, expectant. "I'm sorry for the things I said. I don't know what's wrong with me."

"Listen to her!" I demanded, then held the phone at arm's length towards the heap of my girlfriend. Her keening made my scalp prickle. Tears flooded my eyes as I watched her clutch at her own clothes, pulling them tight around her. I spoke into the phone again. "Can you hear that, you son of a bitch? What did you do?"

"Chick Pea? Is that you?" he asked. And then he chuckled.

"Stay away from us!" I shouted. I slammed the phone down and sank to the floor covering my face with my hands. Through my fingers, I watched Cherise.

Slowly, she quieted, her breathing evened out, and she pulled herself into a sitting position with her knees tucked under her chin. She glanced at me, but wouldn't hold my gaze. I waited for her to speak.

"Kal, I'm sorry. I know you thought—" She broke off and looked up at the ceiling. She took a deep breath and continued. "He gave us a drink. Me and Marc. I think it was drugged."

My heart skipped. "Roofies?"

She nodded. "I think so. I'm so sorry—"

"What do you remember?"

"Not much. A little. I woke up in his bed and it...it hurt." Her face crumpled for a second, but she toughed it out by breathing heavily through her nose. "Kal, I'm sorry. I am so sorry."

I wanted to hold her, but guilt and rage kept me still. She closed her eyes tightly, jamming her knuckles into her brow.

"We'll get him, Cherise. He won't get away with it."

She shrugged and sniffled. "Of course he will."

"What do you mean? We'll go to the police. Marc can tell them."

"Tell them what? He passed out. He has no idea anything happened. He won't believe me, anyway. Dean is his friend." She stood, all business. "I'm not going to the police. It's too late now, anyway. Hungry?"

"What?" I demanded as I scrambled to my feet. "We have to do something, Cherise. What if he does it again?"

"What if he does?" She whirled on me. Her eyes were hard and angry as she shouted at me. "How is that my problem? When did it become the victim's duty to stop rapists? I was stupid. Maybe I deserved it for being so goddamned stupid!"

"What are you talking about? You weren't—"

"It's easy to say *we* have to do something, Kal, but *we* weren't raped. *I* was. Where the fuck were you?"

The shrill question hit me in the face like a bucket of ice water. "You're a grown woman," I mumbled, recalling Marc's words. "I thought you could take care of yourself."

"Bullshit. You thought Marc would take care of me. And the minute you knew something was up, you thought I cheated on you."

"Cherise, how was I supposed to know?"

"You didn't even bother to ask me. How long were you going to pretend nothing was wrong? Until you finished your fucking thesis?"

I couldn't answer her. She was so hard and ugly at that moment, but I knew she needed to articulate her fury. Besides, she was right.

She glared at me, waiting for me to say something. I held her eyes until my own filled with tears and her face dissolved into a blur. She pounded a fist on the counter and howled, then grabbed a cabinet door, flung it open and slammed it shut with all her strength. The dishes inside rattled. A glass fell over. She stopped screaming and dropped her head into her arms on the counter. "I can't do this. I won't. It's over."

"Over?"

"Not us, you big idiot. This anger. I'm letting go of it." She exhaled and lifted her head. Then, with a wink and a smile, she went about the business of making dinner.

We were supposed to pretend none of it had happened. I moved to help her. The only sounds were chopping, sizzling and clinking. My hand brushed her hip and she cringed, stiff and quick before letting out a short laugh and mumbled apology.

We ate in silence and I cleared the table. When I finished, I joined Cherise in the garden. She lit a cigarette, her first in months. She glanced up, expecting me to give her shit.

"Do what you have to, Babe," I murmured and watched the smoke drift away above her head.

"I'll be okay, Kal," she said between puffs. "I just need some time. I have to do this my way."

"Whatever you want, my love."

"Don't coddle me. Don't do anything different. I won't let this change us. I don't want it to be a turning point. If I give it that kind of significance, I'll never get past it."

"Are you sure that's—?"

"I don't want to talk about it. What happened in the kitchen–that's the last time." She threw her butt on the ground and lit another. "How's the research going?"

I told her about the diary and my theory. She chain-smoked while she listened. She smiled and nodded as I laid it out for her and I realized how long it had been since we had talked like this. I felt odd sitting there with her, outside myself, an observer more than a participant. Sadness underlined my words and I knew Cherise could hear it.

It *was* a turning point. We *were* changed, and Cherise would never recover from what Dean had done to her.

~ ~ ~

Andrew Murray

1955, September

In my first semester of law school at Osgoode Hall. Came from a B.MA program at Wilfred Laurier. Corporate law. That's where the money is.

1955, October

School is fine. Don't start articling until next year, but research doesn't hurt. Toronto or Ottawa. One or two look interesting.

Course work: Case study where a man abducted a woman and held her prisoner in his basement for ten days. Tortured her the whole time. Defecated on her and hung her by wrists from rafters. Stitched her cuts himself. No painkillers. Animal.

1955, November

Met a stubborn woman today. Works in the public library, periodical section. Very methodical and level-headed. Should be a lawyer, the way she argues. Bleeding heart says criminals are products of society. Abused children. That very well may be, but these abused children grow up and learn that it's wrong to rob, maim and murder people. Her eyes are green.

1955, December

Christine.

1955, December

Exams went well. Law firm in Ottawa looks promising.

1956, January

Good Christmas. Mother and Dad won't be disappointed when they see how far I go. I'll buy them modern presents for Christmas. No cheap books and dime-store perfume like this year.

Christine suggested I article with a local firm. Small, private with no clear specialty. Quick background on a few of the lawyers. I will not work at the last ditch for bad students.

Christine says they help downtrodden people. She also argues they almost always win their cases. Maybe so, but how will I live?

1956, February

Christine agreed to have dinner with me if I agree to take her little law firm seriously. Bribery! I conceded.

1956, March

Christine believes law is intentionally elevated out of the reach of the people it is intended to protect. She called lawyers a "self-propagating species."

1956, June

Christine has agreed to marry me to keep on me and my kind for the good of the public.

We will be married in a year.

1956, July

Leave for Ottawa in two months to begin work with the firm. Christine is disappointed. She doesn't know that I never spoke to her little lawyers.

1956, September

She won. Turned down the offer from Ottawa for Christine's little firm.

1956, December

I cannot live like this any longer. If I go to Ottawa, in a few short months I will double my income. I haven't told Christine of my decision.

1957, January

Christine has broken off the engagement.

1957, February

Dad is in trouble. Arrived in Ottawa and I'm in no position to leave. Mother has pleaded with me over the phone.

My furniture has not yet arrived.

1957, March

Christine returns my letters unopened.

1957, April

I managed to take two days off work to meet with Dad. I didn't recognize him until he spoke to me. Christine has married another man.

~ ~ ~

Chapter 12

It lay there on the sidewalk all afternoon, spine cracked, face down. Some children on their way home from school kicked it around a bit before racing off down the street. Dappled sunlight hit the cover, but the man could not make out the picture from his house. His breathing was shallow as he peeked out from between the spindles of the porch railing. Only a hint of the sun still glowed on the horizon, the purple clouds above it growing charcoal, then black. He inhaled and gripped the railing a moment before launching himself off the porch and down the sidewalk at a sprint. He stopped in a crouch over the battered book and looked around nervously. A dog barked just as his hands closed around the book. He jumped to his feet and whirled in a circle, frantic. No one was on the street. His legs flexed, as if to run back again, but he stopped himself. He hugged the book to his chest and took careful, measured footsteps back to his porch. His breath was ragged, but his feet were steady.

– Konrad Heuslegger, *The Wait*

The Quiescent

JUST INSIDE THE FRONT cover, a red stamp indicated the book had been left at the library on September 17, 1957. How anyone had ever mistaken it for a library book, I couldn't imagine. The librarian, Katharine Harvey, had apparently realized the mistake after stamping the book, and taped a note to a blank page. I held the note in my fingertips as I waited in line at the circulation desk. Yellowed shards of brittle tape still clung to the edges of the page. Time had robbed the tape of its stickiness and the note now floated loosely between the rippled pages.

"Next," said the middle-aged man behind the desk.

As I approached, he pushed his glasses up on his nose and looked to my hands for the books he expected me to sign out. I cleared my throat and his eyes darted up to my face.

"Yes?"

"I'm looking for Mrs. Katharine Harvey. She worked here in 1957?"

"She died more than ten years ago," he said. "Is there something I can help you with?"

"How long have you worked here?" I asked against hope. He would have been a kid.

"I'm not sure how that's relevant," he muttered, then took the note from me. "But maybe I can help…" He trailed off and tipped his head back to peer at the neat handwriting through his bifocals. He read barely aloud, tongue working against teeth on the sibilants. By the time he reached the end of the note, his fuzzy eyebrows had disappeared underneath his unfortunate bangs. He set the note back on the countertop just as the front door opened. A draft caught the note and it fluttered toward me.

"Did you know her? Or Mr. Bedford?" I said, grabbing for the page as it floated off the edge of the counter. I swatted at it during its descent and snatched it around my knees. When I straightened and looked back to the librarian, he shrugged and said, "Yes, and it was just like her to think that was a library book. I can't help you." A line had formed behind me. I glanced around at the collection of young mothers, the elderly and the unemployed who patiently shifted their weight from one foot to another. He turned his attention from me to the little girl who stood behind me with three books to check out.

"I remember Miss Harvey," said a deep voice to my left. I turned to see an older man pulling himself out of an armchair in the reading nook. He was tall with tufts of white hair sticking out at odd angles over his ears. He strode toward me and held out a hand. "May I see?"

I handed him the note. He smiled when he finished and gave me back the paper. "That sounds just like her," he said as I tucked the note back inside the diary in the place it had occupied for almost fifty years.

"Oh!" he said. "I do remember that book. It was in his lap when I found him."

"Found who?"

"Mr. Bedford." He fell silent.

"Sir?"

"Hm?" He shook his head a little and laughed at himself. "Sorry, I was just remembering."

"Remembering what, Mr....?"

He thrust his hand toward me and introduced himself. "Jeremy Russell. I used to take him books from the library. I thought it was just another library book. His diary, eh?" While he spoke, he led me to the reading nook where we took padded chairs facing each other. My bum hit wood when I sat too hard. The orange fabric of the chairs was worn and stained.

"This is a coincidence," I said, not really believing it. I figured he must be recently retired or widowed and lonely. I was familiar with his type, suddenly finding themselves with nothing to do and hanging around coffee shops and libraries looking for a conversation.

"Not really. This is a nice neighbourhood. People don't move away. I never left, and I've been coming to this library every week since I was eleven. Same with them." He gestured to a group of cronies seated in similar chairs reading newspapers or conversing quietly.

"So you knew Mr. Bedford very well, I guess," I prompted.

He took off his glasses and tucked them into his shirt pocket. "He was a shut-in. The neighbours looked out for him. Cut his grass, took his paper in to him, kept an eye out. My father told me his wife died in a car accident and he stopped coming outside."

"He never left the house?"

"Well, there are stories."

"What stories?"

"Oh, kid's stuff."

"Like what?"

"Some said that on a summer night, Mr. Bedford tiptoed out of his house, picked something up from the sidewalk, then dashed back in."

"What did he pick up?"

"That depends on who's telling the story. Some said a dead cat. Some said he was picking food out of the garbage."

It was the diary. I was sure of it. Someone had left it as a carrot to tempt the rabbit from his hole. It was what the lonely grief-stricken man had been waiting for. It had worked on me.

~ ~ ~

THE WALK HOME from the library was soggy and cold. The rain didn't let up until a block from the house. The black clouds split apart in the west to allow orange rays to hit the trees. The turning leaves blazed against the dark backdrop of retreating clouds. I squinted to see the sidewalk in front of me.

I had considered heading farther east along Bloor to visit the flower shop where the next person to write in the diary worked, but I wanted to get back to Cherise. I hoped to have an early supper together and play a game of Scrabble. The two of us had established a calmness in the past days that we hadn't known for months. Cherise no longer complained of the long hours I spent holed up at the library or in my office, and for my part, I got back into the habit of calling her when I knew I was going to be late. I missed her quick laughter, and her eyes had grown a little duller, but I knew she needed time to reclaim that part of herself. She was healing, and I was doing what I could to help her. When I reached home, I paused a moment to pluck a rain-drenched black-eyed susan from the flowerbed. Then I skipped up the steps to the front door, turned the knob and stepped over the threshold into an ambush.

"Is that the mysterious Kal?" I heard a woman call from the living room. The question was followed by footsteps hurrying across the room and into the hall where I was hanging my wet jacket.

Cherise poked her head around the corner. Her smile faded when she saw me. "You're soaked!" she hissed.

"I forgot my umbrella at school," I said and moved to kiss her. She ducked. "Who's here?" I asked through my aborted pucker, then noticed that she was wearing a sari. "Why are you dressed like that?"

"I have a surprise." She grasped my hand and yanked me into the living room. "Mommy and Daddy, this is Kal," she announced with a nervous giggle.

Cherise's parents jumped to their feet; my stomach jumped into my throat.

"Is this a joke?" asked her father. He was a striking man with silver hair and coffee-coloured skin. His black eyes glittered and thin mouth twitched, wanting to smile.

I swallowed around the cotton in my throat, took a step toward him and offered a hand. "Kal Winters, sir. Pleased to meet you." I glanced at his wife. My smile felt like a muscle spasm.

Cherise's mother sat down hard on the couch. Her jaw flapped before she squeezed out a cold "hello." Her features were a harsher version of her daughter's; her nose was wider, mouth fuller and jaw heavier, though I could detect the same plumpness under her red sari.

My hand hovered in the space between us for a moment too long before I dropped it to my side.

"I told you you'd be surprised," Cherise said lamely from the doorway. I didn't know if she meant me or her parents.

"You can't be serious, Cherise," her mother said. Her disdainful eyes swept over me, head to foot, cataloguing my faults. I imagined the picture I made: spiky red hair curling away from my head in sopping waves, blotchy freckles smeared across my nose and cheeks, drenched T-shirt clinging to sharp shoulders and draping nearly to my knees over baggy, ripped jeans. I looked down and realized that not only were my knees poking out of the holes in my pants, but one toe stuck out of my wet wool sock.

"You said you were dating a professor," her father said. He squared off in front of me and put his hands on his hips.

"I—" I started, but Cherise rushed to my side and interrupted me.

"A grad student, Dad. A grad student. A *grad* student! I've told you that a hundred times," she said, her voice rising. "And we're not dating. We live together."

Oh god.

Her father laughed suddenly. A burst of merriment swept across his features, and he slapped a thigh. His wife smiled weakly, not getting the joke. "You're roommates!"

he exclaimed. "Oh, Cherise, what am I going to do with you? You had us going. So sorry...Kal, is it? My name is Anand and this is my wife, Tira."

I looked to Cherise's mother who fidgeted on the couch. She twisted her fingers into the hem of her gown. The brief smile had left her face. She didn't buy into her husband's desperation.

"No, Dad. Not just roommates." Her eyes shimmered with tears as she drew a shaky breath and released it. She held her mother's eyes and lifted her shoulders, dropping her chin almost to her chest. I felt her fingers at my side, groping for a handhold, and I twined my hand in hers. "Lovers."

Oh fuck.

Cherise's mother erupted. She flew off the couch, spewing a hot, rapid stream of Hindi at her daughter. Cherise dropped my hand and strode forward so she stood nose to nose with her mother, matching the older woman in tone and pitch. Her father bellowed behind them and fell back onto the couch, clutching at his hair.

I stood like stone, my mouth gaping open. I knew that Cherise's parents adhered to Hindu law, but she had made them sound hip to the Canadian way of life. It had never occurred to them, for instance, to bother to arrange a marriage for her. They treated her, their only child, the way traditional parents would treat a son.

Tira demanded that Cherise abandon her life with me. She was shocked to learn we had been together for more than a year already and deeply hurt to have been kept in the dark. She leaned in to her daughter so that the younger woman was forced to take a step back. Cherise threw wild looks from her mom and dad to me, then said simply and forcefully, "No."

Her father let go of his hair and scrambled to his feet to grab his wife by the shoulders. His firm grip silenced her tirade. He murmured to his daughter in his native tongue, quietly with dull eyes, then steered his wife through the room and out of the house.

Cherise drew shaky breaths. She sank into a chair and looked up at me. "They disowned me," she said.

She wanted support. Her eyes pleaded with me to make her feel loved. I couldn't. I was irate.

"What did you think was going to happen?" I said. "I can't believe you right now, Cherise."

I waited until I heard the car pull away out in the street, then I grabbed my coat to go for a fast, angry walk. The rain let up after twenty minutes, about the same time that I slowed my stride. My breath was heavy and hung in a fog in the cool autumn air. I tried to think of what to say to Cherise, but every sentence that bashed around in my skull was too harsh. I wanted to scream, not at Cherise, but at whatever god was responsible for upsetting the peace we had finally found together. I regretted the tone I had used with her, but it was as gentle as I could be after the way her parents had treated both of us. Nasty remarks popped into my head, phrases that I wished I had had the presence of mind to use with Anand and Tira.

Another twenty minutes or so of walking led me to a bar on Dupont Street. I went in. The light was dim, the atmosphere depressed, probably by the gloomy day outside. I took a seat at the end of the bar and draped my drenched coat over the back of it. Two or three old men were scattered about the place. Die-hards, I guessed. Experience told me they wouldn't bother me, which was just what I wanted.

The bartender sauntered to my end of the bar. "Forget your umbrella?" she asked with a nicotine-stained grin. I shuddered from a chill at my back.

"I'll have a pint of that," I said, gesturing to one of the taps. It was a dark beer, just like my mood.

I drank five pints in silence and nobody bothered me. My mood darkened and blurred. The sky outside deepened from dove grey to slate to charcoal. The wind picked up and I watched the odd piece of garbage float past the greasy window. This angered me further as I brooded over the people too lazy to secure their garbage so that bags ended up caught in the branches of trees, drink boxes lodged in shrubs and candy wrappers twisted around the stems of flowers, strangling them.

I left when I ran out of money. I wandered aimlessly, half-heartedly toward my office at the university, but my feet led me to a bank machine. I didn't want to go home yet, anyway. I didn't know what to say to Cherise, and I knew my inebriated state would only make the situation worse. I decided to wait until I sobered up and calmed down. Maybe by then I would think of something to say to her that would make it alright. But first, I wanted to get one more drink.

~ ~ ~

MY HANGOVER woke me. I kept my eyes squeezed shut against the pain. Something felt scratchy against my cheek. I slitted an eye and looked down. Hot pink shag carpet glared up at me. Where the hell was I? I opened both eyes and lifted my head.

I had apparently spent the night face down in a Moroccan brothel. Gold walls were hung with tapestries, beads and mirrors. Rugs and large purple pillows stood for furniture. I dropped my head back to the floor and worked on remembering what I did the previous night.

I remembered dark bars and rain. And beer. Oh, yes, it had been raining beer last night.

"Good morning, Sunshine!" chirped Marcus. He dropkicked a pillow in my direction. "Welcome to *mi casa*. How are we feeling this morning? Oh, does your head hurt? Would you like some juice? Some aspirin? How about a kick in the head? Oh, never mind. You had enough of that last night."

I rolled onto my back. Pain jabbed at my eyes, and my stomach folded itself into a pretzel. I spun back onto my side and curled into a ball, panting. Nausea gurgled in my gut. My wrist throbbed, my back burned, my head ached, my neck was stiff, and one leg was blessedly numb. I opened my mouth to speak, but a split in my bottom lip gaped and sent spasms into my chin and jaw.

Marcus leaned over me and placed a pillow under my head. "Nothing is broken and you don't have a concussion, which proves my theory that your head is made of rubber," he said. "How much do you remember?"

I grimaced, afraid to shake my head. "Wha—?" I stopped, gasped, and made a mental note to avoid words beginning with W until my lip mended. "Nothing."

"The short version is that you got drunk and called me to meet you at a bar."

I nodded.

"Oh, you remember that much, do you? Then, you took a header down some stairs."

I groaned.

"Coming back to you?"

"No," I croaked.

"The manager called an ambulance and you bolted. That's when you fell down again. You puked on the paramedics, but they patched you up, anyway."

"Oh."

"Oh."

"Wher—" Dammit! "My vhag?"

"Your bag? I don't know where it is, Kal. You had nothing on you when you were picked up. Did you leave it in the bar?" His voice seemed tense to me, but I was hardly one to judge.

I thought. No. I'd left it in my office before going to the bar. I sighed and raised my good hand to stroke Marc's fuzzy cheek. "Thanks."

"You're not welcome," he said, but smiled. He turned his face and kissed my palm. "Jesus, Kal."

He disappeared into the kitchen and clanked some plates while I collected myself. I splashed water on my face and armpits and gargled with mouthwash. I surveyed the damage in the mirror. A black eye, scraped cheek and split lip gave me the appearance of a thug. I looked like I'd spent a night in jail. Cherise would freak out when she saw me. From bad to worse, always. Never the other way for Kal Winters.

I slowly ate the breakfast of oatmeal and coffee that Marcus had prepared for me, using a little spoon so I didn't have to open my mouth too wide. I even sat still while he cleaned my wounds with antiseptic. By nine o'clock, he was out the door to go open the store for the day.

I sat down at his computer to check my email before going to the office to pick up my bag. I cringed when I saw a message from Ross in the inbox. The subject line was simple: WHERE ARE YOU?!

~ ~ ~

Simon Bedford

March 27, 1957

Dear Sir or Madam:

Owing to the fact that there is no catalogue number, title or editor for this book, I think I can safely assume that this is not a published book, nor does it belong in this or any other library. From what I have read in these most varied and personal pages, I believe there is a Pattern, although I can't begin to decipher it. The book was found in the death grip of Mr. Simon Bedford. I do not know how it got there. For the time being, I shall have to place it in Lost and Found. I don't know what else to do with it.

Sincerely,
Katherine Harvey

~ ~ ~

Chapter 13

The boy freezes in horror when he sees his mother standing in the doorway. He kneels on the shed floor with his arms raised above his head, holding high the body of a dead rodent. Droplets of blood run down his raised arms and land on the book that is spread open on the floor in front of him. The red beads obscure the childish script on the pages.

– Konrad Heuslegger, *Clearly Departed*

The Daisy Pusher

I FOUND FRANK in the back room of the flower shop. I stepped through the door and was shushed before my eyes could adjust to the dim light. Candles flickered from the corners of the room, placed on shelves among rolls of ribbons and wrapping paper. My pupils expanded and Frank's form seated behind a workbench grew clearer. He waved a bundle of strong-smelling smoldering herbs in a slow circle over the tabletop. He muttered in a language I couldn't identify. With a quick twist of his wrist, he dunked the burning bundle into a vase of water, and let out a slow hiss that echoed the drowned embers.

"I'm in the middle of something," he said. "Can't Linda help you?"

The glass doors of the refrigeration unit behind him reflected the candlelight so that it appeared to form a halo behind his shaved head. I couldn't see his eyes in their darkened sockets.

"Mr. Bosa, my name is Kal Winters."

"Is it? What kind of name is Kal?"

"I don't really know. You'd have to ask my parents."

"You never did?"

"No."

He shifted to rest his elbows on the table and lean toward me.

"How do you know Frank Bosa?" he asked.

"I don't claim to," I said. "But I have something I know you'll be interested in. When you finish your...arrangement, I'd like to show you what it is."

"Well, aren't you manipulative?" We regarded one another in silence. "Have a seat," Frank finally said. I found a stool tucked under the countertop. "*I* have something that might interest *you*. Be quiet and pay attention."

He pulled out an armful of flowers. From the bunch, he separated them out and uttered the Latin names of each as he placed them on the table between us. His movements were methodical, and the flowers, when he had finished, formed a circle. The stems met in the centre of the circle and the blooms formed a multi-coloured cornea.

"When you arrived, I was sanctifying the ground." His eyes flicked up to my face, searching out a reaction. I doubted he could make out my features any better than I could see his, but I put on a neutral mask. "The Western world pretends to understand death. It heaps ceremony onto the heads of participants to one end: the pacification of pant-wetting fear. The ceremonies are largely meaningless, which is ironically appropriate. Death, to the Western world is meaningless. Religion tries to say otherwise, but also calls suicide a sin."

He paused to gauge my comprehension. I didn't know where he was going. Apparently satisfied, he turned to a shelf on his right to take down a chunk of oasis and a container. He plucked the herbs from the bowl of water and dropped the green foam cube into it.

"In its rush to deny that it has no understanding of death whatsoever, the Western world performs rituals that bring carnage to other living things." Without looking at me, he pulled the soaking oasis from the bowl and placed it into the plastic vase. "Flowers, ferns and other greenery. The plant world suffers because of their ignorance."

"The *plant* world?"

He slammed a fist onto the tabletop. The vase rocked and the circle of flowers shook. He gulped a couple breaths and turned his face to mine. I caught my reflection in the glass doors and checked my shock.

"Have you ever been to a funeral?" he asked. I nodded. "Then you've witnessed the massacre that takes place when a human passes. When somebody dies, you don't know why. You're just glad it isn't you. You are ecstatic it isn't you. So you send flowers. The bigger the bouquet, the happier you are that you're not the one in the coffin. It's your way of appeasing whatever gods you fear. You offer a living sacrifice of a creature that won't defend itself."

"Won't?" I whispered.

He shushed me again, then began picking up the flowers, one by one, snipping their stems and sticking them into the oasis. He called each by name and whispered a blessing into its petals. He finished the arrangement this way, and I had to admit the man was talented.

"It's lovely," I said when he turned it around.

"It's an abomination," he replied, then stood to flip on the overhead light. "What do you have for me?"

I squinted against the sudden glare. "That's a tough act to follow. I have a diary that I hope you remember."

He frowned, an expression that was much less menacing under fluorescent lighting. Frank was a petite man, standing no more than five foot four. His frame was angular, but for the delicacy of his hands. He sat at the stool again. "I remember a diary, but the odds of you—"

I dropped it in front of him, open to the pages he'd added at the tender age of fifteen, the anti-climactic height of his psychosis.

"You used to play with dead animals," I said out of revenge for freaking me out. "How did that turn out?"

He laughed at me. Then he picked up the diary and read his old entries. He finished and pushed the diary toward me before standing and turning his back on me. Hands on hips, he breathed deeply twice and dropped his head. When he spoke, his voice was deadly serious.

"My therapist thought that my only aptitude was for ritual murder. He's thrilled that I became a florist."

~ ~ ~

THE FIRST THING I saw was her bare foot on the white tile. The bathroom door was open a crack as I passed. Morning sun sparkled on her silver anklet. I pushed the door open, but it caught on her elbow. She was on her stomach, sprawled on the floor, her face in a puddle of vomit.

I dropped to my knees beside her, and pulled her into my arms. She was cold and limp, but I was sure she was breathing. I rubbed her arms to warm her up, and dragged her up until we were on the edge of the bath. I reached for the tap to splash water on her face. The sink was full of empty pill bottles.

I rocked her and called her name, but I couldn't wake her. I tried mouth to mouth and I searched frantically for a pulse. She was gone. My love had left me. She had given up. Rather than face what had happened to her, my pretty, sparkling Cherise overdosed on pills and slipped away while I slept in the next room.

~ ~ ~

I FOUND HER note the next day as I was getting ready to meet with her parents to go over the plans for the funeral. When I tidied the house, my arm bumped the diary where it lay on a shelf and it dropped to the floor. It landed on the spine and fell open to a page where a pen was tucked in. There, in the middle of the otherwise blank leaf, were two lines of Cherise's tidy, tiny handwriting.

I closed the book and put it in a drawer.

Anand and Tira, dressed in white mourning garb, arrived a few minutes later. We sat uncomfortably in the living room.

"Everything is set," said Tira. She didn't meet my eyes. "Tomorrow, ten o'clock at the temple."

"What about visitation? I'd like to be there for that. And she had friends."

Tira set her jaw and pursed her lips. Anand patted her hand, but she gently pulled her hand away and placed it in her lap. "I am aware of you and your friends," she said. "We have her at our house. The body needs to be cleansed before the cremation. Please don't come."

Anand whispered into his wife's ear. Her forehead furrowed for a second and she ducked her head, blinking. To me he said, "She loved you. You should be there, but you understand that you will not sit with the family."

"Yes."

"And you are not invited to participate in the ceremony. There are rules. Wear dark colours. Do not speak to anyone. Do not cry." He paused to search my face. "You understand, Kal. It's tradition."

"Of course."

Tira stood. "I am going to light a candle in the…room. Please keep it burning until she is cremated." She paused and took a breath. "You cleaned?"

"Of course."

Anand stood to follow his wife upstairs. As he passed my chair, he dropped a hand on my shoulder and squeezed. "I'm sorry," he said when his wife was out of earshot. "For everything."

"Me, too," I whispered.

~ ~ ~

ON THE DAY OF the funeral, I drove the van Cherise and I had bought to the bookstore and picked up Marcus. He jumped into the driver's seat. I noted his outfit–somber colours and no clanking jewelry–and cocked an eyebrow at him.

"For Tira," he said.

"What about Cherise?" I asked. She wouldn't want him to change to please anybody, least of all her mother.

"Fuck her," he said. He had made it clear that he was only coming for my sake. He was angry at Cherise. I knew he was angry at himself, too, but I left him to work that out for himself. Besides, I was having trouble forgiving him for delivering my love to a rapist. As for my part in leaving her there, well, that was something I would think about much later.

The day was overcast and cold. I hoped it would rain. Cherise told me once that it was a good omen if it rained at a funeral. Cleansing.

We spoke to no one at the temple. Marc wanted to sit at the front, but I chose a seat in the back. I didn't hear the service. I stared at the urn that held her ashes, memorizing the details. Beside the urn was a portrait of her dressed in a traditional sari, holding a rose.

The procession to the river took half an hour. Marc hummed as he drove. I stared out the window. The greens, reds and yellows of the trees were vivid against the dark grey sky. Wind turned the leaves white.

Marc and I stood at the back of the crowd of mourners and couldn't see the urn being placed in the water. Just as well. I listened to the leaves rustle above us and raised my eyes to the sky. I heard a splash from the river at the same moment the rain broke. Umbrellas went up around us, but Marc and I were still as the cold drops hit our faces.

We were among the last to leave. I approached the bank and gazed down into the brown water. The urn on its raft turned in the current. I felt a deep, quiet grief that drowned out everything except for the image of her sobbing on the kitchen floor. I knew I should have some parting words for her, but could think of nothing to say. I didn't even have a flower to leave for her.

Anand caught up with us at the van. He handed me an envelope and walked back to his own car. Inside the envelope was an eviction notice.

~ ~ ~

Frank Bosa

March 7, 1959

My name is Frank Bosa. I'm 15 years old and I'm going to die someday. Just like my dog. He was my pet all my life. He was older than me, but only two months. If he can die when he's only 15, then I can go at any time, I guess. I've been reading. I'll copy some stuff down.

> When a Viking warrior died in battle, it was believed that the Valkyries (female warrior spirits) rode onto the battlefield to collect him and take his spirit to Valhalla. Valhalla was a great hall in the afterlife where all the dead warriors feasted every night, then rode into battle every day for eternity.
>
> The warrior's earth-bound body was placed on a ship with all of his armour and gold and furs. The ship was set on fire and sent out to sea. Other dead mortals went to the underworld of Hel, which was believed to be among the roots of the Tree of Life.

Scrappy was hit by a car and killed yesterday. We buried him under the maple tree in the backyard. I think he would have been happier in Valhalla with all those scraps they drop on the floor (Vikings were very sloppy eaters), but my parents say there are laws against setting flaming pets adrift on Lake Ontario.

March 12, 1959

> When a Mongolian died, the face was covered with silk and the rest of the body was left naked. Blue stones were placed in the bed where they died to ward off evil spirits. The body was arranged with one hand behind the head. For the next several days, the family burned incense and watched over the corpse. They tied up all the dogs in the area, then threw the body out onto a steppe or put it on the back of a horse. The horse galloped until the body fell off. It was hoped that wild animals would eat the body allowing other animals to live a little longer.

March 22, 1959

> In Borneo, the dead body was placed in a coffin, and the coffin put in a hut and left there until the body was decomposed. Then, they buried the body, sacrificed slaves bought for the occasion, and hung other slaves from poles to die of hunger and thirst.

March 30, 1959

> The ancient Egyptians built massive pyramids with mazes tunneling underground to place the bodies of their dead kings in. First they mummified the bodies by taking out all the organs and fluids, then embalming them and wrapping them in strips of cloth. They placed the mummy in a coffin called a sarcophagus and painted an image of the king on the outside. The king was buried with all his treasures and clothes and food—and servants and slaves. He was sent into the afterlife with everything he might need there.

There is a dead squirrel that I found on the road on my way home from school. It was smushed by the wheel of a car so I couldn't tell which parts were the organs. I tried to wash it in a bucket of water and bleach and separate the organs, but it turned all mushy. And they never said what the Egyptians did with the organs after they took them out of the bodies. I wrapped it all up in one of my mom's tea towels that I cut into strips. I had to use another one because the first one got all soaked with blood and bleach. Then I put the little mummy in a sarcophagus (I made it out of a shoe box and drew a squirrel on the front.). I dug a hole behind the shed and put the sarcophagus in it with a pile of peanuts and half a loaf of bread, then built a pyramid out of rocks.

I'm getting a new dog on the weekend. Dad told me to try harder to keep this one tied up like it was my fault Scrappy died.

April 5, 1959

> Indian women used to throw themselves onto the burning pyre of their dead husbands as an act of sacrifice and proof that they were loyal to their husbands.

April 10, 1959

I wonder how long my new puppy, Duke has. I've already picked out his grave. It's nice, under a tree. I found Muffin, Mrs. Winslow's cat, dead. Probably a heart attack. His fur was sticking straight out from his body and his tail was all stiff. But other than that there wasn't a mark on him. No blood or bashed up bones. He was pretty old, I guess. So I gave him a proper burial, like the ones they do in Zimbabwe.

I buried him in Mrs. Winslow's garden. That's where he spent all his time. I cut a yardstick to Muffin's height and stuck it out of the grave. I have to remember to go back and pull the stick out, so Muffin's soul can escape through the hole.

April 30, 1959

I pulled out Muffin's stick today. So I have to keep checking for a worm or caterpillar. That will be Muffin's soul looking for a home. When I find it, I'm supposed to do some ceremony, but the book didn't give the details, so I'll just put the worm in Mrs. Winslow's garage and that can be Muffin's soul's new home. That's where he used to sleep, I think.

Duke will sit up now and bark for a biscuit. Next I'm going to teach him to shake a paw.

May 14, 1959

Duke is really good at learning tricks. He sure will impress the other dog spirits when his time comes. I haven't decided what kind of burial to give him yet.

Mom thinks that I spend too much time reading. She wants me to talk to a man she called. They tell us in school that it's good to read, and now I have to have a meeting with somebody who's going to tell me not to read. I don't get it. But I'm going to read as much as I can before that so I can store it all up.

> Ancient Greeks were buried with food and water, and gifts of weapons, jewelry and clothes. An animal was sacrificed at the grave site and another one at the house of the next of kin.

May 20, 1959

Mrs. Winslow was getting her garden ready for spring today, and I thought that she might find Muffin's body and disturb his soul. I still haven't found the worm, so I'm pretty worried. I'll have to come up with something else.

May 21, 1959

Last night I snuck out into Mrs. Winslow's garden to look for Muffin's worm. I didn't find anything, so I decided to dig him up before Mrs. Winslow does by accident and give him an air burial. That's what they do in Tibet. They cut the body into pieces and let the vultures and other animals eat the remains. It's a great sacrifice and keeps the circle of life going. Maybe Muffin would appreciate letting mice and rats eat him, since he ate so many.

Muffin smells pretty bad now, and he was really hard to cut up with the pruning shears, but I think I did a good enough job. I'm going to ride him over to the dump on my bike. That's the best place around here for an air burial, I think.

May 30, 1959

I had my meeting with the man who doesn't want me to read anymore. His name is Dr. Billing. I call him Bill and he doesn't mind. He said it's okay to read, but I should choose different books. He wants me to read adventure stories and spy novels, like other boys my age. I told him that other boys my age think that they're going to live forever.

He was really interested in hearing about Muffin. I wasn't going to tell him about it, but my mom already did. The man at the dump wouldn't let me give Muffin an air burial and he called my parents. What a rat. No wonder he's stuck working at the dump with the other rats. Mrs. Winslow is really mad. She thinks I killed Muffin and wouldn't let me come to the crematorium with her. I told her that I wasn't sure cremation was the best way to go, and she just cried and ran away. I wish she didn't think I murdered her cat. I would never do that. She didn't even miss him until my mom told her where he was. That's why I'm sure now that poor old Muffin starved to death or something. Mrs. Winslow doesn't deserve to bury that great cat. I hope her family cremates her when her time comes and forgets to welcome her spirit back home.

June 20, 1959

Bill says that I worry too much about death. He says I can't read any more books about it. He even called the librarian and instructed her not to let me get any more books about it. Fink.

He's got Mom and Dad watching every move I make. I'm not allowed out of the house after dark any more and I have to tell where I spend every minute.

Nobody understands that I have to live the best I can so that when I die I won't have unfinished business. I promised Mom that I would never talk to her about dying again as long she promises to moisten my lips as soon as she finds my lifeless body. She has to do it before she even tells Dad that I'm dead. I told Dad the same thing. I also reminded them that if I end up being a shepherd that they have to bury me with a lock of wool. Then we talked about me maybe getting a part-time job and they smiled a lot. And I started teaching Duke how to roll over (in case he gets buried face down, his soul will know how to right itself).

August 10, 1959

I have been really busy working at the fruit market. I still talk to Bill every week, too, and he says I'm making progress, whatever that means. Duke has learned all the tricks I can think to teach him. Mom smiles more and Dad grumbles less. Mrs. Winslow has even started waving to me from her garden again. I still know I'm going to die and I still think about it all the time, but I realized that everybody is happier if I pretend not to.

August 20, 1959

Duke died today. He hung himself on the chain Dad made me tie to him. I had let my guard down. I'm not prepared for this. I don't know what kind of burial to give him. I can't remember all the stuff I read and the librarian won't let me have the books again. The stuff I wrote in here doesn't have enough detail. I would buy a book, but Dad makes me account for all my money. I don't know what to do. I don't know who to ask. Poor Duke. I'll think of something.

August 22, 1959

Dad took Duke to the vet and had him cremated and said I can put the ashes in the backyard, if I want. Just planting Duke like he was a flower.

August 23, 1959

I found some old notes on an African tribal burial! It's definitely stylish, but pretty bloody, too. It won't be easy. I'll have to improvise.

> When an African Ibo tribal chief died, the family washed the body, and covered it with palm leaves. The children of the chief sacrificed a dog and cut its head off. Then they drew a circle around the dead chief with the dripping blood. They also killed a cat, an eagle, a parrot, and a goat. Each animal gives the chief a special power to take into the afterlife. Then they killed the wife of a special slave and put her body in the grave beside the chief. The wives of all the other slaves had their arms and legs broken before being thrown alive into the grave to be buried with the chief. The luckiest, strongest men of the tribe were chosen to break the women's bones. More slaves were sacrificed in the places where the chief ate, bathed, slept and entertained. After the grave was closed up, except for a small space, the strongest men of the chief's tribe captured and beheaded a man from another tribe. They placed the head into the last small opening of the chief's grave. The grave was decorated with the skulls of other victims and the whole tribe feasted on the flesh of the sacrifices—both animal and human.

August 24, 1959

I have to go away for awhile. I'm sorry, Duke, for not finishing your funeral rites, but nobody understands. I wasn't going to kill anybody.

~ ~ ~

Chapter 14

She might be pretty, but the angry lines around her eyes and across her forehead make her face severe. The brown uniform fits poorly, too loose in some places and too tight in others. Her stockings have runs, and the running shoes on her feet are smeared with food stains and mud from the street. She bustles around the diner, slamming coffee mugs and plates of food down too hard in front of impatient customers. She jumps too easily when the fat man in the kitchen bellows. She drops a plate on the table. The edge hits the saucer and coffee sloshes onto the eggs and toast. Her face crumples, but the customer touches her hand and smiles. It's okay, he seems to say, and her shoulders relax. After she has left to wait on another table, he takes a package from the bench he sits on and places it on the table. He eats alone, quickly, and leaves.

– Kendra Horne, *Equilibrium*

Serenity

Every material thing I had brought into my life with Cherise fit into the van. The notice from her parents provided a generous thirty days to get my things in order, but once I got started two weeks after receiving the brisk note, it only took me an afternoon to pack my things into plastic bags and the odd box. Clothes, books and the gaudy afghan she had finished just hours before her suicide. Everything else was hers. She hadn't written a will so it all reverted to her parents. I had neither the money nor the energy to fight them, although Marcus encouraged me to do so.

"You were common law, Kal. That gives you some rights," he repeated as he swept an arm across my dresser top, dumping the jumbled mess of combs, deodorant, belts and other small items into a box. A piece of paper fluttered to the floor.

I continued quietly folding shirts from the closet and stuffing them into a plastic bag. He set the box on the bed and folded the flaps shut before stooping to retrieve the page. His thumb partially obscured the University's letterhead.

"You can pay the lawyer out of the settlement," he said. "Jesus, Kal, I can't believe you're just going to walk away from this. I know you're in mourning, but that's why you should have a lawyer handle it. Don't let them take everything. Cherise would be furious with you."

"Cherise *was* furious with me," I said and left the room. I didn't want this confrontation with him. I hadn't asked him to help me and I didn't want to be anywhere near him. He followed me downstairs into the kitchen where I grabbed a bottle of gin from the freezer.

"Well, I'm furious with Cherise for—"

I plunked the bottle on the counter and spun around on him. I grabbed a handful of dreadlocks and felt beads dig into my palm. I yanked hard until he was on his knees and bent over to hiss into his ear, "Don't speak her name."

I let go and stalked to the patio door to rest my head on the cool glass. Black heads of the rudbeckia she had planted bobbed in the wind and knocked against the wooden fence.

"Kal, this letter... Did you get kicked out of school?"

"Get out." I sighed heavily and looked at him over my shoulder. "I'm done here, anyway."

~ ~ ~

I veered the van into a privately-owned parking lot a few blocks from the book store. The attendant, a short, stocky guy in bright pink pants and a bomber jacket waved me to a spot in the back corner. I rocked in the driver's seat as the front passenger-side wheel went up and over the roots of a substantial maple tree that loomed over the lot. What an incredibly shitty parking spot. It would be perfect.

I opened the door and squeezed out the meager space between the vehicles.

"Nine dollars," said the attendant over his shoulder as he jogged to the kiosk. I followed him and stood outside watching him through the tiny sliding window. "What's the plate number?"

I told him and handed him a ten.

"How much for a month?" I asked when he handed me my change. He raised his bushy black eyebrows and whistled through his teeth.

"We don't do that," he said, but he didn't seem convinced.

"Even in that spot?" I asked. "I don't imagine too many Jag owners want to park there."

He thought about it for a minute, pursing his lips and making sucking sounds deep in his cheeks. "What's nine times thirty?" he asked, then grabbed a calculator from a shelf under the counter.

"Two hundred and seventy dollars," I said before he got the result out of his little machine. "That's too much."

"You want to park overnight don't you? And it will cost more for the snow plough to go around you."

"What if I clear the snow for you?" I asked, looking at the size of the lot and mentally figuring what an idiot I was for suggesting such a thing. It would take a whole day to shovel that much snow.

He laughed and came out of the kiosk. "You looking for a job, too? Baby, with those arms, it would take you a week to clear this lot. Besides, I have a contract with another company."

He was friendly, at least. I plunged ahead. "You're the owner? Are you sure there isn't something we can work out?" I needed somewhere to park the van. Without a valid address and insurance, I couldn't get a permit for the street. I could sell the van, but then I wouldn't have anywhere to live until I was again eligible for student loans. Most of the lots downtown were too expensive. This was my last resort.

He stroked his black goatee and sucked his teeth as he sized me up. I didn't like being stared at, but I was desperate so I suffered his scrutiny.

"Tell you what, you work for me, three, four hours in the mornings during the rush and I'll take the money out of your pay." He ducked back into the kiosk and grabbed the calculator to punch some buttons. "At seven-fifty an hour for four hours, minus nine dollars for parking, that leaves you twenty-one dollars a day for walking around money."

"Really?" I asked. Without rent and other bills, that was pretty good, I thought.

"Wait," he said. "I forgot about weekends. The rate is reduced to five dollars, so it'll be ten bucks less a week. That okay with you?"

It was great with me. I would have somewhere to sleep, enough money for food and my afternoons free to track down leads.

"When do I start?" I asked and we shook hands to seal the deal.

~ ~ ~

"FUCK *ME*!"

The smile on the face at the kiosk window melted into a frown. "Ooh, that looked like it hurt," said the lanky man.

I extricated my index finger from the cash register and slid it into my mouth. I sucked hard and loud. "F-huuuck," I said again around the digit.

"Keep the change, and try not to let that ruin such a gorgeous day," he said, smiled again, and left.

With my good hand, I pocketed the loonie. The face of my new boss, Max, appeared at the window. In the week since I had started the job he had left me pretty much alone, but it was a beautiful sunny day and Max was in a good mood.

"Problem?" he asked.

I waved my sore finger at him.

"I guess you're not a morning person," Max said with a huge, irritating grin. "You look like hell."

"You look like you couldn't decide what to wear," I replied, looking him up and down through the kiosk window.

Max was layered and ready for anything autumn wanted to throw at him. The first layer included wool socks, blue spandex pants and a gold-and-green striped turtleneck. Over that he wore nylon sandals, grey cut-off sweat pants and a white T-shirt. The outermost layer consisted of a red down vest, an orange scarf, a yellow toque and wrap-around sunglasses.

I made change for the next couple of hours while Max maneuvered the cars in and out of impossible spaces. The sun warmed the air and Max ducked into the kiosk to peel off the top layer.

"It's gonna be a nice day," he said and tossed his vest on a hook. He grabbed a fold-up lawn chair and hauled it outside where he plunked himself in it and put his feet up on a bumper. I continued balancing the till and sucking on my sore finger.

My only response to the knock at the window was to wave the middle finger of my good hand over my shoulder. I pulled my other finger out of my mouth to study it. It began to throb so I jammed it back in.

The knock came again, louder, with a shout: "Kal, open up!"

I turned to see Marcus. He shifted from one foot to the other as he waited for me to emerge from the booth.

"What?" We hadn't spoken since the day I had moved out of Cherise's house.

"Fine, thanks. How are you?" he replied. He squinted in the bright sunlight. "So, really. How are you?"

"Gainfully employed."

He shuffled his feet, and I noticed that his eyes kept going to the van. "That's good. Making decent money?"

"What do you want, Marc?" I knew he hadn't come here to wish me well in my new career. "And how did you know I was working here?"

"Oh, I noticed the van parked over there." He pointed lamely, then jammed his hand in his pocket. "I pass by here on the way to the store."

"Yeah..." I prompted.

He took a breath and held it for a second. "Where are you living now, Kal? In the van? Because, if you want, I have some extra room at my place. And a computer so you could do your school work. If you thought you would go back to school."

I stared at him, at a loss for words. I felt a mixture of gratitude and suspicion. "I'm okay. I'm...staying with friends."

He nodded. I could tell he knew I was lying. He knew I didn't have any friends. "Do they have a computer?" he asked.

"No, but I use one at the library. I'm trying to get back into school. I've been working on a theory."

He brightened. "Oh. That's just great. Good luck."

"Thanks."

He seemed about to leave, but paused to put out a hand. He almost touched my arm, but stopped. "Come over for dinner tonight. We'll get drunk or something."

"Sure." What the hell? God knows, I liked getting drunk.

~ ~ ~

"MAX, PARK THE blue piece of crap in back!" I shouted out my kiosk window. The owner of the disco-era Impala gave me a startled glance. I smiled. "That will be nine dollars, sir."

The man juggled a battered brief case and dug around in his coat pocket. "Does your boss know how rude you are to customers?" he asked and handed me a ten.

"You're welcome to dock somewhere else," I replied and snatched the bill from his gloved fingers.

Parking somewhere else would mean wedging his wheeled barge back into rush hour traffic. It would take him fifteen minutes to inch the block and a half to the next lot. Once there, the attendant wasn't likely to be any more docile than myself, and the disgruntled customer wouldn't be guaranteed a spot. As it was we had cars parked four and five deep on our tiny lot with one or two spaces open for shifting them around and retrieving them for drivers. Max was a wizard at juggling cars, priding himself on the ability to pry a Volkswagen from the third row in two moves or less.

"Thank you, sir. Have a pleasant day," I said and handed a loonie to my valued customer. "Your change."

I watched him trudge through the muddy parking lot. He pocketed the dollar coin and pulled out a pack of cigarettes. Another man approached him from the sidewalk, gesturing moderately. He was probably asking for a spare smoke or some change for a coffee. The first man didn't break stride.

Around thirty homeless people die on the streets of Toronto every year. The media reports the first death of the winter with up-to-the-minute details about the deceased's identity and circumstances. A week or two later another body is found frozen to death in a bus shelter or park. Experts are interviewed about the homeless crisis. Donations to food banks increase, and newer-looking blankets show up to brighten the winter-grey parks. Then twenty-some more people die from the cold, malnutrition, and beatings while the rest of the city sleeps, unaware of the howling outside its door.

I watched the second man turn on the sidewalk and approach a woman who was waiting for the light to change. She smiled at him and fished some change out of her purse.

The next four hours progressed as normal. The lot filled to capacity by eight-thirty, then started thinning out again by eleven. By eleven-thirty Max no longer needed my help at the cash register to handle the flow so I grabbed a scrap of paper off the dash of the van. I double checked the address and headed for the subway.

~ ~ ~

I VISITED JENNIFER around this time, but she didn't tell me anything I hadn't heard before. She said that there was no mystery. It was hard not to believe the kindly matron, but I had read the words she wrote in the 1960s and there was nothing kindly about them.

Jennifer

February 11, 1961

Dear Fucking Diary:

It feels great to be the first person to swear in this piece of sentimental trash. God! Who are you people? La-di-dah language and oh woe is me. What do you expect when you pour out your pathetic little hearts and pass it around for anyone to see?

Well, let me tell you, my story isn't nicey-nicey with perfect grammar. I don't live in a fairy tale and I'm not about to pretend that I do. I think you're all a bunch of fakes and liars. I'm not stupid and I don't believe half of what I've read. But okay, I'll tell my story and if you don't believe it, then fuck you.

My name is Jennifer Bracknell and I'm 20 years old. I just finished high school last year. I was late in finishing but I had to graduate or my parents were going to kick me out of the house. So I have a so-called education. And I have a so-called job. It's a shitty waitress job in a shitty restaurant. I'm trying to get into a bar where the tips are better. Drunk men will tip anything in a short skirt.

Shit! My boss is yelling at me. I gotta go.

March 1, 1961

I work at a shit job because I didn't get married. If I get married, it's going to be somebody who wants to go somewhere and be somebody. I don't mean a doctor or a lawyer—they're all too stuck on themselves. And I don't want to sit at home and squeeze out babies. I'm not sure what I'd do—not this fucking job, that's for sure. Maybe an artist or something. I'm pretty good at drawing, I could probably paint, too. I remember my mom told me once when I was really little that I should make greeting cards for a living, you know that roses are red crap. I don't think too many people would be comforted by my cards. 'Way to go on getting fired...fucking loser'. Maybe I could get rich making greeting cards with some balls instead of stupid little poems.

Some customer is complaining about her soup being cold and my boss is yelling at me again. Maybe I should dump it in her wrinkled old lap and see if she still thinks it's cold.

April 4, 1961

Okay, I still haven't been fired from my job. As long as I show up every day and don't bitch at the customers, my scumbag boss is happy to pay me shitty wages and holler at me for eight hours. But he's started calling me Shakespeare since I started writing in this damned book. So now I'll only write at home. I don't need to give the fucker ammunition.

I've got a wicked headache today—probably from drinking so much last night. I went to a bar and got pretty messed up. Met this guy, though, who says he's a sculptor. He must be an artist since he didn't have enough money to pick up the tab. We went back to his place and he had some grass. I've never tried it until last night.

It made me all light-headed, but really focused. He showed me his sculptures. They're pretty weird and not very good, but I liked them anyway. They were mostly naked women, but all swirly and fat and bright colours. And they're all small–about a foot high. I always thought sculptures were supposed to be huge. My favourite one looked more like an old curled up tree than a woman, but if you looked really close you could see her arms and breasts and face.

His name is Gene. I told him I'd let him take me out if he promised to pay next time.

May, 1961

I quit my job and now my parents will probably kick me out of the house for good. Maybe Gene will let me stay with him until I find another job. I don't care if people think we're shacked up and call me a whore. I need a roof over my head, don't I? And besides, they'd be right. We haven't done it yet because I don't want to get pregnant, but I've given him blow jobs and he feels me up all the time.

I doubt I'll marry him. He never has money. And he doesn't seem to want to get a job. But I'll move in with him if he'll have me.

June, 1961

The fucker beat me up last night. He wanted me to steal my parents' car so I could take him to some party in Scarborough. I told him to take the bus like all poor people have to. And he swung at me. I ducked and grabbed one of his sculptures. I said I'd smash it against the wall if he tried to lay a hand on me. He picked up another one and chucked it right out the window. Down it went, four stories, just missing the bum that sleeps there on the sidewalk. I called him some names and told him he'd end up in jail for murder and I wouldn't defend him, that he'd get a worse sentence because he tried to hit me. And he threw another one out the window. I didn't see where it landed because he tackled me and started slapping my head and face. But I didn't hear the smash. I was too busy trying to keep him from breaking my nose.

He was yelling like a maniac and I didn't understand anything he said. I think he was pretty drunk. Or worse. I found needles in the bathroom and he said he was diabetic. I think it was heroine, though.

Anyway, he stopped trying to hit me and instead he ripped up my skirt and blouse and took advantage of me. He didn't like me crying either and hit me in the face with the sculpture I had dropped. I passed out after that.

When I woke up, I was lying in the street with my ripped clothes and bleeding beside the bleeding bum that the sculpture had hit. I checked. He's still alive. My purse was beside me, but all the money was gone out of it. This book was still there, and you can see that he scribbled on the pages and ripped some out. My blood is smeared all over it. I'm sorry.

June, 1961

I think it's still June. I'm not sure. It's been a couple of days. I've been sleeping in empty garages. I got cleaned up in the bathroom at the bus station. My mouth was cut pretty bad and keeps bleeding, and I have a black eye. I thought my nose was broken, but now

I don't think so. A couple of my fingers are, though. I wrapped them up with bits of my skirt. I haven't seen Gene since that night, thank God, but I've been hiding.

Well, I said my story wasn't pretty, but I didn't think my life would get this ugly. I've lost everything. All my clothes and money. I haven't eaten for a few days. I have to go home. I will go home, but I'm waiting for my face to heal. I can't tell my parents what happened. I'll get another job. I don't care what it is anymore. I just need to make some money or something.

July, 1961

I met a woman on the street who wanted to give me some money and buy me something to eat. I let her buy me lunch and promised to pay her back when I got a job and some money. She said I could come and use her phone, if I wanted to. I said no.

But she came back the next day and bought me lunch again. And then she brought me a sandwich. Then she finally took me home with her. Her name is Mirella.

She lets me read the paper every day to find a job and she lent me some clothes that she doesn't wear anymore. When I ask her why she's so nice, she just smiles.

August, 1961

I still live with Mirella, but I pay her rent, now. I got a job typing in an office. It's boring, but it's better than the restaurant, I guess.

I called my parents yesterday.

August, 1961

I had a big fight with Mirella. She found a bottle in my room and starting talking about Jesus. I don't know what she did to piss Him off, but she's pretty worried about it. I think it has to do with booze and men because she sure hates them both.

I got my own place. It's a tiny box, but it's close to work. And I haven't seen any cockroaches yet.

September, 1961

This is my last entry. My life has become boring again. You got to see me in my worst moment and I hope that makes you happy. Now all I do is work and sleep and drink and smoke on the weekends. I've made a few friends in the building, and they're all fun. We have dinner together every Saturday then go to a party or a poetry reading and get high together. We take care of each other and talk about stuff, but nobody asks any questions. It's good.

~ ~ ~

Chapter 15

She lies on her stomach on the floor, knees bent, feet swaying behind her head. A cigarette dangles from her lips. She drops the pen, brushes a black curl off her forehead and takes the cigarette out of her mouth. Her eyes droop and her head lolls. The cigarette rolls out of her fingers, across the open book and drops onto the floor. It rolls a few more feet before it catches on a piece of crumpled paper and stops.

– Kendra Horne, *Little Monster*

The Beast

AFTER THE FIRST night of dinner and drinking with Marcus, I ended up spending a few days at his place. There was more room to work on his living room floor than in the back of my van or at the library. We only saw each other in the late evening when he got home from the store, so I had whole afternoons to piece together the puzzle of the diary. I had talked to almost everyone that could be found, but I still couldn't put it all together.

On my third night there, I spread everything on the floor around me, opened a bottle of vodka and looked at my pages of notes, the books, and the printouts through alcohol-glazed eyes. Kimberly Harding, Karl Hanson, Kass Holbrook, Kevin Herbert, Konstantin Horowitz, Kevin Harkness, Kasara Humphrey, Kelly Hopper, Korine Horner and Kristophe Herolde. I was sure that all of these people were one; that they were pseudonyms that Clara had used to tell her story and the stories of David, Daniel, Myrtle and all the people to follow. I realized, of course, that Clara would have to be at least ninety-four years old by now. However, if she had died, what was stopping someone else from picking an appropriate pseudonym and carrying on the storytelling tradition?

I lay down in the middle of the mayhem of information and stretched my arms above my head. My fingers brushed a page. I snatched it and held it in front of my eyes. A shopping list. I sighed and let it flutter out of my hand. Testament to the mess my life had become. I never did get around to picking up the laundry soap that sunny day before any of it had started. Cherise had brought it home, knowing that I would stay late at school and forget. That was the day I had found the diary.

I sat up suddenly and dove on the paper. I flipped it over and reread the web address on the back, a Kimberly Harding fan page I had dismissed. I cast my saturated mind back. I had written down the address for a reason. It escaped me now, but I had nothing else so I stumbled over to Marc's computer and connected to the internet. I opened his browser and typed the url into the address bar.

To my surprise, the very address popped up in the menu bar before I had finished typing. I clicked on it and the website opened up. Why would Marc have this page bookmarked? I was disappointed to find it had nothing to do with Kimberly Harding. And I didn't remember it. Nothing on the welcome page was familiar to me in the least. So why had I written it down?

It appeared to be a blog, an online diary called *Prosperocity*. I browsed through the posts and comments. A surge of dread went through me. My fingers trembled around the mouse, and I had to pause for a deep shaky breath before clicking on the longest thread: *Who is Kal?*

I finished the vodka and switched to beer while I read the comments and impressions of all the people I had met in my search for the secrets of Clara's diary. They all used online personas, but I recognized them. Rebecca, under the pseudonym, *The Diviner*, wrote of reading my palm and hoped that I would soon find a thesis. Myrtle Ellerington called herself *The Mother*. She looked forward to seeing me again. Most of them were there with clever and descriptive handles discussing my mannerisms, cheering my discoveries and mourning my losses. Marc, *The Reader*, was the blog owner and host of the forum. Of course: *Prospero's City*. He provided insight into my character and, at first, championed my suitability for inclusion in the group where others, like *The Expositor* and *The Daisy Pusher*, had their doubts.

I began to understand the nature of the diary, the novels, the strangeness of these people. It was obviously a cult of some kind, or a secret society, and they wanted to recruit me into their ranks. I had not found the diary by chance; it had found me.

~ ~ ~

From: mross@network.ca
Date: November 15, 2004 4:23pm
To: k_win@salut.com
Subject: Re: K.H. lived on
Original Message:
=============
>Dear Dr. Ross:
>Please find attached a copy of my proposal for re-admittance into the program. A recent series of bizarre, but
>related events has led me to the conclusion that the author Kimberly Harding continued writing after the release of
>her alleged final book, Under Her Wing. In fact, I have evidence that indicates that she published sixteen more
>books under various pseudonyms. Her real name was Clara Strachan.
>With the gracious consent of the graduate studies committee, I hope to develop and defend my theory,
>completing the requirements for my doctorate. I look forward to reading your thoughts and suggestions. I do
>hope we can meet to discuss my proposal soon.
>Sincerely,
>Kal Winters.

Kal:
I know you are familiar with the prevailing criticism of Harding's work by much more astute and accomplished scholars than yourself. When you first suggested writing your thesis on fairy tales, I had no inkling that you intended to invent a new one. This work is sub-par. You had the opportunity and the intelligence to contribute something vastly more important and insightful.

I am aware that you have undergone a tremendous amount of strain for the past months, and I am sorry for all that you've been through. However, I think the stress is affecting your reason. I believe I have been patient with you, Kal, but if this is the level of work I can expect from you, I cannot act as your advisor.

Regretfully,
M. Ross, PhD

Fuck him, I thought.

~ ~ ~

BY MY FIFTH or tenth beer, my clammy skin felt too tight for my body. My head pounded and my eyes and brain struggled to focus. Outrage and a little fear boiled in my bloated stomach as the realization hit me: I had been under a microscope ever since the diary had landed in my hands.

Suddenly, an idea popped into my soggy brain. I scrolled to the bottom of the entries and found the *Post* button. I clicked on it, and when the new window opened, I started typing: *New developments. If anyone is interested, meet at* The Plaid Hound *on Front Street tomorrow night.*

I signed it *The Querant* and posted the notice before I could change my mind. I heard Marc's footsteps on the stairs and scrambled to shut down the browser. I jumped out of the chair when I heard the key turning in the lock and the movement churned the booze in my tummy. By the time Marc stepped into the apartment, I had staggered into the bathroom and was heaving over the toilet. Sweat soaked my back and rolled off my face. Marc joined me and pressed a wet washcloth on the back of my neck. He murmured soothing words and handed me a glass of water to rinse the acid from my mouth.

"It's alright, Kal," he murmured. "It's going to be over soon."

~ ~ ~

I SAT ALONE in the corner of the tavern on Front Street, combing the diary for clues when Rachel Murphy entered on a gust of wind. She stood in the entrance and shook out her umbrella against the backdrop of the late fall storm outside. After hooking the umbrella on her purse strap, she wrung out her hair. The wind slammed the door behind her, and whipped around the aged building that sheltered us.

An odd look crossed her face as she let her eyes travel around the room, a cross between exasperation and anticipation. She motioned to the bartender as she strode between the tables. The lights flickered as she passed me. She took a seat at the far end of the bar and smirked into the drink that waited for her.

We made eye contact and she raised her glass an inch. I nodded to suppress a shudder. A waitress circulated with a tray of antique-looking hurricane lanterns, one for each table. She deposited one on my table and smiled as she lit the wick.

"Just use this knob to turn it up or down," she said.

"Who is the woman at the bar?" I asked.

Before I could stop her, she looked over her shoulder to see who I meant. Rachel caught us looking at her and arched an eyebrow.

"Sorry, " said the waitress. "I just started. I can ask Benny if you like."

"That's okay, thanks. Can I have another pint?" I nailed my eyes to the diary, afraid to catch the woman's eye again. So far, no one else had turned up. I thought Marcus would be there for sure, but there was no sign of his blue head.

"Compliments of Rachel Murphy," said the waitress a few minutes later as she set down a pitcher of dark amber beer and two glasses.

"How's the book?" asked Rachel when I raised my eyes. "I've heard chapter fifteen is riveting."

The lights flickered and went out. Rachel took a seat across from me and pushed the lantern from the centre to the edge of the table. She poured our drinks and offered her hand over the tabletop. "Rachel Murphy. And you are?" Her eyes glinted.

"Kal Winters." We shook hands.

"Eerie coincidence," she purred.

I nodded. "Have you heard of me?" I asked.

"Should I have?"

"No."

"Well, then, no I haven't."

We drank.

"You had a colourful childhood," I offered.

"I had no childhood. What's your story?"

"I beg your pardon?"

She grabbed the book and flipped to the first blank page. "You haven't written anything, Kal. Why not?"

I shrugged.

"Do you think that's fair? Reading everyone's stories without adding your own?"

"I have nothing to write about."

"Bullshit," was all she said before draining her glass and topping us both up. She took another gulp, then bared her teeth in a sly smile. "Get drunk with me and I'll give you something worth writing about."

We drank. Four pitchers between us. Then we ran out on the bill.

Rachel clutched my hand and dragged me, panting, behind her for four or five blocks before she slowed to hail a cab. She shoved me into the back seat then tumbled in on top of me.

"Danforth and Carlaw," she said to the driver, and pulled the door shut with her foot. I struggled for a handhold to right myself, but my position was awkward. I had one shoulder on the seat, and the other sagged toward the floor behind the driver. My arm was pinned by Rachel's hip, and our legs were a tangle.

"Help me up."

"Shh," she soothed and pressed her stomach into mine. Her fingers grazed my neck then she lowered her face to brush her lips across my jaw.

"Rachel," I whispered. "What are—"

It was barely a kiss, that brief contact of her teeth fluttering across my bottom lip. I gasped, a short, light intake of breath.

"That's nothing," she murmured, then backed away and sat up in the seat. She held out a hand to help me up. "Take the DVP to Bloor," she instructed the driver.

For the rest of the trip, her only words were clipped directions to the cabby. I felt her watching me as I shifted away from her and looked out the window to the darkened city. We crossed the Don Valley and followed Danforth east, then turned north on Carlaw. I didn't know what to say.

When we pulled up in front of Rachel's house, she took my hand. I turned to her. She pressed a crumpled bill into my palm. I felt the corners bite into the base of my fingers. "You can come in with me, or you can use this to go home," she said. Her face was shadowed and I couldn't detect her preference from her voice.

"What do you want me to do?" I asked with a glance to the driver. He drummed his fingers on the steering wheel. She didn't answer me. I sat perfectly still. Her fingers were hot on my hand and my skin prickled. "It's been a long time. I don't know," I whispered.

Rachel released my hand, leaving the money in my limp fingers. She passed another bill between the front seats to the driver and told him to keep the change. Then she stepped out of the car and sauntered up the front walk to her house without closing the car door. I watch her, paralyzed with indecision.

"Where to?" asked the driver.

"Uh. Nowhere. This is good." I slid across the seat and scrambled out onto the boulevard. I slammed the door and watched the car pull away.

"Oh, goodie," said Rachel from the front steps.

The whole neighbourhood was in a blackout. Dim flickers illuminated a few windows, but most were blank. The rain had softened to a steady drizzle, and the dark sky rumbled to the south. I was soaked through from our mad dash through sheets of rain.

"Why don't we go inside so you can tell me why you think I'm beautiful," said Rachel.

Beauty is a prevalent thing. It surrounds us. A dandelion, yellow and multi-petaled, finds its way between the cracks and casts its swaying shadow across the pavement designed to suppress it. Beauty is everywhere, in everything, shining in the eyes of everyone. Except Rachel Murphy.

Inside, she lit candles and poured red wine into fine crystal glasses. I watched her slim figure traverse the living room, placing candles on shelves, window ledges and the coffee table. She held a match to the end of a stick of incense until it glowed red. Then she blew gently through puckered lips until the ember grew bright and spread around the tip of the stick. With a graceful flicking of her wrist, she waved the incense to disperse the smoke.

She stood in front of the couch where I sat and lifted her arms above her head. Her shadow wavered on the wall behind her and stretched across the ceiling. Her upper arms framed her delicate face when she bent her elbows and slowly, slowly lowered her hands behind her head. In a heartbeat and a shrug, the dark cloud of her dress slithered down her body. I was off the couch, over the coffee table and on her before the dress hit the floor.

The first climax came unexpectedly. Cherise's face hovered behind my closed eyelids. I sighed and a simple statement came out with the breath. "You're beautiful."

~ ~ ~

THE SUN'S GLARE through streaked windows woke me. She had left me alone and naked to sleep on the threadbare carpet over creaking floorboards. I sat up shivering and groped for my clothes. I dressed quickly, kneeling on the floor underneath the bare windows. My head throbbed. I squinted my crusty eyes to take in my surroundings.

The place was a dump. A thick layer of dust covered every inch of shabby furniture, crooked shelves and cracked plaster. Cobwebs hung limp and thick in the corners and pools of hardened candle wax sagged and clung to shelves, books and tables. I knocked around the cruddy house in a half-hearted search for Rachel. The second floor featured a filthy bathroom and a bedroom full of dirty laundry and stained linens. In the kitchen I found an ages-old pot of moldy coffee and the diary. It lay open on the table in the shadow of a vase of rotted roses. Rachel had scribbled a note for me—*Beauty is an illusion*—and her phone number.

I ripped the page from the book and left it on the counter, then sprinted from the house. I heard the clatter of the sagging screen door behind me, but I never looked back.

~ ~ ~

Rachel

He says he can't live with us and take care of us, too. I feel the same about him. At least he cleaned up the broken dishes before he left. Mom cried herself to sleep. Maybe she won't cry anymore now that he's gone.

He came back today while I was at school. Mom must have been asleep since she didn't say anything. She doesn't remember the fight. Doesn't know he's gone. I'm not going to tell her. He left $20, cigarettes, phone numbers, stupid pink teddy bear (I call it the Pink Nightmare), lame note about how he still loves us, bottle of wine. I took the wine back and traded it for gin, flowers which I gave to Mom. I set Mom's hair in curlers while we drank the gin and smoked.

Phone disconnected today. He calls too much anyway and always wakes up Mom.

Trouble at school. Miss too many classes, but my grades are still good. Mom signed note without crying. Getting better.

Doctor gave Mom new prescription. Says she sleeps too much. Blue pills. They give a good fuzzy buzz, instead of edgy. I give her one when I get home from school. Slip the pink ones in a drink if she gets too high from upper and booze.

Dad waiting for me after school. Wants to see Mom. Says she's always asleep. Fine with both of us. Invited him for dinner. Better not burn the food or he'll think we need him. Gave me $20.

Jerry came to dinner, too. Wanted to meet "Sugar Daddy." Boring, but at least there was no fighting. Jerry says Mom's crazy in a good way and that my dad needs to be put out of his misery. He was just joking.

Electricity turned off. Have to pay bills! Candlelight is nice, though.

Mom asked about him today. Told her he's working more to get promoted. She bought it.

Jerry gave us new colour TV. Told Mom that Dad brought it home because he's doing well at work. Went out with Jerry last night. Double-dosed Mom so she wouldn't wake up alone. Did heroine. Found out I'm attracted to beauty. That's what Jerry said. I can find beauty in the ugliest of places. Not sure what he meant, but ugliness always finds me. Too tired to figure it out. Mom is beautiful and she created me. Dad isn't beautiful or ugly, unless ordinary is ugly. What does that make me? Jerry says beautiful, but can't be trusted.

What makes something beautiful? Art books talk about technique and 'inner'. I think inner means that in spite of outside dirt, wrinkles and bad language, you like it anyway. I like things other people think are ugly. Is that inner?

Tried smoking tonight without moving the cigarette. Kept my arm perfectly still and only moved my head and neck. I thought it was sexy, but Jerry said it looked dumb. Especially when I got ashes all over my forearm.

Went to school drunk. Jerry gave me doubles. Teacher didn't notice. Home is really good. Mom smiles way more that when Dad was here. Electricity back on. Told Dad and he forked over more cash. Mom and I laugh a lot. Mostly about my cooking and when Jerry comes over.

Went to Doctor for more medicine. He wants to see Mom. He thinks we're going through too many pills. I told him I lost them. He wants me to find them by Friday. Have to talk to Jerry.

I don't believe what I did. Jerry took me to a pharmacy last night where his friend works. I couldn't remember the name of Mom's medicine, but we took all the pink and blue ones so I could compare. Jerry will take the wrong ones back tomorrow night.

Dad's bugging me again. Can't put him off. OK. He wants a fuckin picnic, we'll go on a fuckin picnic. FUCK. Just realized I'm younger than Clara was. But I've lived more, I bet, you innocent little idiot.

I feel ugly. Where's my inner? Where's my implied? Jerry says it's still there, but he's always high. So am I. Mom sleeps more and more. Had to give her two pink ones for the picnic. He brought a Frisbee and Hula-hoop. Jerk. He whined a lot and asked too many questions.

More trouble at school. I should have skipped, but Jerry said they'd send a truant officer after me. Big deal, I say. Besides, there's no such thing anymore. Instead I went high and got in a fight in art class. Paint everywhere. It was kind of cool, but I'm in a mess of trouble.

Social worker came to house today. Mom was good. Showed him her Hollywood pictures when she almost became a movie star. Dad came over and cooked and cleaned. Jerry said if he frowns that's bad. But he didn't frown or smile or do anything that meant anything. Dad said to me that he'll move home. FUCK HIM!

~ ~ ~

Chapter 16

In the complete blackness, the only sound is heavy breathing and a pounding heart. Soon, the breathing slows a little, and there is a rustle of clothing. Quick grunts and the dull thud of something hard banging against wood. Finally, a deep sucking of air followed by a wild, throaty howl.

– Kevin Harkness, *The Fortress Breached*

The Bastion

I LEFT A FEW DAYS later, in the morning before Marc woke up. The computer had been turned on, I noticed, but I didn't dare check to see if Marc had visited the page. I pulled my stuff together and dumped it in my bag, then quietly tiptoed out of the apartment.

I drove without insurance to the nearest hardware store and bought an armload of spray paint. After sundown, I intended to paint the van, to change its colour so I could move around undetected for a little while. I considered leaving town, but the diary and its secrets kept me back. Besides, this was my home, and I wouldn't be chased out of it. I decided to visit the last person on my list.

I located Dr. Larkin in a nursing home, catatonic. The visit only lasted a few minutes, but I learned from an orderly that the doctor had been a psychiatrist. His state was due partly to advanced age, but mostly to self-medication after a nervous breakdown in the 1970s. Towards the end of our very short visit, I placed my hand over his and gently squeezed his skeletal fingers. He blinked, slow and steady, and a string of spittle slipped over his loose bottom lip. The glistening strand wavered, stretched and broke away to dissolve into the damp whiskers on his chin.

From newspaper archives, I had pieced together the story: he had fallen while hiking in Africa. Mistaken for dead, he was buried for two days before someone dug him up, presumably to rob the grave of the rich white tourist. No one seemed to know the details for sure. Dr. Larkin himself had had only the vaguest recollection of the events. In the diary, he had written about being in hell.

I returned to find the van completely trashed. I rounded the corner and immediately realized something was wrong. The doors all stood open and my clothes were strewn on the road and sidewalk. Two small children on tricycles surveyed the mess with open mouths. I asked them if they had seen who did it, but they just squinted up at me, the sun in their eyes.

I circled the vehicle to assess the damage. The windshield and headlights had been smashed, and the paint cans had been emptied, crude symbols sprayed across the hood and side panels. The tires were all flat, hubcaps stolen, bumpers dented.

I looked around helplessly, but the houses on the quiet street stared blankly back at me. It seemed like a nice neighbourhood. This sort of thing didn't happen in Toronto, did it? Except for the two kids, nobody was on the street so I couldn't ask anyone what had happened.

I began picking up my belongings and throwing them into a duffel bag I found stuck in a shrub. When I put the bag in the van, I noticed the empty overturned box. The diary and all my notes were gone.

~ ~ ~

Dr. Larkin

August 15, 1970

Imagine yourself in a darkness so complete that you can't decide whether your eyes are open or closed. It feels, at first, as though you are lying on your back, enclosed in the darkness in a box. Soon, though, your muscles lose their sense of up and down and you may very well be floating. The only sounds you can perceive are your own breath and heartbeat; the only smell is your own perspiration, shit and piss, growing musty with the passing of time, marked by heartbeats.

Time slows down. Where am I? Why am I here? How long have I been here? How long will I be here? No one answers you, so you stop asking. You let go of the questions.

You remember something–an accident and terrible pain. Flying? No, falling. You recall a long fall followed by a multitudinous crunch. You remember hearing shouting and pounding feet, a woman screaming...

The vastness of the universe is nothing compared to the vastness of eternity and the inability of the human mind to comprehend it. We believe ourselves to be superior because we are self-aware. I think therefore I am? I know I am, therefore I fret. And cling to creature comforts.

What is more divine than a strong cup of coffee on a cold Saturday morning? Or a wonderfully crafted book, painting, or piece of theatre? Consider how a freshly laundered towel feels against your skin after a shower. Ponder the stroke of the soft breeze on your face, blowing in the window to soothe you in your hot bed in summer. Sea water on your scalp. Have you never laughed until your sides ached? Smelled the neck of your lover? Witnessed the very first smile of a baby?

There is no God; there is no Heaven; there is no Hell. We, in our own divine capacity have invented them all. I've been to Hell, and it is as dark and close as you can imagine. There is no morning, noon or night–no sun or stars to mark the passage of time. Those you find in Heaven. In Hell, you are utterly alone.

~ ~ ~

Chapter 17

The plastic bin lays on its side, its contents spilling onto the curb. The roving gang of raccoons is gone now, but the evidence of their riot is scattered all over the sidewalk and street. Rotting vegetables and bones, soiled paper and plastic packaging roll around in the wind, which carries the smell down the street. The corner of a book can be seen jutting out from under a hedge, its pages chewed and discarded.

The protestor shakes his head and sets down the sign he carries. He bends over to pick up the ripped bag and his ponytail falls over his shoulder. It brushes against his cheek as he works. He shoves the scattered refuse back into the bag, using bits of newspaper to pick up rotting food. He finds the book under the shrubbery and stops to look at it.

– Kevin Harkness, *Light*

The Beacon

I LOGGED ON at the library and typed in the url of the blog. I had it all in my head, the things I wanted to say to this group of nut-bars in a post to their demented little forum. They had figured me out. Rachel Murphy had been the only one to meet my challenge and she had left me naked and humiliated on the cold floor. Enough. Time to fight fire with fire without backing down. I didn't need the diary to expose their sick little cult because I had their webpage. All the evidence the police needed was right there on the world wide web.

Except that it wasn't.

The computer returned an error message.

I found a search engine and typed in "Kimberly Harding". All the usual suspects, innocuous pages of literary criticism and quilting bees, but not my prime suspect. I tried the other author names and got similar results. Nothing useful and certainly not what I was looking for.

When I saw the name Kevin Harkness on a personal web page, my mind went back to my meeting with Mary Ann the previous summer. My own ingenuity surprised me now, how I was able to find so many of these people and interview them before they could catch on to what I was up to. It probably helped me that I hadn't had a clear idea of my intentions beyond curiosity.

The first thing I had noticed about her was her bum because it was the only part of her sticking out of the garbage dumpster. It was a pretty bum, round and hugged by patched denim. I had approached and knocked on the side of the metal bin, trying not to startle her. She ceased her rummaging and stood up to find the source of the sound.

I nodded my head toward to the dumpster and asked, "Find what you're looking for?"

She crossed her arms across the bib of her overalls. "Is it yours?" she asked. When I shook my head, she continued, "Then, I guess it's none of your business."

"I guess not," I said to her backside as she resumed her search. "But this might be your business." I held up the diary until I had her attention.

She exhaled sharply when she realized what I had, then climbed out and landed beside me in the graveled alley. She took off her work gloves and tucked them into her bib. "Wow, I haven't seen that in a long time." I handed it to her so she could thumb through the pages. Everyone wanted to touch a piece of their past. "How did you find me?"

"I plugged some lines of your poetry into a search engine. That gave me your last name and the phone book did the rest."

"Why did you want to find me?" she asked.

"I'm not sure," I admitted. "I'm thinking of writing a book."

She put her hands on her hips and stared hard at me. "Have you ever written a book before?" she asked, and before I could answer, said, "I didn't think so. What's it going to be about? A string of interviews with people you barely know who wrote in a diary? Do you have a plot? What holds them together? Do they know each other? Are they in some kind of a club? Might as well write a book about an internet chat room. At least with that you would have some relationships to work with."

Her verbal assault caused me to take a step backward. "I haven't really thought about all that yet," I mumbled.

She took a step toward me and raised a hand. I thought she was going to jab me in the chest, but instead she reached for the diary again. She opened it to a random page. Then she smiled. "I would read a story like that. Make sure you do a good job."

"I'm really just starting to do some research right now."

"So, you're tracking people down to talk to them. Good idea, but you know you could just make stuff up. Nobody would know any different."

"But truth can be stranger than fiction."

She rolled her eyes. "I hope your book isn't going to be full of clichés."

"So do I."

She handed the book back to me and turned to a large canvas backpack that leaned against the dumpster. It was the kind that hard-core campers carry their gear in. She bent at the waist and knees and, using two hands, swung it up onto her shoulder and wiggled into the shoulder straps. Still bent over, she fastened a belt at her waist and across her chest, then stood up more or less straight. She leaned forward slightly to carry the weight with her knees.

"How much does that weigh?" I asked.

"Probably around 80 pounds," she replied. She couldn't have been more than 125 pounds herself. "It's for work."

She hiked up the alley towards the street. I followed her. "I'm sorry, I didn't realize you were working," I said, then realized how stupid that sounded. Who digs through dumpsters for fun? "What do you do?"

"I educate people about recycling," she said. "Are you hungry? Do you want to grab some lunch?"

"Sure, but I don't have a lot of cash."

She looked me up and down and seemed satisfied that I was, indeed, broke. She wore a sunhat with a wide brim that looked like something out of *The Great Gatsby* and huge sunglasses that covered half of her face. The skin of her cheeks and chin were freckled by the sun, and her thin lips shone with gloss.

First she took me to her warehouse loft around the corner. The building was one of the few warehouses in the city that hadn't been gutted and spit-polished for the rich urban crowd. Mary Ann's space on the second floor was tiny, only about 400 square feet, but the ceilings soared to 20 feet. Shelves covered each of the four walls, even the windows, and were piled with books, cookware and an assortment of things I assume she had pulled from the garbage—furniture springs, flower pots, pillows, clothing, coffee makers, bits of wood and many unrecognizable plastic objects. Her bed hung from the ceiling on chains in the center of the room. Beside it stood an antique wooden stepladder.

She dropped her bag, hat and sunglasses and gave me the tour, pointing to each shelf as we circled the room.

"Recyclables, including plastic and metal, paper products; hygiene products, including make-up, soaps and creams; gardening products, home-building materials, fabric and toys." She stopped in front an industrial oven. Beside it stood a kiln. Shelves above and beside it held heavy-duty cook pots and metal utensils. "My lab."

"What do you do with all this stuff?" I asked.

"I recycle what I can–turn garbage into useful stuff. Melt down or otherwise dismantle old stuff and shape it into new. I sell patents when I come across something that works. I sell products that I can get government approval for and give away what I can't. Some of it I have shipped to third-world countries. What I can't recycle, I give to someone who can, like the metal and tougher grade plastics." She turned to me with a big smile. I noticed her eyes were bright green. "It's been years since I bought anything other than food."

I wondered what she was planning for lunch.

"Speaking of food, I'm starving!" she announced and grabbed a bag from a hook by the door. It was a quilted assembly of old jeans, with buttons and what looked like Girl Guide patches sewn on for decoration. I assumed it was one of her creations from other people's garbage. We walked to a nearby restaurant, a small deli, and placed our orders at the counter. As we waited for our sandwiches, Mary Ann rifled in her bag and pulled out two plastic food containers and two cups. She handed these to the teen-aged girl at the cash register and paid for both lunches. The girl handed Mary Ann her change, and took the containers to the sandwich man. He served our lunch in the containers. Neither of them seemed to think this was odd.

"They know me here," Mary Ann said by way of explanation. "It saves them money on take-out containers and they don't have to wash the coffee mugs. It all comes down to money. If you can save a company money, then they don't mind showing environmental responsibility."

She handed me my lunch and a linen napkin which she had also pulled from her bag. I was mildly surprised that she wasn't a vegetarian and said so.

"All environmentalists have to be tree-hugging granola crunchers, right?" she said, exasperated. "I like meat. I'm a carnivore. I eat organic when I can, but when I can't, I will dig into a big steak and enjoy it as much as the fat cat CEO at the table next to me. My conscience is clearer than his, so I probably enjoy it more."

I bit into my sandwich and chewed thoughtfully while she continued to talk around the wad of food in her mouth. She ate like Cherise.

"I'm sorry, but I am so sick of the all or nothing attitude that keeps people from making even the smallest change. If you're a vegetarian, but wear leather, that means you're a hypocrite. If you recycle, but drive an SUV, you're a hypocrite. I've noticed that these arguments come from people who don't lift a finger and they use that as an excuse to do nothing. I tell people in my workshops that even the smallest thing you do for the planet is better than doing nothing at all." She stopped talking long enough to take another bite of her sandwich. "Anyway, you didn't find me to talk about all this. What do you want to know?"

I swallowed and took a sip of my milk. "Who gave the diary to you?"

She stopped chewing to think, and a small smile crossed her lips. "What makes you think someone gave it to me?" she asked.

My lunch with Mary Ann had been very pleasant. Looking back, I wondered at the difference in my own demeanour. I had been polite and engaging–nothing like the angry, rude misfit I eventually turned into. Mary Ann had even suggested getting together again, but I had declined because of my relationship with Cherise.

The diary had been a gift from a teacher when Mary Ann was just 14 years old. That's not all he gave her.

"People said he was a pervert, a child molester. He went to jail and ruined his career over me." We were finished eating by this time. She was leaning back in her chair with her arms crossed casually over her stomach.

"Was he a pervert?" I asked.

She sighed heavily and shrugged. "I loved him and I believed he loved me. After we stopped seeing each other, he started a relationship with a woman his own age."

"When did he give you the diary?"

She smiled and closed her eyes for a moment. I remember thinking how wonderfully gentle and bright she seemed. I couldn't picture her in the throes of raging adolescent emotions. "It was the first time he kissed me. We'd just finished up an environmental awareness meeting for kids in school who wanted to get involved with activism. It wasn't a popular group with the parents, let me tell you. Anyway, everyone else had gone. We stayed and talked for a little while, then he took hold of my hand and kissed me. As far as first kisses go, that had to be one of the best."

"Where did he find the diary?"

"On the street, he said. Weird, huh?"

It certainly was, and it didn't fit with my fledgling theory that it was being passed around on purpose. For that reason, I ignored it, preferring to think later that she must have been mistaken, or even lying.

"Was it near his house?" I asked, determined to make the square peg fit. Someone could have left it there on purpose where he would be sure to find it.

"It was in the trash. I think that was the beginning of my obsession. You can always find something worthwhile in even the dirtiest of places."

I didn't see her again after that. I wish I had. She was one of the loveliest people I have ever met.

I checked email.

The inbox held a single message with the subject line, "Get out of town!" I opened the message from an unknown recipient, but it was blank. I stupidly clicked on the attachment, not caring about viruses because it was the library's computer. The screen went black for an instant before taking me to a porn website dedicated to rape.

Bile burned the back of my throat and I choked it down. My vision blurred, but I blinked hard to clear it. The image was still there. I tried to close the window, but it only opened more windows. I hit the switch on the monitor to turn it off, and put my head down to stop the sudden spinning. It had to be a threat. I couldn't see any other explanation. Sure, it could have been nothing more than spam, but the coincidence was too much. They were obviously referring to Cherise as a warning for me to leave town. Panic hit hard and I frantically searched the faces in the library for one that I recognized. Inexplicably, everyone seemed familiar and menacing. I was going crazy. Getting paranoid.

I bolted. I had to shove my way through the lineup at the circulation desk and knock some chairs out of my way before bursting through the doors and into the street. My panic blinded me. I sprinted into the road, my ears filled with the sounds of screaming tires, honking horns and shouts. I vaguely remember my knees collapsing underneath me as they were bent sideways by a bumper. Then nothing.

~ ~ ~

Mary Ann

My Daddy

When I was just a little girl,
My daddy was the sun.
He warmed me with his tender love,
His laughter and his fun.

When I was just a little girl,
My daddy was the rain.
He picked me up when I fell down
And washed away my pain.

When I was just a little girl,
My daddy was the wind.
He blew away the ghosts and ghouls.
And he would always win.

When I was just a little girl,
My daddy was the earth.
He helped me keep my little toes
Planted in the turf.

My daddy was a giant then
When I was wee and small.
He and nature, hand in hand,
Helped me heed the call.

But now he is a little man,
In this great, big world.
He follows orders from the rest
Forgets his little girl.

The sun grows cold with passing time,
The rain deposits acid
The wind is thick with smog and
fumes
The earth is sick and placid.

Oh, Daddy, can't you feel it, too?
The world is fading fast.
Too many people take too much.
You know it cannot last.

What Child is This?

When you look at the child,
Who do you see?
Her elegant mother
Polished and sleek?
Do her dimples, her freckles,
    her practiced smiles,
The toss of her head and
    feminine wiles
Cast the child
Like the mother
In sin?

When you hear the girl speak,
Who do you hear?
Her eloquent father
Talking down fear?
Do her calming tones and
    well-chosen words,
Her pounding fists and
    passive verbs
Make her voice
Like her father's
Seem thin?

When you look in her eyes,
What do you see?
Do her childish smiles
Beckon to thee?
Do her lazy brown curls and
    skinny arms
And barely-there-breasts and
    giggling charms
Tell you anything
about everything
within?

My Questions

When will love find me
Where will love find me
How will love find me
And will I recognize it?

Meat

Cold and clammy
Red and bloody
Marbling is best
Fatted calves
And unbeaked hens
Eggs thieved from the nest
Veal and pork chops
Youngest beef
Tender and sublime

Babies taken
From their parents
Walk the killing line
It doesn't hurt
So don't you fret
Don't waste your soulful care
Death comes quick
No cruelty here
Dumb creatures aren't aware.

Natural Love

In the clouds in the sky I imagine your face
In the wind in the leaves I hear your voice
The sun on my skin is your embrace
When, my love, will you make a choice?
Your words haunt my dreams, your eyes always see me
Life is perfect, love is right
When together we are dreaming
I'll be yours, through nature's night.

Handle With Care

Your lips touched mine, soft and dry
You pulled away, I started to cry
I wish I wish to relive that day
If I could, here's what I'd say:

Touch me, my dear, softly softly
My tears are not real, my tears are not here
I love you, my dear, fondly fondly
I give you my heart, handle with care.

Little One

A little one loves
With tears and cries
Too young to kiss
Shudders and sighs

His love, she thinks,
Is real and true
Her love, he knows
Is soft and new

The world would frown
To see this man
Touch this girl
And take her hand

But gentle he is
Slow and wise
And eager she seeks
With wide bright eyes

The noblest of men
Might turn her away
Hard words or cold looks
But not on this day

Her mouth was hot
Her temper was high
This little girl blue
Would reach the sky

This bravest of men
Could stand his ground
To an angry mob
And smooth their frowns

He talks of the earth
And of heavenly delights
He urges them all
To take up his fight

The weakest of men
In sun or in rain
Shut out his words
And put him in chains

They look to the girl
And hear her cries
And believe in their hearts
That the noble man lies

They don't understand
When the girl screams
That they've chained her love
And shackled her dreams

She offers her wrists
Small and frail
To be bound and bruised
They take her to jail

The mob shouts and cheers
But they don't understand
This little one's love
Is not for the land.

The Other

If only I'd never heard her name
Her face, so calm, will ever remain
The one you chose instead of mine
To lean into yours, to ever be thine.
Life is harsh. I kiss you kiss you
You broke my heart. I miss you miss you.

Word Association

Earth   Eden   Garden   Dying
Green
is
brown

Alive   Roots   Air   Choked
Life
is
shrivelled

Oil   Smog   Smoke   Smother
Birds
can't
fly

Nowhere   left   to   go.

~ ~ ~

Chapter 18

Sun streams in the window of the warehouse studio, shafts of light illuminating the dust as it swirls, hovers and lands on the paintings that lean against all four walls. Crowded shelves seem about to collapse under the weight of tins and tubes of paints, brushes, rolled up canvases and sketch books. The only stick of furniture in the place is a ratty wing chair, red fabric worn, ripped and hanging from the arms and back.

The book is on the floor at her feet, spine cracked open, pages facing down. The stripes are barely discernible under the blanket of filth. The corners that aren't ripped away roll back, splitting into sheaves of spongy cardboard. She is standing barefoot at her easel, wildly dabbing paint onto a canvas. Her arm arcs over her head to stab the brush downward. Drops of paint loose themselves from the bristles. One lands on her cheek, another on her toe, and a last one on the face of the young hobo. She looks down at her foot and rubs it against the back of her bare calf. When she sees the paint on the cover of the book, she drops the paintbrush and crouches quickly. Balling the hem of her T-shirt in her fingers, she dabs at the face in the picture, smearing the red paint. Most of it comes away on the cotton, but there is a light pink stain left behind.

— Kasara Humphrey, *Howl*

The Hunter

I WOKE UP IN hospital. I tried to sit up, but something restrained me, bound me to the bed. Pain shot through my body from head to foot, knocking the air out of me. When the waves subsided, I struggled again until I could no longer stand it.

I shouted, my cries raspy in a dry throat and short-lived.

A white-clad figure appeared in my periphery and did something with my intravenous.

Then darkness.

~ ~ ~

THEIR FACES FULL of concern and contempt floated before me one at a time. Kind words, tender hands on my face. All of them came to tell me their stories. I could feel Marc beside me. He held my hand, his face buried in the blankets beside my hip. He was there always, even though I couldn't quite see him.

The palm reader with her beautiful hair and sparkling shawls stroked my face as she told me about finding a baby on her doorstep so many years ago. Her friend the matron came, too, with children running around her legs, giggling and tickling each other. The old man was wheeled in by the storyteller. The storyteller read to me from books about quests and dragons. The elderly couple brought the widow with them, flanking her, arms hooked like Dorothy on the yellow brick road. The husband had dirt from his garden under his nails and he whispered to me that he loved his wife. The blind man cried and ran his hands over the casts on my arms and legs. The hermit brought with her the scent of mint. The lawyer told me I had no case, but I didn't know what he meant. The librarian brought books. I cried when I saw the flower arranger and begged him to take his bouquet away. I was afraid to die. The kindly housewife brought a lovely-smelling bouillabaisse. The cold woman pressed her lips against mine until I whimpered for her to stop. She told me with a smile that the psychiatrist was dead at last. The poet washed and combed my hair while she hummed softly. The painter was drunk and she forgot to take the black canvas with her.

I saw Clara. It was nighttime, after visiting hours and the room was dark. I couldn't see her face very well, but her haircut gave her away. She asked me to give her diary back to her. I tried to tell her it was gone, stolen, but she left too soon.

They all came. All of them except Cherise.

~ ~ ~

"COFFEE OR GIN?" the artist had asked while I looked around her studio. Paint splatters had marked every surface in the upstairs apartment. Like bristled bouquets, coffee cups filled with brushes surrounded an ancient metal sink and crowded the counter. Palettes, pots and tubes, oils, acrylics and water colours littered shelves, the fridge top, windowsills and a hacked and leaning worktable. The artist's studio reeked of the chemicals of the trade. A small fan clattered and squeaked through its reluctant oscillations, managing only to lift the corners of an old newspaper.

Last summer I had visited a few of the people who had written most recently. I threaded my way through piles of canvases and easels to lean against the counter top.

"Gin." Definitely gin.

She yanked open the freezer door and grabbed a bottle and handful of ice cubes from inside. She set the bottle down and dumped the contents of two mugs before rinsing them and mixing our drinks with the handle of a paintbrush.

"Your work is really wonderful," I said as my eyes flitted across the paintings hung on the wall.

"It's getting there," she replied with a shrug. "You probably want to see the diary collection. I don't have any of the originals, but I take photos of all my work."

She shuffled past me in fuzzy slippers and open robe into an adjoining room. Betina Finch was fairly well known for a nature series that hit big in the eighties. The water-colour flower and gazebo prints hung in waiting rooms, graced calendars and greeting cards, and even showed up on the odd box of tissues. The paintings that stuffed the apartment were very different.

"This is my best work," she said and handed me a photo album. The spine crackled when I opened the book. I could feel the grittiness of years of dust on my fingertips.

"These are the paintings you described in the diary," I said. Similar to those on the wall in front of me. But different.

"Yeah. The diary series," she snapped, then poured herself another drink. She cocked the bottle at me. I glanced at my own drink, which was three-quarters full, picked it up and downed it, then nodded. She shrugged and refreshed me.

"You sold them?"

"Gifts," she snarled. "I only ever *sold* daisies and lilacs."

I looked away from her portfolio to size her up. At ten o'clock on a Wednesday morning, Betina was drunk and angry. I imagined the two states mutually informed each other, and often.

"You gave them all away?"

"Do you want one? I'll show you what I'm working on and you tell me if you want it or not." She waved her drink as she spoke and didn't spill a drop. I followed her into the next room. I rounded the easel that stood in the centre of the darkened room to look at the canvas. Betina waited in the doorway. She leaned a shoulder against the jamb and jutted a hip.

The canvas was painted black.

Betina flipped a switch on the wall. The brush strokes seemed to jump off the black background as a spotlight illuminated the high gloss against flat finish. Thick crests in black and charcoal sculpted into the shape of a face. Light shimmered on the shiny cheekbones, nose, chin and wide smooth forehead. Black meringue curls raced away from the face to the edges of the canvas. Somewhere between two and three dimensions, the rough subtle face jangled in my memory.

"It's called *The Hunter*," said Betina. "Do you recognize her?"

"*The Hunter*," I repeated. "You mean like the Greek goddess?"

"Could be," she said vaguely. "I still have to add the stars, but I could have it ready next week if you want to pick it up."

"I have nowhere to put it."

She shrugged and turned to shuffle back to the kitchen. "Fine with me," she said over her shoulder. "It's yours if you ever want it."

I followed her and accepted another drink.

"You could get a lot of money for it," I said to her. "Why don't you sell it?"

She slumped into a chair that was jammed between the fridge and counter and put a foot up on the table. Her ankle knocked against a vase of silk flowers. It fell on its side and rolled into her calf. Her robe slid off her thigh, and I noticed that her nightie was hiked high.

"I didn't paint it to sell it." Her head wobbled. "Past my bedtime."

After another look at the haunting face in the painting, I had let myself out while Betina slept in her kitchen.

~ ~ ~

A SHATTERED FOOT, cracked pelvis, internal damage that required two surgeries, two broken arms, and my face pretty well flattened made winter pass in a drugged daze. I was fed pain-killers and nutrients intravenously since my jaw was wired shut. My injuries were no longer life-threatening, but I longed to join Cherise.

Marc came to see me in February.

He stepped into the room, took one look at me and closed his eyes for a moment.

"Oh, Kal," he sighed. He took a breath, straightened his shoulders and came over to sit by my bed. "Can you talk?"

I rolled my eyes.

"Good," he replied. "Now maybe you'll finally listen to me."

I turned my head to look out the window. Black branches swayed against a white sky.

"That's fine," Marc said. "You don't have to look at me, but I'm still going to talk some sense into you. First, I have some news. Dean goes on trial next month."

I looked back to him.

"I thought that would get your attention. I found the pills in his medicine cabinet and went to the police. They can't do anything about him attacking Cherise, but—" His voice cracked and his eyes clouded. He stopped and sniffled. "But three other women came forward. There are probably more. I am so sorry I doubted Cherise. I knew you guys were having problems and I thought—"

I stopped him by groaning. I didn't want to hear Marc say her name again. I closed my eyes against the tears and rolled my head away from him. The pillow grew hot and wet under my cheek.

"Kal, you have to believe me when I say we didn't do this to you. The police found the kids that trashed your van, and the driver of the car that hit you. It wasn't us. I know you think we were conspiring against you, but use your head. What could we possibly want from you?"

A nurse came in to announce that I had had enough. Not a moment too soon.

~ ~ ~

Betina Finch

Near Divinity
I see the spectrum hiding behind the blackness. The light source is weak, but not failing, originating from above, slightly right. Divinity in the near future. Soon, the spectrum will be stronger. The book is there, too (but I'm not sure where to place it). The page is nearly blank, slightly torn, resistance to having the page turned or from having the page turned too quickly. Near the book rests a hard strong hand attached to a long slim arm, not too muscled. The arm reaches from behind a cloak that is the blackness that hides the spectrum for now. The arm is reaching back from right, from the future. Perhaps the light source is a halo? The hand doesn't reach to touch the book, though it lies there, calm, palm up. There is something in the hand but it's not clear to me yet. The left is still blank. I see music, tinny sounds and a girl giggling and a man moaning but the colour eludes me. Is it meant to be muddy or are my thoughts unclear?

Dream Mother
The dream version of my mother is gentle and secretive. She smiles and winks, strokes me, hums and sways. She talks but I can't understand what she says to me. It is soothing. She looks down on me as though she is floating. Her face sways a little, her chin tucked down, her hair falls across her cheeks. It hangs down and I feel as if I could reach it with my fingers. She is young, before the lines added wisdom to her appearance, before her hair turned grey. Her eyes are cloudy, but not from cataracts. She weeps softly as she looks at me, not from pain or sadness, but from awe. My very presence overwhelms her and her tears fall on my forehead. She brushes them away with a hand and I miss her touch when she is finished. No one will ever look at me again with such tenderness.

The Moon in the Man, the Man in the Woman
A pale disk floats in the centre as the focal point. Pales of yellow, grey, pink and blue tease each other within the disc, but do not mingle. The changes in colour are subtle, emphasized only by different lighting, detectable only upon the closest inspection. It should appear white at first, but liquid. Below the disk is water; above it stars. The water and stars are veils.

To get below the surface, the viewer must squint. The ripples appear random, but are not. There is a uterus; in the uterus is a fetus. From the fallopian tubes spring canines, who howl at the moon. Fish swim in the waters, a crustacean climbs ashore, using the umbilical. The umbilical cord appears as the light the moon casts upon the water, joining the disc to the womb; or the womb to the disc. Flowers float on the foam. The water laps at curvaceous rocks, whose shadows and undulations form rounded, dimpled hips. From the rocks spring gentle, fragile flowers. The stars swirl, milky white among cloudy breasts.

The Barefoot Writer
A woman sleeps among books. Are the books of her or is she of the books? Shelves fill the canvas, titles in all directions. The viewer must turn her head this way and that to read the hundreds of titles, all recognizable. The shelves appear about to topple. The viewer wants to reach out a hand to steady them. The woman lies on a chaise lounge,

her face turned away, partially buried in her pillow of books. Her shoulders are square on the lounge, but her hips turn toward the viewer. The pose is sexual like an odalisque, but her demure dress suggests innocence. One arm falls off the lounge to trail on the floor. Slim fingers rest on the blank pages of an open book. The pen she holds rests on end between that book and her fingers. She wears no shoes.

The Innocent—A Series
Children running an office. Children in gridlock. Children on an assembly line. Children at a political rally. Children in the lab. Children anchoring the news. Children at trial. Adults on the swings. Adults in the sandbox. Adults in a tree fort. Adults building a snowman. Adults at story time. Adults playing house.

Second Coming
Viewpoint from above and behind. In the foreground is a shoreline that stretches up onto a desert. At the edge of the desert is an encampment of hunter-gatherers. They camp on the edge of a modern city. Beyond the city are mountains, behind which the sun is rising.
Along the waves walks a figure, dressed in jeans and a simple white T-shirt. The figure, foreground centre, is walking to shore, away from the viewer. The figure is barefoot.
Tiny figures populate and popularize the city. King-Kong climbs a building. Marilyn Monroe walks over a grate. A soldier kisses a woman. Tara is on fire. Charles and Diana wave to the crowd from a balcony. The Hindenburg tilts dangerously. Kennedy slumps against his wife. Ronald Reagan, Hitler and Elvis have coffee in a corner diner. American soldiers in fatigues prowl through a city park. The Pope blesses a crowd of seagulls. The faithful worship an image of Che Guevera that manifests itself on a shopping bag. Insert many, many images of the 20th century.

~ ~ ~

Chapter 19

The only light came from the window facing onto the street. Headlights moved across the wall and the floor, hitting the chair before disappearing off the opposite wall. The book lay in the chair, muddied, bloodied and torn from years of travel, a testament to the wanderers who had carried it with them for a brief time. She almost left without it, but it caught her eye just as she reached for the door. She retrieved it from the chair, flipped through its pages, and dropped it in her purse. Then she went home.

– Kelly Hopper, *Luminosity*

Fire

Her braid had reminded me of Cherise. That was silly, of course, since Deirdre and Cherise were nothing alike. Where Cherise had cappuccino-coloured skin, Deirdre's complexion was so pale it was tinged with the blue of her veins. Cherise's black hair was thick and reached her waist; Deirdre's blonde braid was thin, and so short it stuck out from her nape, moving with her head, rather than finding its own sway against her back. It was something in the way the hair twined and twisted. It also had a lot to do with the fact that almost everything reminded me of Cherise in those earliest days after her death.

I shouldn't have continued my research and interviews, but the distraction attracted me. The idea of her being gone forever was just too much for me to wrap my heart and mind around. I wasn't ready to miss her.

I had lied my way into an interview with Deirdre, the veterinarian, telling her I worked for a newsletter for pet owners. Almost immediately she had seen through my sham and I was forced to explain the real reason for contacting her. The encounter is embarrassing to recall. In brief, Deirdre grabbed the diary from me and read the last entry—Cherise's suicide note. I broke down and excused myself having learned nothing new.

~ ~ ~

Marcus came back to the hospital a week later. A vicious wind threw winter's last blast of snow against the window. He set a vase of sunflowers on my bedside table and a picture he had of Cherise and I snuggled together on a blanket by a campfire. The night we first met.

"David Gaudrault found Clara's diary and fell in love with her. Against the odds, she came into his store to buy another notebook. Toronto was a lot smaller in 1928. He seduced her, but couldn't offer her the excitement she wanted. She left him after two months. Eight months later, he found a baby—my father—on his doorstep. David never knew for sure whether Clara had left the child, but he liked to think so. A bookstore was no place to raise a baby, so Rebecca agreed to help. She named him Daniel Mesinger and raised him. As a teenager, he met Myrtle and started an affair with her."

I raised an eyebrow.

"No, she's not my mother. Daniel told Rebecca about Myrtle, so Rebecca went to retrieve the diary. It was meant to be a family heirloom, a tribute to Clara, my grandmother, but when Rebecca held it in her hands, she got a feeling from it."

I nodded. I knew the feeling.

"She and David thought the diary should go out into the world to collect stories, the way Clara might have. So, they placed it in the store for someone to buy. Derek van Horne's wife bought it shortly before she died. Then, we didn't see it for years until it just showed up one day. People find it and take what they need from it. Not everyone writes in it. Sometimes it disappears for years and just when we think we'll never see it again... well, you get the picture."

He reached for my hand and held it tightly. I looked at him.

"Where is it, Kal? Where did you hide it?"

I frowned at him. He didn't have it?

"Oh," he said and let go of my fingers. "It's gone."

~ ~ ~

Deirdre

Anyone who has spent any time around animals will know that they are capable of vast expressions of emotion such as joy, disappointment, anticipation and dread. This story proves it.

I suspect that it began one October afternoon when I arrived home with two bags of colourful wool. The air was cool and frost had coated the trees that morning when I left for work. It was time to knit new sweaters for the animals. I bustled in the door with my bags and danced from one animal to another. I gave each a kiss and a pat, and dropped the balls of yarn in front of each of them.

"Bosco gets green and yellow plaid. Acrylic, of course, for the little sneezer."

"Ouf," sniffed Bosco. He had been abandoned at the shelter by a breeder who had no use for a beagle with chronic allergies.

"Falstaff gets black and white stripes."

"Eep," squeaked the white rat, who had been rescued from solitary confinement in a lab.

"Wic gets orange and blue polka dots."

"Yow," moaned the psychic Persian. She showed up at the door one day just in time for dinner and never left.

"And lastly, Lex gets a scarlett vest."

"Thcarlett!" screamed the African Grey parrot. Lex had learned to speak from a small child with a lisp.

It all seems so obvious to me now. I never once considered that they didn't appreciate the warmth of the wool. Never a thought that they might feel embarrassed in the local park. Many animals would have hidden the wool, or destroyed it. Not my pack. They were above such destructive behaviour. Instead, they held midnight meetings to come up with a collective solution to their dilemma. The heart of the scheme lay in our morning sojourns to the park. They started by sleeping late, and refusing to leave the house until each and every one of them had finished eating. They picked at their food, they wrestled with each other and they hid under the couch refusing to come out until the sun was well and fully risen. I was late for work every day for a week. And yet, I never suspected a thing.

Suddenly, out of nowhere, came a deep and abiding interest in other people. Not their pets, but the people themselves. They showed a marked preference for men, particularly tall, young, good-looking men with no rings on their left hands.

Monday morning:

Falstaff took a wild leap off my shoulder into a pile of leaves where a cocker spaniel was sniffing around. The dog found Falstaff and quickly pinned him to the ground with her snout. When I jumped to his rescue, Lex lost his balance on my other shoulder and took off flying. He landed on Rick, the dog owner. Bosco wrapped his leash around the man's ankles and Wic planted herself in front of him where she arched her back and hissed at him. The surprised man was completely surrounded.

He yanked hard on the cocker's collar and dragged her away from Falstaff. "Nathty," said Lex and he flew back to perch on my shoulder.

"If you train her to sit on command," I said to Rick, "there is no need to choke her with her own collar."

"You're one to talk about training animals," he replied, but my pack were already dragging me away from the brute.

Tuesday morning:

Using more or less the same method, we all met David, a construction worker who was walking two German Shepherds, Black and Decker. Once I got the animals corralled and safely behind me, we chatted pleasantly about the weather and the joys of owning pets. I gave him some tips on training the dogs and he was eager to show me the few tricks he had taught Decker. Sit, stay, roll over, shake a paw. We were all suitably impressed. Decker was happy with his biscuits. Then it happened. David had Black sit and tip up his snout. Then David took a biscuit and balanced it at the end of Black's nose and told him not to move.

The dog's sides quivered, his tail twitched. He crinkled his forehead and his ears were tight to his head. Other than that, though, he did not move to shake the cookie from his nose. My animals made various noises of disgust. Bosco sniffled, Wic growled, Falstaff squeaked and Lex said, "Eat!" With a quick motion of his head, Black snapped the biscuit from the top of his nose.

"Bad dog," said David, but Black wasn't listening. He was soaking up the empathy of my indignant animals. I'm sure that is the last time Black performed that humiliating trick for David.

Wednesday:

We met Shane, who yelled in Italian at his Chihuahua, Pedro.

Thursday:

We figured out that Roger only bought his Jack Russel puppy, Jax, to meet women.

I couldn't figure out what had gotten into my animals. They were never rough with the bachelors, but they scared more men than they endeared themselves to. They made me look like a crazy woman who knew nothing about the responsibilities of pet ownership. They didn't come when I called, they didn't sit when I commanded. They were noisy and aggressive. They were desperate. At all costs, they had to stop me from knitting those sweaters.

Friday:

Their efforts paid off. The sun was shining brightly, and the frost had burned off the trees by the time we reached the park. Rick, David, Shane and Roger all glared at me from the other side of the park where they waited impatiently for their dogs to do their business. Shane said something to Roger and all four of them laughed.

"Jerk," said Lex.

"Thank you, Lex," I replied and scritched him under his beak.

Then it happened. Falstaff gave a mighty squeal and fainted dead away. Bosco pounced on Wic and wrestled her to the ground. Lex took off flying. I keep his wings clipped, so his flight pattern was a downward trajectory. He landed on the back of a very large, very muscular Doberman.

Not knowing who to attend to first, I scooped up Falstaff, who appeared to be in the most trouble. At a run, I checked to make sure he was breathing and dropped him into my shirt pocket. I trusted that Wic would have enough restraint not to tear Bosco into ribbons, so I left them to retrieve Lex from the surprised Doberman's rump.

I had almost reached the two when a sudden crash landed me on my back in a pile of leaves. I blinked and looked up at the sky, catching my breath. That was how I met the love of my life. We had crashed into each other as we were running to rescue our pets. His name is Paul and his dog is Petunia. No amount of debate will get him to change her name.

As I lay in the leaves, unable to speak with the wind knocked out of me, Paul crouched beside me. He reached forward and I raised a hand so that he could help me up. But he bypassed my outstretched fingers to gently pull Falstaff from my pocket. He cradled the limp rat in his large hands and prodded gently at Falstaff's chest.

The little rat stirred to life. He blinked slowly and rolled over in Paul's hands. Gingerly, Falstaff limped up Paul's arm to his shoulder. The little devil raised himself up on his hind legs and licked Paul's earlobe. Petunia sidled over with Lex still perched on her back, one foot clinging to the stump of Petunia's tail. She turned her head around to sniff at the parrot, and Lex made the loudest, sloppiest, most obnoxious kissing noise of his career. Bosco and Wic strolled back as if nothing had happened at all.

I was still lying in the leaves as the animals gathered around Paul where he crouched and gazed at him adoringly. He smiled at each and patted them all before helping me to my feet. I didn't even know his name when we kissed for the first time.

We all left the park, Paul and I holding hands. Lex chuckled as we passed the spurned suitors with their unfortunate pets.

I donated the unused wool to the community rummage sale.

~ ~ ~

Chapter 20

The angel dominates the scene, white and gold, arms and wings spread wide. It looks down to the woman, man and child who emerge from golden coffins. Their eyes are all cast heavenward, arms reaching towards the perfection the angel represents.

A goose-necked desk lamp throws a glare on the glossy page. He tilts the lamp in order to see the picture better. The scene depicts Judgment Day, but it's a rare interpretation that omits the damned. He checks the caption to see the name of the artist and raises an eyebrow in surprised recognition.

– Korine Horner, *Consequences*

The Reckoning

I DIDN'T SEE MARC for awhile. I still had questions that he was either unwilling or unable to answer for me. The diary, the novels and the web site were all part of an elaborate set-up, but to what end? I believed it all fit together, but I didn't know how or why. I wondered if Ross had anything to do with it besides wanting to steal my work. The thought that I might never know haunted me.

When the trees outside were pimpled with hard, red buds, another spectre rose to torture me: Dean. His face appeared on the news, first as a generic police illustration of a vague white man between 25 and 45 with short hair and squinty eyes; later as something much muddier in both representation and implication. Someone had pulled a web cast off the internet: a blurry, jumpy digital video showed a man hovering over a prostrate form on a bed. When he moved to adjust the camera, his face came into view. Dean's pixilated face leered out from the television screen. Three victims had come forward just as Marc said. Police urged anyone with information to contact them. I thought I might hear again from Marc, but he did not appear.

The sudden intrusion of Dean into my ordered world of convalescence brought the torture of my love's last days to life. I had almost convinced myself that it was a dream, a memory so distant that I could only remember it when others told me. My grief came into sharp focus even as the pain of my physical injuries faded. I had not allowed myself to mourn her, throwing all of my fear, frustration and angst into tracking down the originators of the diary.

I waited during the daily newscast for the story to appear and had orderlies scour the newspapers for me. I debated and discarded the idea of talking to the police on Cherise's behalf. She had made it clear to me that she wanted it to remain a secret. I didn't feel I had the right to drag it out for her parents and make them mourn her again. I still wonder, and always will, if it was the right decision. It wouldn't have changed anything, so I have to content myself with that.

By the time the buds had grown fat and purple, ready to burst into green, my suspicions of Ross and Marc had melted away in shame and embarrassment for the way I had behaved. Faulty logic and repressed sorrow had caused me to search for answers to the wrong questions, to see evil in the wrong people. I had failed to understand an important aspect: random people all had the same need to communicate something of themselves, to shout into the void and listen for an answering voice. Strangers had crossed paths with a diary full of others who had the same compulsion. In my need to find the master narrative, the grand truth, I had missed the simplicity of the game: Read. Scribble a few lines of your own. Pass it on.

In late May, the wires came out of my jaw and the casts off my limbs. During my morning rehabilitation sessions, as I struggled to regain control over my atrophied muscles, I could see the bright yellow daffodil heads bobbing outside the window. Robins hopped across the brown, matted lawn in search of brunch. Back in my room, their songs put me to sleep.

In the afternoons, with the help of a therapist, I struggled to regain control over my atrophied reason. In the evenings, I wrote.

The routine comforted me, but I was starting to go stir crazy. The hospital staff was friendly, but I was still lonely. I felt with each snippet of conversation I engaged in that I was sniffing around like an ant looking for a pheromone trail, some hint that another like-minded ant had passed by. I began leaving random notes around the hospital, scribbled bits of half-remembered poems, hoping someone would pick up my trail. No one did.

Marc came back in June, days before my release from the hospital and took me for a walk. He put me in a wheelchair, wrapped Cherise's afghan around my shoulders and signed me out.

The day possessed the adolescent coquettishness of late spring. Magnolia trees dropped their blossoms like handkerchiefs as we passed beneath their branches. The pale blue sky was made paler by a veil of clouds that drifted in fingers across the sun.

"Nobody meant to hurt you, Kal."

"I know."

"We didn't choose you. The diary did. It was there every time you came in the store. I watched you pass it over."

"Why didn't you tell me sooner, Marc?"

The white wash of clouds diminished the spring sun's fragile warmth. The breeze tickled my bladder.

"Things got so crazy so fast," Marc said. "There is no agenda behind the diary. It's just a platform. Nobody is ever forced to write. Most don't. There are no rules."

"There's one: pass it on."

"Yeah."

"One rule and I managed to break it."

"Not really. It's out there again."

Marc positioned my chair so it faced the bench and sat. He pulled out a bag of bread crumbs and started tossing them into the wind. Soon, we were surrounded by pigeons.

"What about the web site?" I asked after awhile.

"My blog? Just another version of the diary really. No hidden agenda. Just a shot in the dark to find interesting people to talk to. I'm happy with how it turned out. I had to move it to another host with more room."

The warmth of the sun reached my cheeks and eyelids and had just begun to register on my cool skin when a light wind swept through like a breath.

"I thought it was a cult," I admitted, red-cheeked.

"I gathered. Most of the writers have never met except online. I know a few of them from the store, but not many. You and Rebecca are the only ones who know I'm *The Reader*. And everyone knows you, of course."

"Should I pick a handle?" I asked with a laugh, finally able to see the humour.

"Probably."

Marc wheeled me back to my room. He helped me into bed and got a glass of water from the bathroom.

"I'll be back at the end of the week to get you. You'll stay with me?"

I nodded and he turned to leave. "Wait. What about the novels? Who wrote them?"

"What novels?"

"Kass Holbrook, Korine Horner…"

He looked blank. Shrugged. "Never heard of them. See you Friday."

~ ~ ~

"EASY DOES IT," Marc murmured as he lowered me into a wing chair in his apartment. He pulled an ottoman over and propped my legs on it, then leaned my crutches against the coffee table where I could reach them.

"I see you haven't changed decorators yet," I said with a smile, looking around at the cacophony of colours and prints.

Marc powered on the computer and moved to the kitchen. "Tea?"

"Haven't you got something stronger?"

"Sure. Whiskey or mushrooms?"

I thought about it for a moment. My vision was surreal enough these days. "Neither," I finally decided.

"Fuck you! I won't do what you told me!" screamed the computer when the start-up script found the appropriate .wav file.

"Computer's on," I said, just as the kettle began to whistle. "*Rage Against the Machine?* I thought you'd have something more profound."

"Aggressive independence isn't as easy as it sounds," Marc replied. He returned to the room carrying a teapot and cups on a tray. "Black, right?"

I nodded and accepted the cup he handed me. He sat at the computer, alternately clicking, typing and sipping. Before long, his blog page popped up onto the screen. He scrolled through a few entries.

"You have lots of well-wishers," he said. "You can read it later when I go to the store. For now, we need to set up a profile for you. Where do you want to be from?"

We went through a series of questions and answers until I had my new persona: a disgruntled bank employee who gathers intelligence on co-workers and clients. This digital-age Robin Hood used the information to blackmail the offenders, never asking for money, but instead securing a promise to do something nice on a grand scale. Cheesy, but playful.

"All done. Here's your home page. Click this icon to add new posts."

He leaned back so I could see the screen. A banner of gold and green blazed across the top: *The Teller*.

~ ~ ~

Cherise

September 27, 2004

Kal,

I couldn't face the indignity. Please forgive me. Go out and find the root and robustness of your own potential.

Love,
Cherise

~ ~ ~

Chapter 21

They come and go, readers and cover-kickers, alike. Most of them look for what they already know. Now and again, however, they find something different. Something devastating, something uplifting, something life changing. Something amusing. The smiles, the frowns, the shuffling unsure feet that track mud and slush from old paths onto new ones. Most turn back. But a few step forward.

I found the most interesting thing among my stacks the other day. I'm not sure what to make of it, but have decided to follow where it leads. It's a diary, a very old notebook, very worn out. The picture on the front is difficult to make out, but it might be a court jester or a hobo. The background was probably yellow before it left home. If this sounds familiar, please comment below.

– Prosperocity (Posted April 17, 1999)

The Truth

"You're late!" Max shouted across the parking lot as I limped around the puddles, leaning heavily on my cane. "A few minutes is okay, but four months? You are killing me, Kal."

His white teeth glowed in the middle of his brown face in a wide grin. He wore new sunglasses that had wide plastic rims painted in bright orange tiger stripes with rhinestones at the corners. Very Edith Prickly. Over a ratty, bleach-stained navy T-shirt, he wore a yellow tie-dyed tank top. His cut-off jeans were cut a tad too short. Thankfully, he had long johns on underneath them. The look was completed with grey work socks and nylon sandals.

"I see you're still dressing yourself," I attempted to say when I got closer to him, but the last words were forced out of me in a grunt when he pulled me into a rough bear hug. I teetered on my cane, but he steadied me long enough to lift me from my feet and twirl me around.

"It's good to see you, man! We missed you around here. The customers are getting uppity without you to put them in their place." He set me down again. "Wait a minute, I'll get you a chair."

He dashed over to the kiosk and returned with a plastic pail and a rickety office chair that was missing its back rest. He squatted on the pail and I balanced on the office chair–wheels in muddy gravel can be precarious. I looked around the half-full lot.

"Kind of empty, isn't it?"

Max shrugged and sucked air through his teeth. He gestured to the torn-up street where men and women in orange vests stood around laughing and chucking each other on the shoulder. Max had to shout over the beep-beep of the dump-truck that backed up to the group of road workers.

"Road construction. It should be over soon."

"Yeah, when?"

"December."

I nodded and pressed my lips together. I had been hoping to get my old job back, but I knew Max wouldn't be able to afford to pay me with business so slow. A stiff breeze blew dust from the construction into my face and I squeezed my eyes shut.

"Oh shit, Kal. Here." Max dug around in his pocket and pulled out a pair of wrap-around sunglasses for me.

"Thanks," I said, declining comment on the metallic purple frames. I put them on. The purple lenses gave the world an eerie eclipse-like cast.

"Oh, hey, I have your last cheque for you. That should come in handy," Max said before bounding back to the kiosk and digging around in the drawers. He came back and handed me the white business-size envelope. "Listen, about your job…"

"No sweat," I broke in. I didn't want to make him say what I'd already figured out. "I was thinking of maybe checking out some of the book stores."

He frowned and plunked himself back on his pail. "Really? I can't see you selling Tom Clancy, but whatever. We all gotta check out our own path. But, I was going to say, about your…"

"Really, Max, I understand. Business is slow."

"Well, yeah, but that stops being my problem at the end of the month. I sold the lot to a developer, man. That's what I'm trying to tell you. They want someone to manage it until they're ready to break ground next year some time. I thought you might be interested."

"Me? Why don't you do it?"

"Well, they wanted me, but I'm tired, man. Tired of parking other people's cars." He sat with his elbows resting on his spread knees, hands dangling down between his legs. As he spoke, he dropped his chin to rest on his chest. He really did look tired.

"Come on, Max. You know you'll miss it." I punched his shoulder lightly the way I'd seen the road workers goofing around. I didn't like seeing him like this.

He looked up at me again, but his brow crinkled and the corners of his mouth turned down. "No, man, I really won't."

"So, what are you going to do?"

He brightened immediately and hopped up from his pail. "I'm going back to school. Thought I'd like to learn about the theatre, you know, sets and lighting. Make those dancing cats look good, you know?"

Huh.

"That sounds…really great, Max. Good luck with that." With a steadying hand from my exceedingly strange friend, I stood up from my chair. "I guess you might as well give my name to those people. Use the book store's phone number."

"Done."

I took a few halting steps away and stopped. "You know, Max, theatre usually happens at night. You'll have to stay up past eight o'clock. Are you sure you're cut out for it?"

He held his arms out from his sides and beamed at me. "Hey baby, I can howl as good as the next cat." And then he did.

Later, when I opened the cheque from Max, I nearly passed out. I had been expecting five days' pay, but instead got a substantial bonus. 'Thanks for the laughs' was all he had written in the memo field. There was enough for a down payment on a small house, if I were inclined to buy a house. I wasn't. Instead, within the space of an afternoon, I found an apartment in the classified ads, put down first and last month's rent and moved in. It didn't take long; all I had was a duffle bag with a few clothes and my notebooks.

An hour after the landlord handed over the key, I sat cross-legged on the floor of the small living room. The apartment was the second-floor of a house in Kensington Market. Rent in the trendy neighbourhood was a bit steep, but with Max's gift, I could afford it for at least a little while. The space was a one-bedroom that included a small kitchenette and living room big enough to fit a dinette set. I, of course, had no furniture, so every sound I made echoed back to me from the bare walls.

I grabbed a scrap of paper and started making a shopping list of the items I would need to set up house: plate, bowl, glass, fork, knife, spoon, pots, table, chair, bed, sheets. That should do it.

~ ~ ~

HARD-COVER NOTEBOOKS of every size and colour lined up along the shelf. I pulled one after another, hefted them in my hand. Most of them had cutesy motifs like kittens, daisies or teddy bears. I rolled my eyes when I found one with unicorns frolicking under rainbows on every page. I was hoping for something a tad more elegant. And I didn't want the pages to be lined or dated. I was indifferent to gold edging. It would wear off anyway.

Finally, my fingers brushed against a soft leather cover. It looked like a day timer, but I picked it up anyway. The leather was dark brown and butter soft. The word 'Journal' was embossed in the bottom right corner of the front cover. Very tasteful. I flipped it open to find around 200 pages of high quality paper. Every page was blank. It was perfect. I checked the price and gulped. It was very expensive, but surely it was worth it.

The sales woman smiled at me when I told her not to wrap the journal in tissue paper. "Save a tree today," I said. "I don't need a bag, either."

I took my purchase to my new home.

~ ~ ~

"LIFT, KAL!" Marc grunted from under the desk a few stairs below me.

"I am doing my best," I groaned. "I'm in a bit of pain here. Or did you forget I broke my pelvis?"

The desk, although not large, was heavy. It was also beautiful. Solid oak with a roll-top. The scratches and peeling layers of paint only added to its character. I was lucky to have found it at the curb only three blocks from my apartment. Marc and I had wheeled it down the street on a makeshift dolly, and now struggled up the stairs with it.

"How long are you going to play the broken pelvis harp?"

"As long as it still hurts."

With a monumental effort, we dragged the desk up the last few steps and into my living room. We positioned it under the one large window and fell gasping onto the floor. Marc looked around while he caught his breath.

"Cozy. Bit Spartan, though."

"That's the idea. If I don't own anything, I have nothing to lose." I struggled to my feet and went to the kitchenette. "Drink?"

"Yep."

I poured some wine into the two tumblers I had picked up second-hand and limped back to the living room with them. I was getting around without my cane a bit better, but I would probably always limp.

We drank our wine and Marc left an hour or so later. The setting sun cast a red-gold glow on the room and the patterns of the stained-glass window lit up the opposite wall. I decided never to hang anything there.

Seated at my desk with the last of the wine and a pen clenched in my hand, I stared at the blank page of my new journal. Soon, the sun was gone and I had to light a candle. It was easier than limping across the room to turn on a light. I was sore from the afternoon's exertions. Finally, I put pen to paper: *Thursday, June 16, 2005*. It was a start.

~ ~ ~

I NODDED TO the security guard as I stepped through the door into the library. Not much had changed. A few chairs had been moved around and the first-year students looked younger than ever. I weaved my way through the rows of study carols and work tables to the circulation desk. A familiar bum wagged back and forth on the other side of the counter. Its owner straightened and turned to face me.

"Can I help you?" Debbie asked.

"Not usually," I replied with a grin.

She frowned a moment, then her eyes widened in recognition. "Kal?" I bowed as low as I could with my cane. "I heard about your accident. Wow, you look different."

I had lost a substantial amount of weight in the hospital and had my hair buzzed close to my scalp. "I feel different," I replied.

"Are you back in school?" she asked with discernible trepidation.

"No," I assured her. "It turns out I'm not much of a scholar."

"Amen," she said with a loud guffaw. Someone from a nearby carol shushed her.

"I wonder if you could help me with something, though." I opened the bag and pulled out the leather-bound journal. I placed it on the counter before Debbie. She reached for the book with one hand and her scanner with the other. She flipped open the cover and stopped when she realized there was no bar code.

"This isn't a library book?"

"No, but can you date stamp it anyway?" She did and looked quizzically after me as I limped away.

I found the place down some stairs in a dark back alley. The store seemed to be more of a landfill for discarded words; its patrons the gleaners of the chaff. Patiently, they sifted through piles of tomes, looking for nothing in particular, many coming away empty-handed. The promise of treasure, of truth and of beauty kept them coming back. The smell of musty old paper warmed my heart. The old man behind the counter barely lifted his head when I entered, preferring to wave his acknowledgment rather than pull his attention from the rare books in front of him. I perused a few titles, passing by volumes I would have found useful once upon a time. With my back to the proprietor, I quietly slid the leather-bound journal in amongst a pile of vintage *New Yorker* magazines and slipped out the door without a backward glance.

~ ~ ~

Kal

Thursday, June 16, 2005

There is no truth. If you can get over that, you can concentrate on living.

Kali Hiver

~ ~ ~

Epilogue

The cemetery was deserted but not empty. I felt, more than heard, the crunch under my feet as I wandered the rows between the white mounds of the snowed-over grave markers. A hush embraced the place, the wind muffled by the high wall that surrounded the consecrated ground. The frozen tangle of tree branches high above my head swayed and clicked against a pale grey sky, but the sound was barely louder than my own faint breathing. Coldness crept into my airways, crystallizing the moisture in my nose and mouth. I placed a hand in front of my lips, exhaled, then inhaled the brief warmth.

I was on common ground, the final destination for the few uncommon people who remained unclaimed. Under my feet, under the January whiteness and the black soil beneath lay the unidentified remains of the nameless and loveless who passed almost completely unnoticed from the world. A stray ribbon of wind ruffled my hair. My ears stung and my bare fingers ached. I trudged on. I kneeled and brushed the snow from modest grave markers. I paused at the various graves of Jane Doe, checked the dates, and moved on.

Then I stopped. I looked around, and squinted watery eyes against the cold air. I looked back to the small, white concrete marker. It was almost obliterated by plastic funereal flowers and trinkets. This grave was the only one adorned by the bereaved.

I dropped to my knees and uncovered the lettering. Jane Doe, passed January 17, 2006. I had found it.

I placed my offering of flowers—the only real ones, I noticed—among the pile. I felt a sudden stab between my eyes as a sob struggled up from my gut. It punched through my tight throat and elongated into a wail. The white snow and black trees absorbed the sound, and the hush of death prevailed. I swallowed, but the action did nothing to stop the tears.

I had come to this place to express solitary pity for a forgotten woman. I had come here to restore my own sense of dignity and decency. As usual, my intentions were pale, paler than the backdrop of ice, snow and death. For the first time in two years, self-pity oozed out of me. I had always known it was there, pummeling bloodied fists on the door I had slammed shut after losing Cherise, but I had never dared to look at it. I slumped forward and buried my face in the snow on the homeless woman's grave. I cried into it and let it freeze the skin on my forehead, calming the heat of my bitterness.

Soon, a sound caught my attention. I sniffled and caught my breath. Footsteps. The rhythmic crunch and thud drew closer. I pushed myself up onto my haunches and wiped at my face with a soggy sleeve. The footsteps stopped just behind me.

"I'm just leaving," I said without turning.

"Stay as long as you need to," a female voice said. "But don't get too cold."

I didn't answer. I stared at the grave and the offerings on it. Besides the plastic and silk flowers, there were figurines, mostly lambs and porcelain globes, a glass bottle with herbs and oil of some kind, a lock of hair braided and tied in a ribbon, and a laminated card. I picked up the card. It bore the same picture as the cover of the diary.

"Who was she?" I asked of the voice behind me.

She came closer and I felt the weight of her hand on my shoulder. "Don't you know?" I covered my eyes with numb fingers and shook my head. After a pause, she patted my shoulder and whispered, "Oh, yes, my dear, you do." Her hand left my shoulder as the sobs took me over again. I didn't hear her leave.

~ ~ ~

Acknowledgments

With thanks to my husband, Steve, for his years of patience and attention; and also to Elizabeth Cassar, my enabler, BFF and sister I never had. Thank you also to friends who read early drafts and provided honest feedback: Dave Culhane, Laila Farrell, Kathryn Hales, Myriam and Steve Pelletier, Bill Mark and Darryl Burgwin. Special thanks to Shaun Proulx for convincing me to just put it out there. And, of course, to everyone who listened to me go on and on and on while I worked on this book, I can't thank you enough.

About the Author

 Karen Hoffman lives and works in and around the rattle and hum of Toronto. Aside from *In the Fool's Footsteps*, she has also written a play called *It Just Is* that was produced in 2007 at the Junction Arts Festival in Toronto. Karen is also an avid blogger and hatcher of plans. To learn what is currently incubating, follow Karen on Twitter at @foolsfootsteps or visit www.prosperocious.wordpress.com.

Made in the USA
Charleston, SC
08 March 2016